FIGHTING *for a* SECOND CHANCE

NIKKI ASH

Never stop fighting for love.

To my two beautiful miracles...

Always follow your heart.

One

LIZ

Graduation Day

AS I SIT IN THE AUDITORIUM OF MY HIGH SCHOOL surrounded by three hundred of my fellow classmates I've gone to school with my entire life, I look through the sea of maroon and white caps and gowns in search of her. I finally lock eyes with Kayla, the best friend a girl could ever ask for.

How we became best friends is anybody's guess since we're polar opposites in every way. While she has naturally blond hair that is long and pin straight, I have mousy-brown, wavy hair that spirals halfway down my back. She has striking blue eyes to my boring light brown. Her pale skin looks like she has never stepped foot on a beach despite living in Florida and surfing the waves her entire life. My skin is naturally a caramel brown even though I can't stand the beach in spite of living so close to it all my life.

Where Kayla is outgoing and always the life of the party, I'm soft spoken and reserved. We've both been cheerleaders for our local high school for the last four years, but I'm only one because Kayla begged me to try out and I gave in, afraid of losing my best friend to the popular crowd. She made team captain, so it was a given I would be on the squad as well.

I truly enjoy school, and while reading is my favorite pastime, Kayla spends her evenings partying it up and the mornings copying my notes.

When our eyes lock, I smile at her and she smirks back. Words don't have to be spoken to know what we're thinking. After being inseparable for the last thirteen years, we can practically read each other's minds without saying a word.

In about four more hours we'll be on our way to Miami Beach to party it up for the next seven days, courtesy of my parents as a graduation gift. Now, I'm far from a partier, but even I'm excited to spend a week in South Beach. I might be a bookworm, but I'm still a teenager.

The principal begins to call us up by last name and I'm one of the first people to step across the stage since my last name is Browning. As I walk across the stage, I hear Kayla holler my name at the top of her lungs. "Go Liz!" she yells. I also hear my parents and brother cheering me on.

I smile wide and stop at the end of the stage, so the photographer can snap my picture. I'm extremely excited to finally be done with high school and ready to begin my journey as a college student in a few short weeks at the University of Las Vegas. Kayla and I will be going to the same college and living together just off campus. I was accepted to ULV on a full academic scholarship to major in business and accounting. Yep, not only am I a book nerd, but I also love math and I'm really good with numbers. I have no idea what I want to do with the numbers yet, but I know I want to spend my days with them and my nights with a good book.

Kayla's parents are just so happy she's actually going to college, they've insisted on paying her tuition as well as our rent while we're there. She has no idea what she plans to study, but I don't think they care as long as she goes. Since my parents are so thankful to Kayla's for paying the rent since my scholarship doesn't cover room and board, they're paying for Kayla and me to go away for a week before we head to college.

I'm excited to do some shopping and lounge by the pool with my latest romance novel on my iPad. Kayla has bookmarked and sent me every hot spot imaginable she insists we must check out. That girl would seriously have us partying twenty-four hours a day if it were possible. I'm hoping she'll get completely partied out and pass out, allowing me to sneak out and do some serious reading by the pool. With the stress of finals behind me, I have too many books calling my name.

The principal announces Kayla's name and just about the entire auditorium of students cheer. I wasn't kidding when I said she is the life of the party. I don't think there's a single person here who isn't friends with her.

She walks across the stage and when she gets to the end, where the photographer is waiting, she raises her fist and yells, "Yeah, baby!"

Everybody can't help but laugh at her enthusiasm. When Kayla smiles and laughs, you have no choice but to join in.

What feels like several hours later, everybody's names have been called and the principal congratulates the graduating class. Throwing our caps high into the air, we all celebrate our freedom. We are officially high school graduates. I find Kayla, and we make our way to our parents who are waiting just outside the auditorium. After taking several pictures by ourselves, with each other, with our parents, and with our brothers, who are good friends and will be sophomores next year, we make our way to the exit to go out to dinner to celebrate.

"I can't believe my baby is all grown up! It feels like yesterday you girls were coming home from kindergarten and begging to go on your first playdate." My mom can't stop crying while we enjoy our Crème brûlée at our favorite Parisian restaurant downtown.

"Oh, Mom, stop," I mumble back. I swear she's cried more this week than I've ever seen her cry my entire life.

"But it's true! You're going to be so far away in Nevada. Promise me you'll come home and visit often. I'm so afraid you'll get over there and never come back."

I love my mom to death, but I think moving away will help me spread my wings. We're extremely close, but because of that, I always live in fear of not wanting to do anything to disappoint her, not that she would judge me in any way if I screwed up. My mom isn't like that—she has always been more of a friend than a mother. She had me at eighteen years old after my dad and her had been dating for four years. They met their freshman year in high school and it was instant love. I've personally never been in love, but I find it hard to believe one can fall in love with somebody they just met; however, I would never tell her that.

As soon as she found out she was pregnant with me, she decided to stay home and be a full-time mom instead of going to college. My dad worked nights delivering pizzas and went to college so he could get his degree in business. Immediately after graduating, he started his own business and still to this day runs a successful window cleaning company here in South Florida. We aren't rich by any means, but we have always had everything we could ever want or need.

After the business took off, my parents bought their first house in Jupiter, Florida right across from the beach, and that is where I met Kayla on our first day of kindergarten. Kayla, on the other hand, comes from an extremely wealthy family, but they're also the least loving family you'll ever meet. Kayla and her brother aren't really close. He is always getting into trouble, and Kayla's parents are rarely ever home.

Kayla and her brother have both practically grown up at my house and she's always saying she wishes her mom was more like mine. It seems like while Kayla's mom chose the career, my mom chose the family. I just don't understand why people feel like they have to choose one or the other.

I know my mom loves being home with my brother and me, but I also know she wishes she would have attended college before having us. She was so focused on raising us and helping my dad run his business, she never went to school. She always tells me to make sure I follow my dreams and passions. I think it's because she never got to follow her own.

Which leads me back to not wanting to disappoint my mom. I've been so focused on school these last four years to make sure I follow my dreams and passions, I haven't even so much as dated. I am looking forward to finally going out on some dates once we're up at ULV.

"I can't wait to leave tonight to Miami," Kayla whispers in my ear. "It's going to be so lit down there. So many clubs and parties going on. You better be ready to get your groove on, girly." I laugh as she shakes her ass in her seat. Kayla is forever looking forward to the next party.

"Yeah, yeah," is all I can come up with as a response. I have no idea how I'm going to make it seven days with Kayla in Miami partying it up. At least here in Jupiter she has to keep it tame since the town is small and boring to say the least.

We decide to drive Kayla's Volvo SUV down to Miami. It's a graduation gift from her parents and is really comfy. We get to the Miami Beach Resort, valet park the car, and check-in to our room. Looking around, Kayla and I grin at each other, thinking the same thing. *My parents did well.* The resort is literally right on the beach. I inhale deeply and can smell the ocean breeze coming off the waves. I may not like the sand between my toes or between other places, but I still appreciate the beautiful scenery. We walk to the back of the resort and see a beautiful pool surrounded by lounge chairs. Right behind the pool is a cute tiki-bar that separates the resort from the beach.

Once we get to the room, I slide the key card in and open the door. Immediately, we start squealing while throwing ourselves on to the white plush mattresses of our queen beds. Looking around, I notice our room is overlooking the ocean. The balcony hangs directly over the sand, and since we're ten floors up, I can see everything down below. The sun is starting to set and it's a gorgeous pinkish-orange. There hasn't been much rain the last few days and I hope it stays that way, but you just never know in Florida.

"Oh. My. God!" Kayla is still bouncing on her bed as I walk back in from the terrace and lie down next to her on her bed.

"Liz, your parents booked us an amazing room. I can't believe we get to spend seven days here, on the beach, at the pool, and it is literally right near every freaking club we're going to be checking out. Thank goodness I got us those fake IDs that say we're twenty-one. We're going to seriously have the best time before we have to go back to boring books and classes."

I stifle my laugh. Since when has Kayla ever let books and classes bring her down? Never. There is no stopping this girl and I'm sure once we're in Las Vegas, she'll be right back to being the life of the school. Although, if we get arrested for the fake IDs she had made, we may never make it to school.

"Ugh, Kayla. Do you really think it's wise to go to clubs that we shouldn't be in, right before our parents let us fly across the country to go to college? What if the bouncer realizes the IDs are fake and we get arrested? We will be so screwed. My mom will be so disappointed."

"Liz, stop! It's all good. They totally look like the real deal. Trust me, the guy I got them from assured me nobody would be able to tell the difference. Stop stressing over nothing. We're going to have an amazing time this week, then you can go back to your book-loving self next week once we're at ULV. I can't believe you decided to start classes this summer. There is no way I am stepping foot in a classroom until August."

Yes, I'm starting school this summer. I don't know what the big deal is. I can take three classes and get a head start. It's the smart thing to do. I didn't bust my butt the last four years in high school to screw up now.

"Okay, okay. So, Miss Miami, where to first?"

Giving me a look that says she's up to no good, Kayla says, "First we get changed. Then we part-ay!"

Two

LIZ

AS WE WALK UP TO ONE OF THE HOTTEST CLUBS IN MIAMI— according to Kayla—we immediately see the line going down the street and around the corner. There is no way we're going to get in there. Not even as hot as Kayla says we look. I look down at my dress, remembering earlier today when she surprised me with this outfit.

As we opened up our suitcases, I realized Kayla had been shopping without me. I should have expected this, as none of my clothes are up to club standards as she puts it. Of course, she had us both completely taken care of and wasn't taking no for an answer. When she pulled out the dress, I thought for sure it couldn't be for me because that dress didn't have enough material to be something I would wear. I was wrong. Between the dress, heels, makeup, and hair, I prayed we would both pass for twenty-one.

Once we make it to the end of the line, I look down at myself wondering what the heck I was thinking letting Kayla play dress up with me. Remember when I said Kayla and I are complete opposites? Well that extends to our body types as well. Kayla is wearing a silver sequin dress that is way too low up top and way too short below, but of course she looks hot. She's skinny but toned in all the right places thanks to her many years of surfing, and she has perfect size breasts that are spilling out of the top of her dress, which is completely formfitting and shows off her amazingly long legs that go on for days. She has topped off her outfit with matching silver fuck-me heels that have got to be at least five inches tall. I have no idea how she is even walking in them.

I, on the other hand, am curvy all over with large breasts, and while I'm not fat, I'm definitely on the thick side with an ass and hips. Kayla surprised me with a simple spaghetti strap black dress, telling me every woman needs a LBD (little black dress) for her first time in the club—it's apparently a rite-of-passage. Thankfully, she provided me with a pair of cute heels that aren't nearly the height of hers. My feet will definitely be thanking her later. Still looking down at myself, I must be frowning because Kayla immediately snaps me out of my own head.

"Stop overthinking the dress, Liz." She looks at me with one brow raised, giving me the *I know what I'm talking about* look that she always gives when I begin to doubt something she thinks is amazing.

"You look hot as hell! Every guy in here is going to want to dance with you. Maybe tonight you'll finally live a little and do the dirty-dirty with someone." She waggles her brows, and I can't help but laugh at her silly facial expression and the fact that she's referring to having sex as the dirty-dirty.

"I'm not going to lose my virginity to some strange guy here in

Miami," I whisper-yell while looking around to make sure nobody overhears me in line. Yes, I'm still a virgin. I know, how cliché. The nerdy girl graduates from high school with a four-point-five grade-point-average and has never even been kissed by a guy.

While I spent the last several years focusing on school, Kayla spent them being a social butterfly, and that includes having plenty of casual sex she has no problem describing to me in full detail. Let's just say I've been living vicariously through Kayla the last few years.

Don't get me wrong, she isn't a slut by any means, but she's definitely had her fair share of guys in her bed when her parents are away on business. She has mentioned numerous times she doesn't want a relationship and makes sure to keep it strictly casual.

Unlike my stay-at-home mom, Kayla's parents are both attorneys for a large firm. According to Kayla, her parents' relationship is more of a business partnership than an actual marriage. Because of their demanding careers, they're rarely ever home, which means Kayla has plenty of time and opportunity to have fun. You know what they say, when the parents are away the kids will play. Hell, if it were possible, Kayla would major in playing.

Just as I begin to think we're going to be stuck in line all night, the bouncer comes walking up to us. He's huge. I'm talking muscles on top of muscles, and he's wearing shades even though it's dark outside. I'm going to assume it's a scare tactic, because otherwise, why would someone wear shades when there's no sun?

In a bored, flat tone he tells us one of the VIPs has invited us to join him. Looking around to make sure he's speaking to us, I begin to ask if he has the right girls, when Kayla immediately jumps in.

"Sounds fabulous!"

He walks us to the podium and puts wristbands on us after barely checking our IDs. He notifies somebody over his walkie-talkie to escort us to VIP, and Kayla is practically jumping out of her skin with excitement. Before we go in, she asks the bouncer to please thank whoever invited us in for the invitation.

"His name is Cooper and you can thank him yourself once you get up to the VIP area." With that, he points us in the direction of the hallway and goes back to manning his post.

We're immediately hit with the pounding bass of David Guetta and Akon singing the lyrics to *Sexy Bitch*, and I can't help but sway my hips to the music as we walk toward the dance floor. Dancing is my guilty pleasure. We dance at the house parties our friends throw, but I love nothing more than to turn the music up in my room and get lost in the lyrics and rhythm.

The hostess attempts to show us where the VIP area is, but Kayla and I head right toward the gyrating bodies. On our way toward the center of the club, I take a second to look around and am enamored with the scene in front of me. To the left is a huge bar that wraps around the corner with the entire back wall full of mirrors, stacked with at least three levels of liquor. *I wonder how the bartenders get the liquor down.* Up ahead on the second floor is a huge deejay booth with a young guy spinning a turntable. Surrounding the dance floor are high-top tables for people to stand at with their drinks.

I look up and spot what must be the VIP section. My eyes trail to the ceiling to find strobe lights everywhere in various shades pulsing over all the bodies. It's all so mesmerizing. I can easily see how people can get addicted to the clubbing scene. This is nothing like the house parties we've been to throughout high school.

Watching the sweaty bodies rubbing up on one another has me getting this tingly feeling in my stomach. I know we should go thank whomever this Cooper guy is, but all I want to do is dance.

Kayla takes my hand and we move through the sea of hot bodies that are grinding one another to the center of the dance floor. She begins swaying her arms above her head to the rhythm of the song while moving her ass back and forth as I do the same. Locking her eyes with mine, she gives me her signature wink. We both turn around, facing away from each other, and as Akon sings about the girl's booty and not being able to take no more, she grinds her ass against mine while we continue to sway our hips and dance like nobody is watching. She turns back around and grinds her pelvis into my ass with one hand in the air and the other resting on my hip. I grind back while swaying both my arms above my head.

The song ends and the next one begins. The sound of Snoop Dog fills the club, along with The Pussycat Dolls as they begin to sing *Bottle Pop*. I crouch lower and begin to pop my ass out, loving this song. I feel Kayla's hand move from my waist, but I don't bother to turn around—I'm in my zone.

Suddenly, I feel hands on my hips once again. I'd assume they're Kayla's except the hands feel too large and too strong, holding me too tight to be her tiny hands. I feel the front of this person's body up against my ass and it confirms it's definitely not Kayla, as this body has a bulge in the front. As it rubs up on my ass, I can't help but softly moan at the feeling of this man's body rubbing up against mine. It just feels so good.

Angling my face, I see the most beautiful bright green eyes staring down at me while still holding his hands tightly on my waist. He's also sporting one hell of a smirk, as if he knows exactly what he's doing to my body. *I would bet my life this man is no virgin.* Because of how far I have to look up, I would say he has to be a good six foot three at least. Once he lets go of this pull he has on me, I'm able to look at his entire face, and it feels like my heart stops, then begins to beat again at a rapid pace.

His piercing green eyes aren't the only beautiful part of him. This man is downright gorgeous. He has golden-brown hair that is styled like he just got out of bed and ran his fingers through it, but it works. His skin is golden-brown like he's been in the sun recently. His nose is crooked, like it's been broken and wasn't set right, but it fits him and for some reason it makes him even hotter.

As I move my head down, I notice how big he is. Not big like fat, but big like built. He's not overly muscular like the bouncer, but fit. It's pure perfection. His shirt isn't tight, but it still accentuates his muscles. He's wearing a light blue button-down collared shirt with the sleeves rolled up, and as I run my eyes down his body, I can see the muscles in his forearms. I'm not a tiny girl, yet it feels like he dominates me as he stands over me, continuing to check me out.

His top teeth pull at his lower lip, releasing it, and his smirk gets even bigger while he raises a single brow. Oh yeah, he definitely knows what he's doing to me, and it doesn't help that he just watched me totally check him out while my ass is still rubbing against him.

I attempt to step forward, out of the line of his dick, but before I can, his hands grip my waist tighter as he pulls my ass closer to him. I don't know what it is about this guy, but I let it happen. Turning my head to face forward, I raise my arms up and continue to dance against him. We dance together for some time, our bodies rubbing against one another. I'm getting sweaty from the warm contact and the lights hitting down on us, and it feels good.

After a little while, his fingertips glide from the top of my arms, slowly trailing a path down the inside, toward the side of my body, stopping just under the curve of my breasts. His face is so close to my ear I can feel his breath on me. It smells like whiskey, making me want to suck on his tongue to see if I can taste it.

He whispers the lyrics into my ear, asking if it's true that I'm wet, and that is all it takes. My nipples pebble through my bra and dress, and I swear my panties are instantly soaked. This man is a walking billboard for sex. He continues to dance slowly and sensually against me, until the song ends and the next one transitions into the mix. Once again, he whispers into my ear, calling my 'baby girl' and telling me he could dance with me all night. I know he's only repeating the lyrics, but it doesn't stop the butterflies from fluttering in my belly.

Taking me by my hand, he leads us off the dance floor. I look around for Kayla and see she's still dancing her ass off with a couple of cuties. She makes eye contact with me, grins, and gives me two thumbs up. I smile and look back at this sexy creature who's holding my hand and pulling me toward a set of steps.

The guard standing in front of them gives him a small nod and he raises his chin in response. As we begin to ascend the steps, I realize this must be the VIP area. I glance back at Kayla to make sure she sees where I am heading. We once again lock eyes, and I know she knows where I'm going, which makes me feel a lot better. I am completely out of my comfort zone right now. While this guy is sexy and makes my body tingle all over, I have no idea who he is. He can be an axe murderer for all I know.

Once we get up to the VIP area, I look around and take it all in. It's similar to the bottom floor, but definitely not as packed. There is a small dance floor in the main area with several booths surrounding the outside perimeter that are roped off so people can sit and relax.

As he drags me along the outside of the dance floor toward the booths, I'm able to check him out from the back, and let me tell you, his backside is as sexy as his front. He's wearing jeans that fit perfectly across his nice ass and has on dress shoes, which are clearly expensive. He's wearing a silver watch with a logo I've seen before but could never afford. Looking at his rolled-up sleeves, I spot a bit of tattoos peeking out. *What I would give to take a closer look at those tattoos.* He's dressed nice, yet still casual, as if he takes pride in how he dresses but isn't out to impress anybody.

When we finally come to a stop, there are several people hanging out. I count three large men similar to him—all of them good looking, dressed up, and full of tats as well. With each guy, there are at least two women—that I can tell right off the bat are out of my league—hanging on to each of them. These women are dressed to the nines in tight, sexy dresses, and have the sex appeal I could only dream about. My little black dress looks like something a nun would wear compared to what these women have on.

Spotting a couple of the women giving the guys lap dances, I wonder if they're getting paid, but then I really look at these guys and see how hot they are—there's no way they would need to pay any woman to dance for them. There are several bottles of liquor covering the table with tumblers and shot glasses all over. One of the guys—who has only one woman dancing on his lap while he grabs her ass with one hand and drinks something that looks like vodka from his other hand—sees us walking over and nods his head to the guy I'm with.

We approach the booth and one of the other guys pats the girls on their asses to move them out of the way so he can let my guy sit down. *Hmm...my guy? That has a nice sound to it.* What the heck am I thinking? I'm only here for seven days and this guy is way out of my league. I have college to focus on for the next four years. Sure, I would like to date, but something tells me this guy is nothing like the college guys I'll be meeting at ULV.

He wraps his arms around my waist and settles into the booth pulling me into his lap with him. I fall willingly and cuddle up close, crossing my legs the best I can so nobody gets a peak up my dress. He begins to nuzzle his face into my neck, and a shiver goes down my spine. He must feel it because he laughs softly. Moving my hair off of my neck, he presses his mouth against my sensitive skin where my shoulder meets my neck. I feel the soft brush of his cool lips against my warm skin, and I sigh outwardly. If my panties get any more drenched, I'm going to need to excuse myself to go remove them in the bathroom.

"Yo, Coop. How's it going?"

The guy who's lap I'm in pauses what he's doing to me to look up at the guy speaking to him. *Coop? Is that short for Cooper? Where have I heard that name before?* Holy Cow! This is the VIP guy...the special guest who invited us in.

Looking around at the women once again, I wonder why in the world he'd invite us up here when he already has women like them surrounding him. Maybe he invited Kayla up. She's pretty hot, but even she isn't at the same level as these girls, though I would never tell her that. As he goes to respond to his friend, I cut in, giving voice to my thoughts.

"Did you invite my friend Kayla up here?"

"Whose Kayla?" He looks at me with genuine confusion. God, he's so beautiful. A girl could easily get lost in this man.

"The girl the bouncer invited in by a VIP guy named Cooper."

"I don't know who Kayla is, but I did ask the bouncer to invite you, and whoever was with you, in. As I was getting out of my car, I saw you walking to the end of the line."

"Did you see my friend Kayla? She was in the silver dress. Are you sure you didn't mean to invite her in?"

He chuckles and moves his hand to my chin to bring my face closer. He smiles slightly and stares deep into my eyes. God, his eyes are hypnotizing. *Focus, Liz!*

"No, baby girl. I meant to invite you in. To be honest, I didn't even notice your friend, but she's more than welcome to join us up here. I thought you would come up here when you walked in, but when I saw you head straight for the dance floor, I realized if I wanted you with me, I'd have to come get you myself and I'm damn glad I did."

He situates me closer on his lap and pulls my legs up and over his thighs while keeping his arms around my waist, and then looks back at his friend.

"What's up, Kaden? Didn't see you here a little bit ago. Did you just get in?"

His friend nods, and they start talking about some fight they went to a few days ago. I attempt to listen to their conversation, but it's hard to concentrate, because while Cooper is talking, his fingers are rubbing across my stomach in a way that's giving me butterflies. He moves his other hand up to my face and pushes my hair from out of my eyes like it's the most natural thing in the world.

They stop talking and he looks back to me like he has something to say. His mouth opens then closes, and then he makes a face that has me falling into a fit of laughter.

"You're looking kind of confused. Are you trying to think hard about something?" I can't stop laughing. How is it possible that a man so sexy can also be absolutely adorable at the same time?

"I just realized I know your friend's name, but I don't know yours." His brows are furrowed and he's giving me the cutest pout with his bottom lip jutting out just a little bit. With this look alone, I bet he could a woman to do anything he wants.

"My name is Lizbeth, but everybody calls me Liz," I say, still grinning at his facial expression.

"Are you from around here, Liz?"

"Um, kind of. I live a little farther north, about two hours from here." I decide not to tell him exactly where in case he is an axe murderer after all, and I also don't mention the fact that after this week I'll be living in Las Vegas. It doesn't really matter at this point since I won't see him again after tonight.

"How long are you in Miami for?"

"My friend Kayla and I are here for week. We're staying right up the road at the Miami Beach Resort. It's a graduation present from my parents." I don't mention it's my high school graduation since I'm supposed to be twenty-one to be in this club, and if he knew I was only eighteen he might be completely turned off. I'm already in shock that he would want me when he could easily have his pick of women in this club.

While we continue to make conversation, the entire time he's touching me in some way—his hands caressing my arms, massaging circles into my thighs. They aren't meant to be sexual touches, but they still cause the same reaction from my body. He looks past me at somebody walking over and tells me that I have company. I look behind me and see Kayla is walking over and sporting a huge knowing grin across her face.

"Well, hello there handsome. I take it you're the nice gentleman that invited us up here."

"That would be me," he confirms. He moves his hand off my

stomach to shake her hand, and I immediately miss his warmth.

"My name is Cooper and my friends here are Kaden..." He points over at a guy sitting nearby who he gives her a chin nod.

"Bentley." He points over to the guy who no longer has the two women giving him a lap dance, but is sitting by himself and staring right at my best friend like he wants to devour her.

"And the guy over there is Caleb." He points to the other guy who had gotten up to give Cooper his seat earlier.

He glances over at Kayla and back to me with a smile. "Guys, this is Liz and her friend Kayla. They're down here for the next week celebrating their graduation."

"Nice," Kaden shouts over the music since the song that is now playing has serious bass going on.

Bentley walks over to Kayla and asks her to dance and of course she says yes. As she is walking away with him, she turns around and gives me a huge, over exaggerated wink. I wouldn't be surprised if they're having sex by the end of the night. Hopefully they make it out of the club first.

"Would you like something to drink?" Cooper asks, pointing to all the bottles on the table. I probably shouldn't drink since I'm technically not twenty-one, but how ridiculous will I look not drinking at a club? After saying yes, he grabs the bottle to pour us each a shot then shoots his back. I follow his lead and shoot mine down quickly. It burns like a bitch the whole way down, and it takes everything in me not to cough.

Four shots later, and I'm definitely feeling more than good. Kayla has come back over with Bentley and is drinking right along with us.

We're currently dancing our asses off on the table to Beyoncé's remix of *Single Ladies* while taking another shot of whatever this yummy vodka stuff is. The other women are dancing with Kaden and a couple of other guys who have shown up during the last couple hours. Bentley and Cooper are sitting in the booth below us laughing while they continue to drink.

Every time I look down at him, I catch him staring at me with what I think is lust in his eyes. The song ends and Cooper stands to help me off the table while Bentley helps Kayla. I realize just how drunk I am, when the room starts to spin.

When everybody decides to head out, I know I have a decision to make. Do I have sex with Cooper tonight? Kayla has clearly made her decision but still asks me if it is okay since it means I'll be going back to the room by myself. I am not about to pussy-block my best friend, so of course I tell her to go. We're eighteen and heading off to college. We're not babies anymore, and if she wants to hook up with Bentley that's up to her. Since she's going back to Bentley's room, they tell me they can drop me back off at our room on their way.

Cooper texts somebody, and it must've been to let his driver know he's ready to go, because when we walk out to the front his expensive and shiny SUV is waiting for us. We all pile in and he gives the driver the name of the resort I'm staying at.

The entire car ride he sits with his hand in my lap, his fingers rubbing over my knuckles. When I look at him, his lips curl into a small smile. He takes my chin in his hand and places soft kisses all over my face. I try to focus, but his lips brushing across my temple, my cheek, the corner of my mouth are distracting me.

I'm still attempting to debate whether I should invite him up, when the SUV pulls up. He tells his driver he's going to walk me to my room and helps me out of the vehicle. Kayla gives me a smile when I turn around and hug her goodbye, whispering in her ear to be careful.

We get to my room and I twirl around, coming face to face with Cooper. I'm now up against the door and he's using his palms to hold himself up and over me. I glance up at him, wanting to invite him in, but knowing I'm too drunk to want to sleep with him. I really want my first time to be memorable and I can't imagine remembering any of this after all of those vodka shots.

Cooper looks into my eyes and, with the next words he speaks, makes the decision for me. "If I come in, it would only be to sleep next to you. You have drunk too much for us to do anything else. When I take you, I want you to be clear headed and remember everything my body makes yours feel."

Unsure of how to even respond, I simply nod. He pulls out his cell phone and texts something to someone, probably to his driver, letting him know to go ahead.

We enter the room and I excuse myself to rinse off and change into my pajamas. I brush my teeth and blow dry my hair so it's not soaking wet. As I exit the bathroom, I see him lying in my bed in nothing but his boxers and holy Jesus does he look hot. For a second, I'm frozen in my place, but I quickly gather myself and walk toward the bed to join him.

"Hope this is okay. I didn't plan to spend the night out, so I don't have any clothes to change into."

"No, I mean, yeah, that's cool," I say, trying not to sound like the inexperienced teenager I am and pray he doesn't notice.

I walk around to the empty side of the bed and climb in, wondering if he can tell this will be my first time sleeping with a guy. I can only imagine how many women he has slept with. I shake off the thought because it really doesn't matter.

Not quite sure how I am supposed to lie down, I awkwardly roll onto my side away from him. He doesn't seem to notice how nervous I am as he pulls me closer, spooning me from behind.

"Are you tired?" he asks softly.

Being wrapped tightly in this man's arms makes me feel protected. I can feel his bulge again through our clothes and I know he's turned on. I feel my cheeks heat up. Thank goodness, it's dark in here and I'm facing away from him or my blush would give away just how inexperienced I am.

"I'm exhausted but feel energized at the same time. I want to go to sleep but feel like I could stay awake all night. It must be the alcohol."

He laughs softly into my hair. "What do you usually do when you can't fall asleep?"

"Okay, don't laugh at me. I usually count."

"Count?"

"You know...sheep or pigs or some other farm animal until I pass out."

He closes his arms around me, kisses me softly on my temple, and begins to count.

"One sheep, two sheep, three sheep, four sheep…"

I can't help but laugh at this man counting sheep to help me fall asleep. My body relaxes and eventually I hear Cooper whisper in my ear, "Goodnight, Liz."

Falling asleep in this man's arms feels better than I could have ever imagined. I never thought I could feel so safe and wanted by a man to the point I feel choked up and can't even respond. With his soft breathing in my ear, I let sleep overtake me.

Three

COOPER

I WAKE UP AND LOOK AROUND, TRYING TO REMEMBER where I am. I feel warm skin under me and I look down at her. I can't help but smile at her rare innocence. She was so adorable last night when we got back to her room. I doubt at her age she's a virgin, but she's definitely inexperienced. I'm not a manwhore by any means, but I've definitely had my fair share of women in my bed. What red-blooded twenty-two-year-old male hasn't?

My mind goes back to when I first saw her walking to the end of the line at the club. I knew I had to have her in my arms. The way she smiled shyly made me want her to smile like that at me. I didn't even notice who she was smiling at because I couldn't take my eyes off her. The way her beautiful curves shown through the tight yet modest little black number she had on, leaving everything yet nothing to the imagination. It was a tug-of-war between sexy and innocent. She doesn't even realize how banging her body is.

When I watched her dance—the way she moved like she has no

idea how fucking sexy everything about her is—was a complete turn on. And when I got closer and her brown eyes connected with mine, I knew I was done for. I would give this girl anything she wanted. I wasn't looking for love. Only here for a UFC conference for a few more days, I was just looking for a hook-up, someone to help me forget about all the stress of my real life, but this girl could never be a simple fuck. She's meant to be cherished, adored, and loved completely, something I'm not capable of. It isn't in my DNA.

I glance back down at her and she's still snoring softly with her backside rubbing up against my dick. I groan at the feel of her perfect ass up against me and reluctantly get up to take a piss.

While in the bathroom, I decide a quick shower is necessary. Afterward I put back on my clothes from last night because I don't have any other clothes with me, and if I don't put something more on I'm going to be tempted to take hers off. The truth is I never stay the night with a female. Staying leads to commitment, and commitment isn't something I'll ever be able to give a woman, and I don't want to lead anyone on.

Since she's still sleeping, I order room service for breakfast. Unsure of what she eats, I order a little of everything and give them my credit card to cover the bill.

I pull out my phone and check for any messages. There are a few texts from Kaden reminding me of when our flight leaves and asking if I got laid. I ignore those. There's one from my mom congratulating me on my win. *A little late mom, that was almost a week ago.* She's probably drinking again. The last text is from my dad, asking if we need anyone to come by to help with the move. I text him back to let him know it's all taken care of and I'll see him in a couple days at the new training center. Just thinking about my dad puts me in a foul mood.

I shake off the aggravation I feel brewing from just the little contact I had with him and put my phone back into my pocket. I notice Liz starting to stir awake as she begins to stretch her legs and pull her arms over her head. The sheet that was wrapped around her entire body starts to move downward.

By the way, she's totally a bed and sheet hogger.

Under the sheets, she's wearing a cute, light pink tank top with her nipples poking through the thin material and tiny, cotton polka dotted matching shorts. Everything about her screams innocence. Her eyes come into focus and after a second, a small, shy smile spreads across her face. I'd like to think she's remembering last night.

"I ordered us breakfast. It should be here any minute."

"Oh, thank you."

She gets up to use the bathroom and, while she's in there, the food arrives. After the guy wheels it inside, and I give him a tip, I grab the various plates and move it all onto the outside terrace so we can eat and enjoy the Miami ocean breeze.

We enjoy breakfast in companionable silence. It's insane how comfortable I am around this girl, like I could just stay here in this fake cocoon forever with her. I can't remember a time I felt like this around a woman. Usually, I'm out the door before the sun comes up. I only have until tomorrow, but I think I would really enjoy spending some more time with her. I decide to bring it up, figuring the worst she says is no.

"I was wondering..." At the same time, she says, "Do you think..."

We both look at each other and laugh.

Like I said, it's just so damn comfortable with her.

"Go ahead, you first," she says, the corner of her lips quirking into a half-smile.

"I was wondering if you might want to spend the day with me. My flight leaves early tomorrow morning, but I'd love to spend what time I have left here with you."

Her face falters for a split second, and if I weren't staring at her, I wouldn't have even noticed. She immediately catches it, though, and gives me a wide smile.

"Yes, I'd love to spend today with you."

I'm not sure if her fallen smile was because she's unsure about wanting to spend the day with me, or because I said I'm leaving tomorrow. I'm obviously hoping for the latter, but either way she's on board for spending the day with me, so I'll take it.

In another lifetime, this would be the start of something new and beautiful, but this girl is just starting out in life. Having just graduated, she has her whole life ahead of her, and she definitely doesn't need to be bogged down by the drama that is my life. From the little I know of her, I can already tell she's the whole package and deserves the whole *happily ever after* bullshit all women want.

I can't give her the happily ever after, but I can give her today. When we part ways, I'll be moving forward toward advancing my pro career as a UFC fighter in Vegas, and Liz will have the entire world at her fingertips. With the grueling training days ahead, there's no room for anything but fighting. I have worked my entire life to get here and, with all these recent wins under my belt, I can finally see the light.

Fighting is all I have.

When I leave here, I'll be going back into the devil's lair. I spent the last four years away, but in order to advance my career, I've finally come to my senses and made a deal with the devil himself. My dad might as well not even be my dad. He's the owner of one of the most elite UFC training facilities and has decided to open one up in Las Vegas. I've been training at a smaller facility in Colorado for the last few years, but now, with my recent wins, my current trainer isn't pushing me the way I need him to, and that's where my dad comes in. Kaden is a huge trainer at one of my dad's gyms and my best friend.

My dad has transferred Kaden to the Las Vegas location and I will be moving to Vegas to train at my dad's facility with him. Bentley and Caleb have decided to make the move as well. I know it is the right move but the thought of being this close to my parents again is making me sick to my stomach.

In my dad's eyes, I am just a fighter that can potentially make money now that I have proven myself. My mom has been drunk since my dad caught her cheating and left her ten years ago. My dad was a fighter back in the day and rarely ever home. Since the day, he caught my mom cheating, he has drilled it into my head that fighters shouldn't be in relationships and they definitely shouldn't be married.

According to him, you can't have both and be successful. Fighting isn't a nine-to-five job. Some days I'm in the gym for thirteen to fourteen hours, whether it's to workout, train, or just to watch fights and learn about my opponent. I go home to eat and sleep, and then I'm back at it again the next day. Watching what my parents went through years ago, I'll never put a woman or myself in that position.

"So, what are you in Miami for?"

Her question breaks me out of my thoughts. I look at her and realize she has no idea who I am. I'm not in the top ranking in my weight class yet, but since my wins recently and the fact that I'm undefeated, people are starting to notice me when I'm out in public. Women are definitely starting to notice me. It's nice to be around a girl who doesn't just want me because I'm a fighter.

"I'm here for work." I tell her vaguely in hope that she won't ask any more questions. She seems content with that answer, so I quickly change the subject.

"You mentioned you graduated. What's next for you?"

She thinks for a moment and replies just as vaguely.

"Kayla and I are moving in together."

We finish up our breakfast and decide to start our day at the pool. While she's changing into her suit, I run downstairs to the resort shop to purchase one.

When I get to the resort shop, I notice the cutest stuffed animals for sale that remind me of her counting sheep. None of them are farm animals, but there are a few I think Liz might like. I grab one, along with a swimsuit, and head to check out.

When I get back up to the room, I knock since I don't have a key and she answers the door in her bright blue two-piece polka dotted bikini that instantly has me hard. *What is with this girl and polka dots and why the hell do they turn me on so much?* I knew she had a hot body in that dress last night, but now that it's all on display I'm speechless.

After running my eyes over her body for the second time, I finally speak up so she doesn't think I'm nuts just standing here staring at her.

"God damn, Liz. Are you sure you want to go to the pool in that? I hear skin cancer is on the rise. Maybe we should stay inside. I can think of a better use of our time in this room where the UV rays won't kill us," I choke out, while trying to adjust myself without making it look obvious.

It takes her a second to catch the meaning behind my words and then she starts to laugh, and not just any laugh. No, she's practically doubled over with tears rolling down her cheeks.

I didn't think it was that funny. I was just trying to save her life... and my dick from remaining painfully hard all day.

"You're silly. Go get changed and we'll head down to the pool. I hate the beach." See. Fucking innocent.

"Wait a second." I hand her the stuffed animal. "I saw this and thought of you. Something to remember our time together by."

She stares at the flamingo. "Um, okay, you're going to have to explain."

"It's a flamingo. You said you count animals. So, the next time you can't sleep, you can count flamingos and think of me."

Her smile widens as she hugs the flamingo close to her and proceeds to give me a kiss on the cheek.

"Thank you, Coop."

As I get changed in the bathroom, I almost consider taking a quick cold shower, but she knows I already took one earlier, and I really don't want to have to explain that.

Four

LIZ

WE GET DOWN TO THE POOL AREA AND LUCKILY IT'S NOT too packed. We find two lounge chairs side by side and lie down next to each other. I didn't even think I would see Cooper after last night and now I'm spending the entire day with him. He didn't mention anything about tonight but, I'm hoping he'll spend the night again.

Last night I had way too much to drink and he was so sweet not to take advantage, but today I have no intention of getting drunk, and I'm not planning on leaving here a virgin. I know Cooper isn't my forever, but like Kayla says, *There is nothing wrong with having a damn good for-now.*

We spend the day lounging by the pool, and I can't get over how delicious Cooper is in his bathing suit. He is amazingly fit. The way his suit hangs down just right, exposing that perfect V in a way I thought was only found on guys in my romance books, makes me want to attack him right here. Whatever he does for a living must involve him staying in shape which makes sense because he did mention he works an obscene number of hours leaving him barely any time for a social life.

We order drinks by the pool: he orders Jack and coke and I order those cute fruity frozen drinks with the umbrellas in them to keep me hydrated. They're so yummy, I doubt they have much alcohol in them.

I'm watching Cooper swim laps in the pool while I'm reading my latest romance novel, when he comes over to the edge and splashes me just a little.

"Hey! Watch out for my iPad. If it gets ruined, it will be the death of you as well," I say jokingly as I turn it off and put it back into my beach bag.

My phone goes off and I check it to see if it's Kayla. It is, and she's confirming that she's spending the day with Kaden and Bentley and will see me later. I type back a quick okay and then join Cooper in the pool.

Putting one foot into the water, a chill runs up my leg from the water being freezing cold. I thought it would be warm in Miami in the middle of May. This is exactly why I stay away from the water. Cooper laughs and explains a huge rainstorm came through recently, which caused the pools and oceans to get colder.

He grabs a hold of me by my waist and pulls me into the water, holding me close. I use him as my human buoy to hold myself up. My legs are wrapped around him as we float lazily in the water. His hands gently massage circles on my ass as he holds me close to him, nuzzling his face into my neck. I'm so relaxed in his arms I almost start to drift off when I can feel the same bulge from last night push between my legs.

Needing a distraction, I ask, "What's your favorite color?"

He looks at me like I'm crazy but then responds. "Um, if I had to pick I would say black, I guess."

"Black isn't a color, silly. It's a shade."

He chuckles at my fact. "Well, then black is my favorite shade."

I let him keep his answer and ask another question.

"What's your favorite food?"

He thinks for a moment and responds with a bit of a frown. "Definitely my mom's lasagna when she used to cook."

I get stuck on the part about his mom but choose to leave it alone. I've noticed he doesn't like to talk about his parents or his life outside of right here and now.

"Yum, lasagna is good. What's your favorite movie?"

He stills his hands from rubbing on my ass and gives me a smirk. "Are we playing twenty questions? Because if we are, I'm pretty sure it's supposed to work both ways."

"I'm just trying to get to know you. My favorite color is pink and my favorite food is Crème brûlée. Now what's your favorite movie?"

He gives me a soft kiss to my lips, one that I hope will continue but ends too quickly. "*Batman*. My favorite movie is *Batman*. I could watch it every day."

I laugh at that.

"What's so funny?"

"Nothing." I shrug. "Just imagining a grown man watching *Batman*."

"Hey, now! Have you seen *Batman*? *Batman* is not just for kids. He's a grown man himself who saves Gotham from all the bad guys."

I laugh even harder. "Okay, okay. It's a grown man movie, and no, I haven't seen it."

"You've never seen it? Then you don't get to judge."

"Ha ha! Okay, Coop. I'll take your word for it. What do you like to do in your free time?"

"Wait, first, tell me what your favorite movie is."

"Okay, don't make fun of me, but *Love and Basketball*."

"So, you like basketball?"

Oh boy, he's totally going to make fun of me. "No, I just love how the girl is so strong, and how over years, through all their crap, they love each other. And in the end, even though the ends were against them, they end up together. Okay, now tell me what you do in your free time."

He doesn't even think about it when he says, "Work out. I love to work out and do MMA."

"What's MMA?"

"Mixed Martial Arts."

"Oh! Like *The Karate Kid*?"

He bursts out laughing. "So, you've seen *The Karate Kid* but not *Batman*? Yes, like that movie, I guess. What do you enjoy doing?"

I have to think about this because I don't want him to realize I'm an eighteen-year-old, recent high school graduate, with no job. I decide to just be honest but vague. "I enjoy reading, but books can be expensive, so when I find a book I really like, I usually read it several times."

"That's commitment right there," he says with mock seriousness.

"Oh hush!" I move out of his arms, getting just far enough away to splash him with the water. His face is drenched and the water is dripping down his hair. Cooper's gaze heats with intensity, causing me to back up a little more. I'm not sure what he's going to do, so I wait in anticipation. As soon as the words *"it's on"* leave his mouth, I take off, but before I can even swim two feet away, he jumps at me and grabs me by the waist, spinning me around. I close my eyes tight so when the chlorine hits me it won't burn my eyes, but no water comes.

Suddenly, I feel his lips on mine, but once again, he pulls away quickly, leaving me with nothing more than a tease. It can barely count as a kiss, but it makes me want more.

Several hours, questions, and drinks later, and I'm beat to death by the sun and ready to go back up to the room. Cooper agrees, and we head back up. When we get inside, I start to head to the bathroom to change out of my bathing suit and rinse the greasy sunscreen off my body when Cooper stops me. He rubs his hand down my arm and looks into my eyes like he's dehydrated and needs me to personally rehydrate him. He moves toward me, closing the distance between us as his lips crash into mine. I gasp softly into his mouth because *holy shit!* I'm finally going to experience my first real kiss.

First softly, then more roughly, our mouths move against each other. His tongue glides across my lips seeking entrance and I willingly open them to allow him access. His mouth tastes similar to what it did last night, sweet with a hint of spice. It must be the Jack he keeps ordering. His hands rub up and down my arms smoothly causing goose bumps to rise across my skin. My hands wrap around his neck and then move further up to grab ahold of his hair as I continue to kiss him back. He groans softly and tugs my body closer to his but stops the kiss way too soon.

"Let's take a shower," he whispers into my ear. Before I can answer, he's grabbing my hand and pulling me into the bathroom. He turns the handle for the water and gets in with his bathing suit still on. I know he is doing this for my benefit, not sure where I stand in this situation, and that makes me want him that much more. He puts his hand out to take mine and I follow him in, still in my bathing suit as well.

The water is warm and feels good against my sun-kissed skin. I turn around to face away from the water and allow it to massage my body. When I open my eyes, Cooper is towering over me, giving me a heated look that tells me exactly what he wants from me.

He grabs the soap from the sidebar and squirts some into his hand, turns me around, and begins to rub it onto my shoulders and down my arms, untying the top string around my neck. It causes me to shiver and he stops, turning my head to face him. He gives me a look with one brow up, silently asking *is this okay?* Unable to find my voice, I nod eagerly.

He continues to rub the body wash all over my body. When he gets to my back, I can feel him untie my last bathing suit string, causing my top to fall to the floor of the shower.

He moves his hands toward my front and begins to rub circles around my nipples, palming my breasts. The stimulating sense I feel from his touch causes me to let out a whimper.

He takes my noises as a cue to continue, slowly sliding my bikini bottom down my thighs as I lift each foot up just enough for him to remove it as it joins my top on the floor.

His hands go back to massaging my breasts and it feels unbelievable. He squeezes more soap out of the bottle and begins to soap up my entire body, moving to my stomach and then to my mound. *Thank god Kayla made me get a full Brazilian before we left.* I think he's going to stop there, but he keeps going.

He soaps up my thighs, and when he gets to my feet, he lifts my foot up and kisses the insole. If he's trying to drive me crazy with want, it's working. He moves back up the inside of my thigh until he reaches the apex between my legs. I can't take my eyes off him as he pulls my pussy lips apart with his fingers, then inserts one into me. I moan quietly at the fullness I feel. *Why in the world did I ever wait so long to be touched by a guy?*

"Damn, baby, you're so tight," he says, pushing his finger in and out of me.

I should tell him I'm a virgin, but I don't want him to stop. Kayla told me she barely bled her first time, so if we have sex in the shower hopefully he'll never know. Plus, I got on the pill a few days before we left, so I'm covered.

He inserts another digit into me, and even in the shower, I can feel how wet I am around his fingers. He pumps in and out of me, causing my body to tremble at his touch. His other hand reaches up and starts pulling and tugging on my nipples. His fingers are bringing me to the edge of insanity and I don't know what to do.

His fingers begin to move faster, delving deeper, and suddenly they hit a spot deep inside of me that causes me to clench. My climax is building, and my body is shaking with the need to release. "Let go, baby girl. Come for me." When I hear those words from him, I have no choice but to let go as the most intense orgasm I've ever felt overtakes me. The ones I've given myself are nothing in comparison to what I'm feeling now.

With a beautiful smile on his lips, Cooper moves the sopping wet hair from my face. His list filled eyes lock with mine and then his mouth crashes against mine. This kiss is different from the first one. This one screams of want and desire. His tongue finds mine, and they move in a rhythmic motion, swirling around each other. It reminds me of how close we danced together last night. Every part of me just fits with every part of him.

As I come down from my orgasm, he removes his fingers and I immediately want them back in me. He sees my face turn to a pout and he kisses it away before he takes the fingers he just had in me and puts them into his mouth. *Holy shit!* My vagina pulses as I watch him lick my essence from his fingers.

"You taste damn good. I'm going to need to taste some more of this soon."

When he removes his fingers, my eyes stay glued to his mouth. It's then I realize he's removing his bathing suit. I watch as he unties the drawstring that holds them up and pushes his shorts down, exposing his long thick dick. He continues to push the shorts farther down and then steps out of them, dropping them on to the floor on top of my bathing suit pieces.

My eyes move back to his hard length as he takes it in his hand and begins to stroke it a few times, never losing eye contact with me. I know it sounds crazy, but I'm seriously wondering how in the world that thing is going to fit inside me.

He must sense my nervousness because he lets go of his dick and moves closer to me, gripping my chin so I'm looking right into his beautiful green eyes. Keeping eye contact with me, he whispers, "Wrap your arms around my neck, baby."

I do as he says. Then he grabs my ass in his hands and lifts me against the shower wall. It's cool against my back but feels good against my overheated flesh.

"I plan to take you in the bed, but right now I can't wait to have you. Are you on birth control? I'm clean."

He continues to look into my eyes, searching for what, I don't know. This is where I should tell him I'm a virgin, but instead I simply murmur, "I'm clean and on the pill."

As soon as he hears those words, without any barriers between us, he presses the head of his dick to my entrance and, in one fluid motion, buries himself inside me. At first, I feel a burning sensation as he rips through my virginity, but after a few minutes, it begins to feel good. *Damn good.*

I hold onto his hair with my arms around his neck as he moves in and out of me. His hands are holding my ass cheeks tightly as he pulls his dick out slowly, then pushes it back in with more force.

"Fuck, Liz. You're so tight. It's like you're choking my cock." He pulls out and then thrusts back in. "Fuck, I don't know how long I'm going to last. It's never felt this way."

My orgasm builds higher, until it's teetering on the edge, as Cooper fucks me with abandon.

"C'mon, baby, give it to me one more time," he growls.

All too soon, my orgasm slams into me. My walls clench around his dick, and he pumps into me relentlessly, chasing his own release. My head smacks against the shower wall, but I don't even care. If I die from a concussion from this, I'll die a very happy girl.

His mouth moves to my neck, sucking hard like he needs an outlet to release all his built-up tension. His thrusts get choppier and his cock begins to swell inside of me as his hands and legs shake from the intensity of his orgasm.

He comes to a complete stop, breathing heavily, and moves his face from out of my neck, giving me a small smile as he carefully sets me on my feet. I'm pretty sure this man just ruined me for every guy whose to come in the future. After we finish washing ourselves, we venture out of the bathroom in our plush towels.

After we get comfy in my bed, he orders room service for dinner, and we watch some television. As we lie together, he rubs up and down my arms absentmindedly. I don't even think he realizes he's doing it. It's like he has to be touching me in some way at all times. As he watches some sports game, I take the opportunity to try to burn every beautiful feature of him into my brain for later, which makes me want him all over again. If tonight is all I get, I need to make it count.

When I start moving down the bed, Cooper looks over at me with a confused expression across his face, but I don't say anything, letting my actions speak for themselves. I get down to the bottom of the bed and pull the sheets off him and staring right at me is his big beautiful dick.

I'm not sure if a dick is supposed to be called beautiful, and I've never seen one until today, but looking at it up close, I have to say Cooper has one mighty fine looking dick.

He stares down at me, wondering what I am doing, probably wondering why I'm staring at his dick. Taking his hard length into my hands, I stroke it up and down. It feels soft like velvet yet rough. I can't believe this was in me a little while ago. I kiss the tip of the crown, feeling the smoothness of it across my lips. I look back up, and his brows are raised, but he still hasn't moved a muscle. I wonder if he realizes this is my first time touching one.

I lick my lips in anticipation before putting the head of his dick between my lips once again. I swirl my tongue over the tip, tasting the little bit of precum that surfaces. I do it once again and Cooper groans out loud. Knowing that I'm causing this reaction from him spurs me on.

I go up higher onto my knees and place my mouth over the entire length and slide it down to the back of my throat, coating it with my saliva. I begin to bob my head up and down, stopping at the top to swirl my tongue around the head.

Cooper takes my hair and moves it out of my way, gripping hold of it tightly, while I continue to deep throat him. Down, up, swirl. Down, up, swirl. I can feel his body begin to tense and feel his grip on my hair go even tighter. The way his dick swells, tells me he's getting close to his release, so I start going faster, taking him as deep as I can go.

He tries to pull my head off him, but I figure if I'm going to do this I might as well fully commit. I keep going, and if it's even possible his dick gets harder and thicker, and within a few seconds I can feel the warm, salty, liquid shoot into my mouth and coat my throat. He groans my name as I continue to suck and lick him through his orgasm, swallowing it all down.

When he's done, I look up at him, hoping it was good for him. His wide smile is confirmation enough that my first blowjob was a success. I get up to wash my mouth out and come back to bed to cuddle with him. I hate that when tomorrow comes this will be the ending, when in another lifetime this would be the beginning.

The food arrives, and after Cooper takes the cart from the guy, he brings it all into the bed.

"I want some of your burger." Cooper goes to grab a piece and I give him a look that says he's crazy. He pouts and I laugh, figuring it will be funny to tease him with my juicy burger.

"Mmm...I bet it's going to be delicious. Maybe you shouldn't have ordered a salad."

I take a huge bite of my double bacon cheeseburger, all the condiments packed inside of it dripping down my face. Of course, he starts laughing at me.

"I don't think your mouth can handle all that. You need to share with me." He swipes his finger up the side of my mouth, removing the mess I've created and puts it into his mouth.

"I handled you just fine, didn't I?"

"Damn right you did. Now share some of that burger with me." I give in and bring the burger to his mouth, allowing him to take a bite.

Once we're finished eating—and Cooper has finished eating almost half my burger—he grabs the empty trays, puts them on the cart, and rolls it outside the door before climbing back into bed. As he gets situated, I'm able to sneak a closer look at his tattoos since he isn't wearing a shirt.

I notice the tattoo on his arm is of a huge dragon that begins at the top of his shoulder and covers his entire arm with the tail extending to his forearm. There's writing in the tail, but I can't make out what it says.

Cooper notices me staring and gives me a wink, moving closer to me. "The dragon symbolizes strength." He points to the dragon. "And him breathing fire symbolizes me breaking free from my parents' constraints. I got it a few years after my parents split up and shit got bad. I was working with my dad and ended up leaving to go work on my own. I'm heading back home to work with him again and have no idea how I'm going to deal with him. In the tail, it says, 'I breathe in my courage and exhale my fear.' It's to remind myself that I'm strong enough to stand up to him and be my own person."

"It's beautiful," I whisper without realizing I'm running my fingertips along the words of the quote he just read to me. I can feel goose bumps rise up, and I look at him and see he's staring at me like he's about to devour me. His look of want causes my lady parts to tingle and I instinctively tighten my thighs to seek relief. He leans forward and begins to kiss me with such passion it's as if he's making love to my mouth. His lips mold to mine, his tongue battling with my own, and it's official, Cooper has ruined me.

We make love a few more times throughout the night, until I once again fall sleep with his body wrapped around mine, wishing tonight would never have to end.

I wake up to the door unlocking and then opening and realize the space next to me is empty. The clock reads five in the morning. Kayla is tiptoeing into the room in a shirt and cotton shorts that reads Miami, Florida. She must've bought them from one of the tourist shops. She has her dress and heels in her arms, and I can tell she's trying not to wake me.

When she looks over at me and sees I'm awake, she giggles and lies down in her bed, patting the spot next to her for me to join her. I get up to crawl across the bed when I feel the crinkling sound of paper. I look down at it and see my name scribbled along the top. The only person it could be from is Cooper, and my stomach falls at the realization that it's a goodbye note. I knew this was coming, but I didn't realize how much it would hurt.

Liz, I had to catch an early fight and I didn't want to wake you. You looked so peaceful lying in bed wrapped up in my arms. I wish I could hold you like that forever. Thank you for the most amazing thirty hours of my life. I will never forget them and will

probably fantasize about them for years to come :)
Stay sweet, baby girl.
— Coop

I take the note with me over to Kayla's bed so she can read it. "Do you regret sleeping with him?" she asks after reading the letter.

"No, it was perfect. I knew going into this it would be a one-night stand, or a thirty-hour stand as he put it. We're just starting college and I'm not about to try to start a relationship with somebody right now. Did you get Bentley's number?"

"Nope, we had fun but agreed what happens in Miami, stays in Miami. Let's get some sleep and enjoy the rest of our week. And don't think I'm letting you off the hook. After I get some shut-eye, you'll be giving me all the details."

"Yeah, yeah." I laugh, and we curl back up into the sheets and fall asleep. My thirty hours with Cooper were amazing and I'll never forget our short time together.

My first day without Cooper is a bit depressing. I can't stop thinking about him and Kayla seems a bit down as well. She hasn't really said what happened with Bentley, but I think—like Cooper did to me—he took with him a little piece of her heart.

Kayla and I spend the day lounging by the pool. She's listening to music while I'm reading my book. Then, by the late afternoon, we decide to go back up to our room to shower before getting a bite to eat. When we walk inside our room, I see a thin white rectangular box wrapped in pink ribbon on my bed.

Kayla gets excited and tells me to hurry up and open it. When I pick it up, there's no card stating who it's from. I pull the ribbon off, and when I open the box, I don't know whether to laugh or cry.

"What is it? I'm dying over here," Kayla says, coming closer to see what I'm looking at.

"It's gift cards to Barnes and Noble, Amazon, and iTunes."

Kayla cocks her head to the side, her eyebrows shooting up. "Um, okay. Am I missing something here? Why do you look like you're about to cry over them? And who sent them?"

I take the gift cards out and find a small piece of paper with typed words.

I wasn't sure where you get your books. Whenever you buy a new book, think of me.
— Coop

"I made him play twenty questions to get to know him and told him I love to read but that I don't always have the money to buy new books, so I reread my favorites."

Kayla's eyes go glossy at my explanation. "Oh, Liz. That is so romantic."

"Yeah, it is. Too bad I can never thank him."

The next day Kayla and I check out some of the sites in Miami. We take a taxi to the art district and check out the graffiti walls while having lunch at a delicious Cuban restaurant. When we get back there's another box on my bed.

"Get the hell out of here!" Kayla shouts when she spots it at the same time I do.

I open the box and this time inside is the entire collection of *Batman* movies. I burst out laughing and look for a note. Sure enough, there's another one.

For your viewing pleasure. Only once you watch all of these can you judge Batman. – Coop

Kayla reads it silently over my shoulder. "Another twenty questions fact?"

"Yeah, it's his favorite movie."

"Did you by any chance tell him you love huge houses and expensive cars?" Kayla jokes and we both burst into a fit of giggles.

Day three post-Cooper and I haven't received a package yet. I wonder how he is doing all this. If he is sending them daily or if he did all this before he left. To be honest, I don't even want to know. It feels magical and I don't want to lose that feeling.

Kayla and I decide to go down to the restaurant in the resort for dinner. When we're done eating and ready to get the bill, the waiter brings me out a Crème brûlée. Before he walks too far away I call him back over.

"Excuse me. I didn't order this."

"Yes, I know. It was supposed to be delivered to your room this evening, but since you're dining with us, I thought you might like it now."

It hits me that I told Cooper this was my favorite dessert.

"By any chance is there a note to go with it?"

"Yes, ma'am. I was supposed to attach it to the receipt. I can go get it now."

A few minutes later he comes back with the note and hands it to me.

I wish I were there with you sharing this dessert. I bet it tastes delicious but not half as delicious as you. – Coop

Kayla slowly shakes her head after I hand her the note to read. "Geez Liz, this guy clearly has it bad for you. Maybe one of these will include his number."

I don't want to get my hopes up, but in the back of my mind I've been thinking the same thing.

The last two days of our trip pass by quickly. The day after I got the dessert, a huge blanket for the beach is delivered to our room with a note that says *To keep the sand away.* No phone number.

The last day of our trip I wonder if there'll be a gift. We're checking out at ten to head home and say bye to our families before we head to Las Vegas, so it would have to be delivered before we leave. At ten, nothing has arrived yet, so we go to the front desk to check-out and that's when the woman asks which one of us is Liz.

"Um, I am."

"This is for you."

I grab the box and pray there'll be a number inside. Removing the top, I find a beautiful white gold necklace and charm. I look closer at the charm and it's a pair of boxing gloves. I lift them up to look for a note and find it, only there isn't a phone number.

To always remember me xo – Coop

"Boxing gloves?" Kayla asks. "Another question?"

"It must be. He said he likes mixed-martial-arts."

I hand it to Kayla and ask her to put it on me. Once it's on, I grab the boxing gloves, bring them up to my lips, and think to myself, *I will never forget you, Coop. I don't even think that's possible.*

Five

LIZ

FOR THE THIRD DAY IN A ROW I'M BENT OVER THE TOILET throwing up everything in my stomach while Kayla holds my hair back and earns her best friend title.

"Ugh! Do you think it was something we ate at the Chinese restaurant last night?"

"Liz, if it were food poisoning, you wouldn't be throwing up for days. I really think you need to go see a doctor. It could be the flu."

I know she's right. It's time to make a doctor's appointment. I stop throwing up long enough to go to my room to find my insurance card and locate a doctor in our area.

Our apartment is so cute and bigger than we expected. Kayla's parents went all out renting us a three-bedroom apartment walking distance from campus. We both have our own room and the third bedroom is used as an office to do our schoolwork. It has a computer desk and a super cute futon that can turn into a bed if we have somebody stay over.

It has been over a month since we've left Miami and I'm not going to lie, Cooper has been on my mind. But it doesn't matter because only knowing his first name means I have no way of finding him, and since he doesn't know my last name, he isn't going to be locating me any time soon either. As much as I wish things had ended differently, there's no point in regretting something I can't change. All I can do at this point is just chalk it up to an awesome experience and move forward.

Kayla made me dish out the details and said I'm lucky I was with a guy who actually knew what he was doing. Orgasming the first couple times she had sex didn't happen for her and she was in shock at how many times he got me there. Any guy who comes after Cooper will definitely have a lot to live up to.

I've started my classes at ULV and Kayla has found a part-time job at a cute bistro right down the street from our place. Her parents are covering all her expenses, but Kayla is too much of a social butterfly to sit at home all summer while I'm in class. She's already met several people there and has attended a few parties.

I make an appointment for this afternoon, hoping the doctor can shed some light on why I've been throwing up for the last few days. When I get inside the room, the nurse has me give a urine sample and asks me to explain what's been going on. Then I change into a gown and wait for the doctor to come in.

"Hello, Lizbeth. It's nice to meet you. My name is Dr. Lee. If you don't mind me asking, other than throwing up, have you had any other symptoms?" I think about it for a second and conclude that other than throwing up, I haven't felt all that bad.

"Not really. Nothing else feels wrong except I keep throwing up. I'm thinking food poisoning, but would it go on for days? My friend Kayla said it might be the flu."

She looks down at her notes and gives me a small smile. I feel like she's preparing me for something bad. "Lizbeth, your urine test shows high HCG levels. In other words, you're pregnant, which explains why you're throwing up every day. Unfortunately, those symptoms can vary depending on the pregnancy. I take it you didn't know you're pregnant."

Every part of me begins to shake, and I suddenly feel like I need to throw up again. I jump off the medical bed, making it to the trashcan, just in time to empty the contents of my lunch into it. Dr. Lee hands me a wet paper towel and I dab my mouth. It doesn't make any sense.

"Doctor, there has to be a mistake. I started taking the pills over a month ago, and I only had sex a couple of times after I started the pill."

"How soon after you started taking the pill did you have sex? The pills should be taken with another form of protection for the first seven to ten days to be on the safe side."

I do the calculations in my head. I started the pills four days before we left for Miami and we had sex a couple of days later. *Shit. Shit. Shit. It had been less than a week.*

Dr. Lee gives me a sympathetic smile. "Judging by your reaction I'm taking it this was unplanned."

"Yes, it is. I didn't realize it hadn't been a week since I began taking the pills."

"You know, Liz. Some of the best parts of life are unexpected miracles." She smiles and continues on. "I'm going to write you a referral to see an obstetrician and they can tell you how the baby is and how far along you are."

She types up the referral and hands it to me. "There are many options these days. Until you decide how you wish to proceed, make sure you stay hydrated and start on prenatal vitamins. Make an appointment to see the obstetrician as soon as possible."

I thank her and walk out feeling like I'm in some crazy dream, until another bout of nausea hits, reminding me I'm not in a dream at all. This is my reality. I'm pregnant with a baby from a guy I lost my virginity to, and I wouldn't know how to get ahold of him if I tried. When I said I would always remember him, I thought it would be from memories, not from a baby growing in my belly.

I get home and Kayla's in the living room watching some ridiculous reality show while munching on popcorn. She looks up at me and immediately knows something is wrong.

"Hey, sweetie. How did the doctor go? Do you have the flu?"

"Yeah, I have the flu all right and it'll be over in about eight months."

Her eyes widen as she soaks in what I'm implying. She grabs my hands and sits me down next to her, closing her arms around me tightly. The tears begin trickling down my cheeks as she hugs me close. We don't need words to say what we both know. My life is about to change. Apparently for me, what happened in Miami, didn't stay in Miami.

Six

LIZ

Five years later

HE GRABS HOLD OF MY HIPS AND PULLS ME ONTO HIM, PUSHING *his massive cock deep into my core. I feel so full. I grip his chest with my hands and begin to move up and down as his hands palm my breasts. "C'mon, baby girl. Yeah, that's it. Come for me." I'm so close, just a few more thrusts and I'll...*

"Mom...Mommy...Wake up, please. Auntie Kay is making us yummy pancakes."

Slowly, I open one eye, recognizing I was once again dreaming. Five years of no sex will do that to a woman. I open both my eyes to find my four-year-old daughter sitting on my stomach, smashing my cheeks together with her tiny hands while trying to wake me up. I can't help but smile when I see her bright green eyes looking at me like I hold the golden ticket to the chocolate factory. It's then I remember what today is.

"Mom, I see your eyeballs. I know you're awake."

I laugh as I grab hold of her waist and throw her onto my bed, tickling her. Her giggles bounce off the walls and hit me straight in my heart. As I look down at her, she's smiling from ear to ear and the same butterflies that always take over my stomach when I see that smile invade me once again.

She'll never know her daddy or what he looks like, but when I look at her, he is all I see. Same green eyes, same beautiful smile, same golden-brown hair, and the same naturally sun-kissed skin. She's a spitting image of the man who gave me the best memories I could ever ask for, my daughter. If I didn't have the stretch marks to prove it, I would swear Isabella Faith wasn't even carried by me but by her father instead.

I continue to tickle her belly as she begs me to stop. "Mom, I'm gonna pee myself! You better stop." I'm definitely not taking a chance of that happening. It's too early in the morning to be washing sheets, so I stop tickling her. In return, she huffs and rolls over to sit across from me in my bed.

"And to what do I owe this pleasure of you waking me up at..." I glance at the clock. "Seven o'clock?" I know why she's up and ready to go, but her excitement is so infectious I want to hear her tell me herself.

"Mommy, how could you forget? Today is the bestest day ever! I start preschool today. Duh!" She glares at me with such seriousness I have to hold in my smile.

"Oh my goodness." I pretend to suddenly remember. "How could I forget the most important day of Bella's life?"

She stares at me without blinking, trying to figure out how in the world I could ever forget something so important. As funny as it is to watch her reaction, I know in a few seconds she's really going to believe I forgot. One thing I often wonder is if her father has a temper, because I have no idea where she could've gotten hers from, but my sweet angel can go from zero to sixty in the blink of an eye.

"Of course I didn't forget what today is. You're so silly, Bella. Look at you all dressed up and ready for your first day of preschool. Okay, let me get up, jump in the shower, and get dressed, and I'll meet Auntie Kay and you for pancakes before we head out to take you to school. Tell Auntie Kay to save me at least two pancakes!"

Bella beams at me, shaking her head up and down excitedly. I smack her bottom as she jumps off the bed and runs down the hall to the kitchen, yelling to Kayla to save me two pancakes.

I can't even begin to imagine what I would have done without Kayla in my life these last five years. When I found out I was pregnant, I lost it. How in the world was I going to go to school and raise a baby? Kayla was amazing from day one. She held my hand through my entire pregnancy and delivery. We transformed the third bedroom into a nursery, and Kayla became Auntie Kay. Although, she's more like a second mom to Bella.

The first year was the hardest. After Bella was born, I thought about Cooper constantly. It was almost scary how much she looked like her father. I cried for weeks after I found out I was pregnant and then for weeks after Bella was born. Kayla tried to look up Bentley and Kaden's name while I tried to look up Cooper's, but it was pointless.

We didn't even know where to begin. We didn't know where any of them lived, their last names, or any of their personal information. I did look up MMA and Cooper but wasn't able to find anything.

Kayla was the glue that held all my pieces together. She made sure we took classes at opposite times and on different days so somebody could always be home with Bella. We both also worked part-time shifts at the Bistro to pay for her necessities. So many times, I felt weak and Kayla was there to be my strength.

It took a little longer than planned, but a few months ago we both graduated from ULV. I received my bachelor's in business and accounting and Kayla received hers in physical therapy. Luckily, the sports complex where Kayla did her internship had a spot available and hired her the day she graduated. I was able to take the summer off to spend time with Bella before she starts preschool, but now I need to find a job.

After showering and getting dressed, I make my way to the kitchen, following the delicious aroma of Kayla's homemade chocolate chip pancakes. She doesn't make them often but when she does, I eat them until I'm so full I can barely button my pants.

As I sit at the table and begin buttering my pancakes, I notice my daughter is scarfing hers down. "Whoa there, Angel. You're going to get a tummy ache if you don't slow down. What's the rush?"

She stops chewing and looks at me, her eyebrows furrowing in the same way I can still remember her father doing. "I don't want to be late," she says matter-of-factly through her mouthful of food.

"Bella, school starts at nine o'clock. You're not going to be late.

Please slow down. You won't be going to school if your belly hurts."

She must agree with my reasoning because she immediately slows down eating her food.

I start eating my pancakes, when I look over at Kayla, who is giving me her *I'm up to something* look. The last time she gave me this look I ended up meeting Cooper and got knocked up, so this look seriously scares me.

"I haven't seen that look in a very long time. What are you up to?" I raise my brows in hope that she'll see I'm serious and back down.

"I'm not up to anything. How dare you jump to conclusions?"

"Kayla, let's not beat around the bush. What's going on? I need to get Bella to school and I have a couple potential jobs I want to check out."

"Okay, hear me out before you say no." I go to cut her off, knowing where this is going, but she doesn't allow me to break in as she continues speaking a hundred miles an hour.

"We did it, Liz! We graduated college. We got our degrees. I think we have done a pretty good job with Bella so far. She isn't completely traumatized and she's alive and in one piece. One night with a sitter isn't going to kill you or her. You deserve this. You've focused on school and Bella for the last five years. Please come out with us Friday night. Hayley has tickets to this cool UFC fight and also has an open invitation to the after-party. It's supposed to be off the hook. Please!"

Kayla and I met Hayley while working at the Bistro. She was also going to ULV but a few years ahead of us and majoring in sports medicine. We all instantly became friends and she is over here so often

Bella calls her Auntie Hayley. She got a job a few months back at a UFC training center and is always begging us to come to the fights.

"Kayla, you don't even watch UFC. Why do you want to go to a fight so badly?" I shake my head, trying to figure out her motive. With Kayla, there is always a motive behind her madness.

"Um, hello! Have you seen their hot bodies? I don't care what's going on with the fight. I just want to see their sweaty bodies and maybe do the dirty-dirty with one of those hot guys I'll meet at the after-party," she says, waggling her eyebrows up and down.

Well, that makes more sense. Where there are hot guys, you can you bet Kayla will find them.

I try to keep a straight face, but when Bella cuts in and asks, "Auntie Kay, what's a dirty-dirty?" I can't help but laugh.

Raising my brows, I join in the fun. "Yeah, Auntie Kay, What's a dirty-dirty?"

Kayla's eyes go wide when she realizes what she just said in front of my very impressionable four-year-old and attempts to back slide by telling her it's when people play in the mud together.

Now, I'm laughing so hard tears streaming down my face. Kayla isn't laughing, though. When I look at her through my blurry eyes she's glaring at me.

When my precious daughter responds, I completely lose it.

"That sounds like fun! I wanna go play in the mud! Can Tristan come play with me in the mud? He loves to jump in the puddles and get all dirty!"

Kayla's eyes completely bug out as she looks to me for help. I give her a look that says, *Nope, ain't gonna happen. You got yourself into this mess, now get yourself out.* Now she is full on shooting daggers my way, which is making me laugh even harder.

She looks at Bella and says very calmly, "No, you may not play in the mud with Tristan. Not until you've graduated from college, have a good job, and are married."

Bella looks at her completely confused and begins arguing when I decide to help Kayla out and change the subject. "Oh, Bella, look at the time. If you don't want to be late we better get you washed up so you can be on your way to preschool."

Hearing the word preschool, she immediately forgets all about playing in the mud and getting dirty with boys. Kayla shoots me a look of gratitude and begins to clean up the dishes from breakfast. I mouth to her, "*you owe me.*"

After dropping Bella off at preschool—and crying my eyes out at the fact that my baby is growing up—I head to a couple places to apply for an accounting position. I love numbers so it was a given I would major in business and accounting, but I never imagined it would be so hard to find a job in this field.

After filling out several applications, I make my way to the coffee shop on the corner near our apartment to get a cup of coffee and continue looking for a job. Right after getting my coffee and pulling out my laptop, I get a text message. I check it and sigh. I should've known she wouldn't drop this.

Kayla: Please, Liz. Friday night 7 p.m. UFC fight

Me: Not happening

Kayla: One night out isn't going to make you a bad mom. Pleeeeaaasssseeeee!

Me: I don't even have a sitter.

Kayla: I already spoke to Tristan's mom and she said she'd watch Bella for the night. No excuses!

Me: All night? You know how I feel about leaving her with someone overnight. I barely even let my mom take her.

Kayla: Your mom lives in Florida! You can't compare the two. One night. Bella will love staying up and watching movies with Tristan. You've known Ashley for three years and she's a mom just like you! Plus, she's a teacher! C'mon...do this for me!

Me: Fine.

Kayla: Seriously? You're really going to go?

Me: Yes

Kayla: Your one-word answers are scaring me...

Me: Good, you should be scared. I'm not happy about this.

Kayla: Yay!! I'm so excited. I will be home around 3 so we can go buy new dresses for Friday. C-ya later!

It's Friday night and I seriously can't believe she's talked me into this. I should be immune to the craziness that is Kayla, but I'm clearly not. For starters, I haven't worn a little black dress since before I got pregnant with Bella, and if I remember correctly, it was that damn LBD that got me into that position in the first place. Although, I can't really be upset about it because it got me Bella, and I wouldn't trade her for anything in the world. But that's not the point.

The point is, I don't want to be wearing this dress and going to this fight when I can be home hanging out with Bella until she goes to bed, and then reading one of my romance novels that I live vicariously through since my own sex life is non-existent. *Well, except for in my dreams.*

After our mini-shopping trip, we pick Bella up from preschool, where she explains to us the entire way home in detail every second of every minute of every hour of her first day at school.

"Mommy, I love preschool so much I I've decided I'm going back tomorrow." *Well, that's good because she doesn't really have a choice.*

I do my best to stifle the laugh I have building up because she's being dead serious right now. I guess it's good she's decided she's going to continue her education on her own because trying to force Bella to do something she doesn't want to do is like pulling teeth.

After dropping Bella off at Tristan's house with my friend Ashley, we head over to the stadium. I met Ashley through a mommy-and-me class we attended with our kids and she's probably the only person outside of my family I trust to watch Bella. As luck would have it our kids also ended up in the same preschool class.

Since Hayley had to get there early, since she's working the event, she left us tickets at will-call. We take our tickets and head to our assigned seats.

As I sit here, in my little black dress and heels, looking around at this madhouse of an event, I wonder why I'm so gullible that I let Kayla talk me into this shit. The entire place is packed. Music is pounding through the speakers, women are everywhere dressed to kill, and everybody is clearly pumped for the event. I never realized how popular the UFC is.

It appears Hayley has hooked us up with decent seats. We're sitting pretty close to the front—or the middle I guess? In the center of the arena is a huge stage looking thing with a fence that runs around the perimeter. From where we're sitting, the guys can practically sweat on us when they're fighting. To our left is a black carpet that leads from what looks like the dressing rooms or is it fitting rooms? Shit, I don't even know. It's some type of room where the guys will come out of and walk down the carpet to get to the stage.

One by one the fighters get announced, along with their opponents, to fight. They each have their own song and they walk out almost in a trance. Most of them have an entourage accompanying them, and many of them are wearing headphones.

Each fight goes a few rounds, until one guy either gets knocked out or they both last and the judges tally up the points, and then a winner is announced. I have no idea what they're fighting for, but it must be something major because these fighters are taking this entire thing extremely personal.

Fortunately for Kayla, every guy who comes out of the...locker room (Oh! Maybe that's what it's called.) has to walk by us and she's definitely taking advantage of the situation by snapping pictures left and right.

The fights are crazy to watch. These guys are seriously no joke. I wouldn't last a second in that ring. At the end of every fight they both walk away beat to shit—bleeding everywhere—several parts of their body bruised and broken.

I'm starting to wonder how many of these fights are going to take place tonight—*there's only so much blood and gore a girl can take*—when the lights dim down and it's announced that coming up is the main event of the evening.

The first guy enters to Imagine Dragon's *Radioactive*. He has a hoodie on and is surrounded by a bunch of guys. He is shaking hands and smiling wide for everybody to see, like he knows he's got this shit in the bag. *And hot damn he's a big guy.* I don't know who the other guy is, but I can't imagine anybody beating this guy. Heads are going to roll, and I doubt it'll be this guy's head. He walks to his corner of the ring and his entourage starts getting him ready for the fight.

The music ends and the next song begins. This time, the guy is walking out to Eminem's, *'Til I Collapse*. Like the first guy, he's wearing a hoodie, but unlike the first guy, he keeps his head down and doesn't shake anybody's hand. It's not that he isn't sure of himself...it's more like he doesn't feel the need to be cocky about it like the other guy. He's focused and his song matches his mood perfectly. His entourage following him acts the same way. They walk out determined like they're here to do a job. I take it back, this guy will be the winner. There's no doubt about it. He's about to fuck this guy up.

"Oh. My. God, Liz! Is that Kaden? Wait, is that Bentley?" Kayla starts tapping on my arm, while jumping up and down, trying to get a closer look.

Everything in my world goes still as I finally catch a good glimpse of the guys surrounding the fighter. A loud gasps escapes my lips—not loud enough for anyone to hear over the music and cheering, but loud enough I can hear it. That's when I take a look at the fighter, like really look at him, and I see it, on his right arm is the dragon tattoo I'll never forget.

Holy mother of God, it can't be. There's no way.

My fingers go up to my necklace. The boxing gloves he gave me. He told me he practiced MMA.

Well isn't that an understatement of the year.

Kayla continues to shout at me, but my mind is all foggy and I can't focus on anything but the man walking away from me toward the ring. It feels like the boxing gloves resting on my neck are suddenly burning a hole through my skin. The music stops and the guy on the loudspeaker introduces the two fighters.

"And now three rounds in the UFC Middleweight division. Introducing first, fighting out of the blue corner, this man is a valid judo fighter holding a professional record of twelve wins and zero losses, standing at six feet two inches, weighing in at 165 pounds fighting out of Los Angeles, California. He is The Ultimate Fighter season winner, Damian The Massive Garcia. And now introducing his opponent, fighting out of the red corner with a record of eight wins and zero losses, he stands at six feet three inches, weighing 170 pounds, fighting out of Las Vegas, Nevada, he is Liam The Raaaaaage Cooper."

Holy hell. I can't believe it. A few things come to mind when I hear his introduction. First, Cooper is his freaking last name, not his first name. And that makes me wonder if maybe I did come across him online but didn't realize it.

Second, he's a famous fighter. That explains why he has to stay in shape.

And third, *Rage?* Well, goddamn that explains our daughter's temper.

Kayla and I lock eyes, having an entire conversation without having to say a single a word. What the hell are the chances of running into my daughter's father here?

Seven

COOPER

I STEP INTO THE OCTAGON AND TUNE EVERYTHING OUT around me. I need this win. Not only will it keep me undefeated, but it'll also ensure me a place in the title fight in a few months at the MGM Grand. This is what I've been working my ass off for for the last ten plus years. This is why, after five years of hell from being around my father, I'm still in Las Vegas.

I look around and see my dad in the corner, along with Kaden, who's still my trainer, and Bentley, who hasn't left my side all these years. I know Caleb is out there watching. I don't know what I would do without these guys. They're my fucking rock. I'd never have been able to deal with my dad all these years without them pushing me.

Three rounds. Three. Fucking. Rounds. If I can beat this guy, I'm one step closer to the title fight and everything I've been through will be worth it.

I look out into the crowd like I do before every fight. Watching them scream my name is a complete ego boost, not to mention their enthusiasm helps to get me pumped up. I hear someone shouting Cooper, which isn't something I normally hear. Normally, the fans are yelling Rage. I look toward where the voice is coming from and my eyes lock with hers. I realize it isn't her voice screaming my name but her best friend's.

It takes me a second to make sure I'm not hallucinating. This girl has been in every fantasy of mine for the last five years. The guys have a bet as to when I'll mention her name again. *She's my girl who got away.* There have been times when I was walking down the street and could've sworn I saw her, only to come face to face with a stranger who has a similar skin tone or hair color or the same curvy body. Well, not the exact same, because everything about Liz is one of a kind.

For five long years, I've lived with the regret of walking away and not taking her number or giving her mine. When we first got back and I couldn't stop thinking about her, I asked Bentley if maybe he had gotten her friend's number, but when he said he hadn't, I knew there was no way I would ever find her again.

Kaden screaming my name knocks me out of my fog and our connection is lost. I want to try to find her, but right now I need to focus on this damn fight.

"Bro, what the fuck is wrong with you? Focus," Kaden says, while wiping Vaseline on my face to prevent too much bleeding.

I look over at my dad and see him scowling at me. He can tell I've lost my focus and is wondering what the hell just happened. The few times he overheard the guys and I talking about Liz ended with us arguing. If he knew she was here, he would definitely lose it. I can't even imagine the lengths he would go to ensure my focus remains on fighting.

I know better than to mention anything about a woman to my dad, not if I want to remain on his good side. So, I shake it off for the moment and get my head back into the fight.

Three rounds. Three. Fucking. Rounds. I just need to get through this fight and afterward I'll find her. There is no way I'm letting this girl go again.

Eight

LIZ

SOMEBODY PINCH ME BECAUSE I MUST BE DREAMING. I REMAIN standing, staring at this guy that looks even more like my daughter than I've imagined over the last four years.

I look over at Kayla and she's in just as much shock as I am. No words are spoken. We just watch in silence while the majority of the crowd chants, "Rage, Rage, Rage." Some of the women are holding up signs that say things like "Marry me, Rage" and "I love you, Rage". *Eww!* One sign even says, "You can take your Rage out on me." *I think I just threw up in my mouth a little.*

I'm in shock. I don't even know what to think right now. The many sleepless nights when Bella was first born and would wake up with Colic, I would hold her in my arms and rock her back and forth while I imagined what it would be like to have Cooper by my side. I'd make up scenes in my head where I'm out with Bella and we run into him. I tell him about his daughter and we ride off into the sunset. Okay, not really ride off into the sunset, but you get the drift. Not in any of those scenes did I ever imagine I would run into him at a UFC fight where he's fighting in the main event.

In all reality, does it really matter how I found him? The fact is, we're both here, and I'll finally be able to tell him our short but amazing time together created the most perfect, beautiful, little miracle.

The bell rings, and the fight begins, and Cooper owns up to his name. He goes after the other guy in pure rage. They both go back and forth swinging punches. I wince several times at the hits they're each getting in. The other guy gets him good in the eye, causing it to bleed, but Cooper doesn't even seem affected by it. It's like he's in a zone.

The fight can't be more than a couple minutes in when Cooper throws a punch straight to the guy's chin that knocks the guy to the ground. The referee jumps in front of Cooper to stop him from continuing his attack on the guy who is now motionlessly lying on the ground. The medics run over to the guy to check him out. *Holy shit!* Cooper must've knocked him out cold because the guy still isn't moving. The crowd goes wild. They're screaming and chanting his name. The arena is a damn nut house.

The announcer declares Cooper the winner and raises his arm in the air. He doesn't even crack a smile, but I notice he's scanning the crowd, and when his eyes meet mine once again, he raises his two fingers to his eyes and points at me. Kayla nudges me, a grin spreading across her face. I'm in such shock I can't even move or respond. I try to make my head shake up and down, but I have no idea if it's working.

The other guy finally gets up with the help of the medic and walks out of the fighting ring, leaving Cooper there with his entourage.

I recognize his three friends from the club that night. Time has definitely been good to all of them. Also with them is an older gentleman who looks to be in his late forties, built like Cooper, with the same color hair and eyes. If I had to guess, I would say that has to be his dad or somebody related to him. He doesn't smile like Cooper's friends do. While his friends are patting him on the back and shoulder and giving him hugs to congratulate him, the guy just stands there and stares, the look on his face sending chills up my spine.

Once Cooper is done with his interviews, they all head out of the fighting ring back toward the room they came from. He whispers something into Bentley's ear and Bentley's head shoots up, looking around until he spots me. He smirks and nods his head. While they all head to the back, Bentley stops right in front of us.

"Well, God damn. If it isn't the girl who got away."

His grin gets wider as he looks me up and down, clearly checking me out. Then he turns his head to Kayla and his face morphs from humorous to full-on lust. Kayla never admitted to what happened between them, only that they had sex and moved on, but looking at his expression, I swear he's reliving it all over again, and I'd bet there was more to them than just a wham-bam-thank you-ma'am.

"And her best friend," he adds. "Never thought we'd ever see you two again."

Because I'm still stuck on *the girl who got away* part, I don't hear anything Kayla and Bentley are saying. *The girl who got away? Could that mean he's thought about me?* It doesn't make any sense because he's the one who left that morning without leaving his phone number.

I catch what must be the tail end of the conversation—Kayla telling Bentley we will be there. *Be where? Where are we going?* Oh! She must be referring to the after party. That would make sense since it's for the fighters and Cooper is a fighter.

Bentley nods at Kayla, then at me, and then walks away. This is too much to take in. To think, if I wouldn't have come tonight, I would've missed running into Cooper. This whole time we've been living in the same city. What are the odds?

Nine

COOPER

HOLY. SHIT. MY WORLD FEELS LIKE IT'S JUST BEEN TURNED on its axis. No, more like picked up, shaken every which way, and flipped the hell all over the place. I've spent the last five years imagining what Liz would feel like beneath me again, but I never thought it could become a reality.

I just won my fight. I should be focusing on the fact that I've ensured myself a spot for the title fight. I've worked my ass off to get here. Thinking about this girl is not going to help me get ready for this fight, that's for damn sure. She would be nothing but a distraction if I let her in. Plus, I'd never be able to devote the time to her that she deserves and where would that leave us? All I have to do is take a look at my drunken, cheating mother to remind myself what women are capable of when they don't get enough attention. But damn, when I think about Liz and our short time together in Miami, it feels so different, like the connection we shared could possibly mean more.

Out of nowhere a wet rag smacks me right in my face and I'm

brought back to the present.

"What the fuck was that for?" I ask, looking around to see who threw that shit at me.

"Get your fucking head in the game, boy!" my dad shouts. His face is beet red and a couple veins in his forehead look like they're about to bust open.

"My head is in the game," I tell him, dropping the rag on the ground. "I just won my damn fight, didn't I?"

"No, it's not! I can hear that shit running through your head about that girl. I heard Kaden mention to Bentley that she's here. You want a championship or do you want a piece of pussy?"

I just shake my head—there's no point in arguing with him. I've learned the hard way to just let him say his peace and walk away. He's never going to change his way of thinking and he definitely doesn't care what I think or how I feel.

"I asked you a fucking question, son. You gonna answer or just stare at me?" And at this simple question, I lose it. All the years of keeping it all in finally rises to the surface and boils over.

"Of course I want a championship. Haven't I made it clear over the last five damn years that I've been working my ass off at the gym every goddamn day? Will anything ever be good enough for you? I'm twenty-seven years old and other than having a very rare one-night stand or a drink with the guys, I've spent every waking moment at this gym. I get that mom cheated on you. I've listened to you tell me for the last fifteen years that women are no good. Ever think maybe she cheated because she couldn't stand the way you treat her or your family? And that maybe not every woman is like mom? I've chosen this career over everything. What more do you want from me?"

He stares at me in silence like he is contemplating how to respond to my outburst. For a second I think maybe he gets it, but then he says, "I'll ask you again. Do you want a championship or do you want that piece of pussy out there in the crowd? You can't have both. If you want her, then go—go after her, but don't bother showing up at the gym tomorrow."

I can't even respond. I just simply look at him and laugh humorlessly to myself while I walk away. It feels like for the first time I'm seeing him in a whole different light. I've always known he doesn't see me how a loving father should see his kid, but I never realized how truly unhappy and bitter he is.

Ten

COOPER

I JUMP IN THE SHOWER BACK AT MY HOUSE AND GET dressed. Normally I'd shower at the arena, but I left so quickly I forgot about needing to get ready for the after-party. Bentley and Caleb are meeting me back here and then we're going to ride over to the Kaden's for the party. I head downstairs to see Caleb and Bentley already in my living room waiting on me.

"Are Liz and Kayla coming to the party?"

Bentley is the first to speak up. "Yeah, apparently, they're friends with Hayley, the chick that works as the on-site doctor at the gym. Hayley invited them to the fight and after party. When I went to go invite them, Kayla told me they were already planning to go. What are the odds, man?"

"Seriously, this whole situation is surreal. Get this shit, my dad told me if I go to the party tonight to see Liz, not to show up at the gym tomorrow. I'm done with him running my life. I get I can't be in a committed relationship. Between the fucked up crazy DNA running through me and the insane hours I put in at the gym, I know it'd never work, but I'm not going to just *not* see her. I've thought about this girl for years. I'm twenty-seven years old and he's still trying to run my life."

"I'm going to say this for the millionth damn time, Coop. The shit your parents put each other through and continue to put you through has nothing to do with you. You're just the collateral damage. You deserve to be happy. You don't realize it now, but one day you're going to wake up and wish you would've went after more than just a title. I'm not saying you shouldn't work hard, but find a balance and let someone in. Just because your parents are both unhappy doesn't mean you have to be as well. Fuck them both."

"Bentley, I get you come from a home with two loving parents and all, so you honestly believe what you're saying, but me and you aren't the same. You're okay with where you stand in your career. You fight and enjoy it, but you don't care whether you win or lose. On top of that, cheating isn't in your DNA. I'm already set up to fail in any relationship, and that's without adding my fighting to the mix."

He slowly shakes his head with a sad smile that tells me this conversation clearly isn't going anywhere so he's giving up. And it's for the best, because yeah, Bentley is one of my best friends, but the truth of the matter is we come from two completely different worlds.

I look at Caleb to see if he's got anything to add and he just shrugs. That's one of the things I like about Caleb. He doesn't throw in his input. He does his thing and let's everyone else do theirs. I grab my keys from the bowl near the garage and we head out in my SUV.

The entire ride none of us says a word. I know for me, I have a lot to think about. Liz's going to be there tonight, and judging by the way she looked at me, I think she might have missed me as much as I missed her. But is it right to be with her again, knowing I can't give her anything more? Maybe if I explain it to her, she'll accept me the way I am. I know it's wrong to ask this from her, and I know she deserves more, but I am a greedy fucking bastard and I want her.

We pull up to Kaden's house and can hear the music thumping from the road. He has some nice ass neighbors to ignore all this, that's for damn sure. If I so much as sneeze too loudly in my community, somebody is all over me hitting me up with fines and citations. I've thought about moving to somewhere with more land, but I don't really see the point. It's just me and most likely will always be just me.

For about four years, when we all lived in Colorado, Kaden, Bentley, and I were roommates while Caleb was living elsewhere. When we all moved out here to Vegas, Kaden and I decided to get our own places, and Bentley and Caleb decided to rent an apartment together. I'm actually shocked Caleb agreed, because while he's one of my best friends, he's definitely more of a loner. Nobody really knows much about his life except that when he fights it's like he's chasing off some demons.

I moved into a four-bedroom townhouse in a gated community only a couple miles from the gym while Kaden decided to move a little further out of the city and into a more rural area where the houses are a bit more spread out, which is why the parties always end up taking place at his house.

I park my vehicle along the road but away a little bit so I don't get blocked in, in case I want to leave early. Walking around back to where the bonfire is going, I immediately start looking for Liz. I look over at Bentley and I can swear he's looking for Kayla as well.

After we left Miami, I asked him about her, and he said she was a cool chick but wasn't the girlfriend type. When I asked him what he meant by that, he just shook his head and changed the subject.

There are people scattered everywhere. I walk around the fire pit, over by the patio, and around the side of the house, getting stopped every five seconds by another person congratulating me on my win. I don't want to be rude, so I force a smile and say thanks but try to keep moving along to find her.

When I don't see Liz anywhere outside, I head inside to look for her. Generally, Kaden tries to keep the party outside. He even has people use the bathroom in the guesthouse near the pool instead of in his house. I'm hoping he's made an exception for her because if she isn't inside that means she might not be here. The thought of not seeing her again makes me feel ill. *How did a girl I only spent thirty hours with manage to turn me into such a damn pussy?*

I get inside and go straight to the living room, where I find her sitting on the couch with Kayla and Kaden. I watch her for a second as she throws her head back in laughter, her thick head of curls flying around her face as she continues to laugh with abandon and all I can think is that I want to be the one to make her laugh like that. *C'mon Coop, get that shit out of your head.*

I make my way over to her and it as if she can sense me getting closer. Her back goes straight and she stops laughing. Maybe she hasn't missed me after all. But then I crack a smile and her face completely lights up, telling me she feels something of what I'm feeling.

She stands from the couch and brushes down her dress. It reminds me of the one she wore that night at the club. I take a minute to check her out and notice that time has been good to her. Her looks have matured. While she still has the same beautiful curly hair and amazing tan, her face appears to be less girlish and more woman, her body is still curvy but again womanlier. She's filled out more in all the right places. Don't get me wrong, she isn't by any means fat. She's still fucking perfect. It's just that something is different about her.

Realizing I'm checking her out, she blushes the most adorable shade of pink while covering her front by wrapping her arms around her stomach. I close the distance between us and pull her into me for a kiss. She must be shocked by my actions because she tenses up as I wrap my arms around her waist and seek entrance into her mouth with my tongue.

She finally gives in and gives me access, and in this moment, it feels like all is right in the world. I want this reunion to be soft and sweet, but the moment she exhales into my mouth and relaxes into my arms, I can't hold back. I attack her mouth with mine, nipping at her bottom lip and then the top one. I move my tongue back into her mouth to taste her.

Her hands come up to my head and tighten around my short hair. *God, I've missed this woman.* I run my hands down her back and over her perfect ass, to her thighs, grabbing hold of the back of them and lifting her up. She can feel it happening and immediately wraps her legs around my waist, locking her ankles together.

She pulls her head back and looks into my eyes, smiling, and I know I would do anything to keep that smile on her face. I vaguely hear our friends in the background chuckling and somebody says to get a room. I can't help but laugh at that. This girl could easily become my entire world.

"Kaden, guestroom?" I can't stop looking into her beautiful brown eyes as I ask him for permission to get this girl alone.

"Yeah, yeah," he replies through laughter.

Not taking my eyes off Liz, I walk her down the hallway and kick open the guestroom door. Once inside, I make my way to the bed and sit on the edge with her still wrapped around me.

"Baby girl, do you have any idea how often I've thought about you over these past five years? How many times I wished I had gotten your number? Too many times to count."

She smiles brightly. "I feel the same way, Cooper...or is it Liam? Or Rage? I thought Cooper was your damn name! What the hell do I call you?"

I chuckle at that. "Baby, you can call me any name you want as long as you are naked and in my arms." I wink at her and she shakes with laughter. *I could never get tired of hearing this girl laugh.*

I bring my lips to hers again and kiss her. It starts out soft and slow. I can smell her vanilla shampoo. It's the same smell from five years ago. She continues to kiss me back and then begins to move her body closer, like she is trying to climb up me. It's then I realize she's tightening her thighs and trying to grind herself against me for relief. My girl wants this as much as I do.

Without stopping the kiss, I grip her thighs and flip us over, so she's lying under me. As our kiss becomes ravenous, I take one of my hands and move it down her side to the bottom of the dress and roughly lift it up. When I get it right above her panty line, she puts her hand over mine to stop me from going any further, and I still my movements, wondering if I read this all wrong.

Eleven

LIZ

A few minutes earlier

I'M SITTING IN THE LIVING ROOM OF KADEN'S HOME, talking to Kaden and Kayla. Hayley is around here somewhere, chatting with everyone she knows since she works with a lot of these people. I'm not really paying attention to the conversation because I'm too busy looking around for Cooper. I hear Kayla tell Kaden that he needs to introduce her to some of his hot UFC friends because sharing is caring and I can't help but laugh at my crazy best friend.

And then I feel him before I even see him. When I look over, he's standing ten feet away from me just staring. I don't know what to do, so I stand and look at him. He's checking me out and it makes me uncomfortable. Not because it's him who's checking me out, but because I know my body isn't the same as it was five years ago. I worked hard to get back in shape after I had Bella, but I'm not delusional about my post-baby body. My breasts got larger during the pregnancy and never went back to my original size. My stomach is much softer now and there's a permanent little pooch from the emergency caesarean I had to have when Bella's heart rate decreased during labor.

Luckily, he can't see the stretch marks that, if after four years haven't completely faded, will probably never fade. Thinking about all the hot women who were chanting his name today, begging him to marry them, and wanting the chance to sleep with him, I can't imagine why in the world he would want me now. Instinctively I wrap my arms around my stomach as if that's going to hide anything. Before I can say anything, Cooper's right in front of me, his lips on mine.

At first I'm in shock, but when I feel the way his lips move against mine, I can't help but give in to him. It just feels right. After a few seconds, he lifts me into his arms and I wrap my ankles around the back of him. Words might be being spoken, but I can't hear a damn thing that is being said. The only thing I can focus on are Cooper's hands on my ass and the delicious smell of his cologne invading my nostrils and hitting me right between my legs.

The next thing I know, we're moving down the hallway and into a bedroom. Cooper sits on the bed with me still in his arms and tells me he's thought about me often and regrets not getting my number. Hearing this from him sends my heart soaring. It gives me hope that when I tell him about our daughter, he'll be accepting of her. Not a day has gone by that I haven't thought about this man. I know I haven't spent enough time with him, but when I'm with him it feels like all the pieces of the puzzle are put together.

When I tell him I've thought about him as well and make a joke about not knowing what the hell to call him since he has so many names, he laughs and then tells me I can call him whatever I want as long as I'm naked and in his arms.

Watching him go from the intense fighter in the ring to this sweet, funny guy makes me laugh. I love the many sides of Cooper. He graces me with the most beautiful smile before we go back to kissing. The need between my legs is getting so intense I can't help but try to relieve some of the tension by rubbing up against him. Jesus, I'm like a damn dog in heat! He must realize what I'm trying to do because he flips us both over and pins my body under his.

While continuing to kiss me, Cooper moves his hand down my body and grabs the material of my dress to pull it up. Once it makes it almost to my stomach, I remember that if he looks at my stomach he'll see the scar from my cesarean as well as my stretch marks. As much as I know I need to tell him about Bella, I just want a few minutes for whatever is happening to be just about Cooper and me. Once he finds out about our daughter everything will change.

Afraid of him seeing what's under my dress, I grab his hand to stop him and he stills. I must've sent him mixed signals by doing this because he completely freezes and drops his gaze to mine. Needing to save this without explaining, I do the only thing I can think of and take control.

I slide out from under him and push him down onto his back. He looks confused, but once I move my hands down his shirt and to his pants, his expression goes from confused to pure want.

I move his shirt up enough so I can undo his belt and unbutton his jeans. I unzip his pants and look up at him, silently asking him to lift up so I can pull his pants down. He understands what I want and lifts up while I grab the top of his jeans and yank them down, taking his boxers with them.

Once his cock is free it springs up hard as steel. So many times, I got myself off remembering the taste of this perfect cock in my mouth.

Taking his shaft in my hand, I wrap my lips around it, taking the entire member into my mouth until it hits the back of my throat, causing me to gag for a second.

He goes to stop me when he hears me gag, but I shake my head and go back down again. I start bobbing my head up and down, getting it soaking wet with my saliva. His dick is hard as granite, and I know he must be close because I can taste the precum on my tongue.

Entwining his fingers into my hair tightly, he pulls my face up to his. "Slow and easy, baby. I've been fantasizing about this very moment for too damn long for this to end so soon. I need to take my time and get to know your body all over again."

When he says shit like this, my body comes alive.

"I need to be inside you, baby girl. Please."

His words have me dripping wet. I remove my panties and get on top of him, bunching my dress up so it isn't in the way, but is still covering my belly and scar.

Since I haven't been with anybody but Cooper I know I'm clean, and although I don't consider Bella a mistake, I decided that getting on the shot would ensure I never get pregnant until I'm ready to again.

I hover above his dick, waiting to see if he wants to use protection, when he grabs hold of my waist and slams me down onto him. My core expands and stretches, taking me a few seconds to adjust to his size.

"Fuck, Liz! You're so tight. It is like you were made for me."

If he only knew that he's the only guy who has ever been inside me.

I lean forward, putting my hands on his shoulders to steady myself, when Cooper stills and then raises his hand up from around my waist to my neck.

"You're wearing it. You're wearing the necklace I gave you five years ago." He says this with such amazement in his tone.

"Yes," I choke out. "I've worn it every day since the day I received it."

Pulling my face down to his, he kisses me with such passion that when he pulls away I swear my lips are bruised.

He moves his hands back to my waist and uses his ass to lift up, pumping into me from underneath. The feeling of him in me is amazing. I don't know how I went five years without this.

"Baby girl, you're too tight and too wet on my cock. I'm not going to last. I need you to rub on your clit. I need you to come for me."

I move my thumb to my pussy and gather up the wetness he's created and move it to my sensitive nub. I begin rubbing it in circles while he hits some crazy spot deep within me with the tip of his cock.

"Oh, my God. Right there. Please don't stop." Between the friction of my finger to my clit and his cock filling me so completely, I know I'm about to have a huge orgasm. It keeps building, and what feels like seconds later, I lose it. My body tightens before it releases, and it feels like I'm going to blackout from sensory overload. I scream out Cooper's name over and over again, clearly forgetting where we are.

He must suddenly remember because all too quickly, he's pulling my face down to him and swallowing my cries with his mouth.

Cooper waits for me to ride out my orgasm then flips me over onto my back, his hands on either side of my face, as he starts drilling his cock into me with a punishing rhythm. Within minutes, he finds his own release, pulling out, and coming in his hand.

I look down at him and he chuckles. "We didn't have the whole protection conversation so I didn't want to assume you're covered. I wouldn't be much of a gentleman to knock you up the first time I get back between your legs."

He gives me that damn wink and stalks off to the bathroom that's attached to the room. A few minutes later he comes back with a small, wet washcloth and wipes between my legs to clean me up. I feel myself blush at this action, as if him doing this is even more intimate than what we just did.

"C'mon baby, don't get shy on me now."

I smile at him and then get up to go use the bathroom. I grab my panties and put them back on while I go pee. I flush the toilet and wash my hands. Looking in the mirror I see my reflection. My face is flushed, my hair is a mess, and my eyeliner is smudged, but I can honestly say I can't remember the last time I looked and felt this content and satisfied and...taken care of. I know what, or I should say who, caused this look and this feeling in me. Cooper. He invokes these feelings inside me that nobody else ever has.

I just want to cuddle up in his arms and never lose the way I feel in this moment. Now I just have to pray when I tell him about Bella he won't run the other way.

I walk out of the room and find him sitting on the end of the bed dressed again. I take a second to watch him and notice his head is in his hands and he's slumped over. My initial thought is, *did I do something wrong? Does he regret this?*

He must sense my presence because he looks up and tries to play it off by smiling way too big, but it's too late because I already saw. I wait for him to explain, and when he doesn't, I go over and sit next to him. I want so badly to put my arms around him or take his hand, but I have no idea where his head's at so I sit close but refrain from touching him.

I swallow the thick lump in my throat and summon up the courage to ask what I'm thinking. "Cooper, did I do something wrong? I mean, do you regret what we just did?"

His head flies, and his eyes meet mine, his expression softening. "Why would you even think that? Of course, you didn't do anything wrong. I could never regret being with you. It was perfect. You're perfect."

I hear the words he's saying, but the thickness of his voice tells me something's wrong regardless of him trying to convince me otherwise. Now my mind is running all over the place. *Does he have a girlfriend? Did he just cheat on her? Oh, God. Am I a homewrecker?*

Going against my initial instincts, I take his hand and put it into mine, needing to touch him in some way. He looks at our joined hands and gives me a small smile.

"Liz, there's something..."

"Cooper, I need to..."

We both laugh, but I can feel the uneasiness between us. It's like a wall is being put up and I can't get over it fast enough to get to his side.

"You go first." He's clearly upset and I think I'll explode if I don't find out why he's done a complete one-eighty.

He sucks in a deep breath and releases it with a sigh. *This can't be good.* My heart feels as though it's going to implode in my chest while I wait impatiently for him to speak.

"Liz, when we met five years ago I wasn't looking for love. As you can see now, I'm a fighter. It's my entire world. I told you a little bit about my dad during our time together, but there's so much more to it. I won't get into all the details, but what you need to understand is, I can't give you what you deserve."

My hands begin to shake and the lump in my throat is back. I can see where this is going, and it's clear we're not on the same page at all. Even if he doesn't want me, all I can hope for is he'll at least want our daughter. I hope he doesn't think I was trying to trap him. What if he doesn't want her? How will I tell her that her father doesn't want her? I need to calm down. I'm getting ahead of myself. He hasn't said anything yet.

"I never thought in a million years I would ever see you again. The connection we shared in Miami ruined me, baby girl. You ruined me. If I was looking for love, I'm pretty damn sure you would be it. No, I am damn sure you would be it. You're beautiful and sweet and so damn innocent. How you're still single is crazy. Some guy is going to figure out how amazing you are one day, and when he does, he'll grab hold of you and never let go. The problem is I'm not looking for love and I'm not the guy for you. I don't do commitment and I'm not husband or father material. I don't plan to ever be in a relationship where the girl requires either of those roles from me."

The entire time he's saying all this, his head is down like he's ashamed of himself and can't look me in my eyes. Finally, he looks up and gives me the saddest smile I've ever witnessed, and my heart plummets into the pit of my stomach. My heart beats erratically, making me feel as if I'm having a mini heart attack. He doesn't stop there though, so I try to remain calm to hear him out.

"When we hooked up in Miami, we both knew it was a one-time thing, but then when I saw you tonight at the fight, my head started to spin. I never thought about what I would do if I saw you again. I reacted without thinking. What we did tonight was wrong. The fact is you deserve the entire world. You deserve the husband and kids and goddamned white picket fence and the happily ever after, and I can't give you any of that. I never should've touched you knowing I have no intention of being with you in any way but physical."

"Why can't you?" That's the only thing that comes out of my mouth in response to what he just said. Is it that he doesn't want any of that or is there something stopping him from being able to have it all?

He lets out long sigh and says the words I was praying he wouldn't say. "I don't want any of that." I can feel a panic attack coming on, my heart shattering into a million pieces. The air is leaving my lungs, and it's hard to breathe. I need to get out of here before he sees me lose it.

He doesn't want it.

He doesn't want me.

He doesn't want our little girl.

He doesn't want to be a part of our lives.

I get up slowly from the bed and will my body to hold back the tears that are forming. "I understand."

As I head out of the door, I pray he doesn't try to stop me because I don't think I can hold my emotions in much longer.

As I run out the door, I hear him calling my name, but I don't stop. I can't stop. I don't know how I read this all wrong. I'm definitely no expert in the love department, but I was way off. We aren't just on different pages...we aren't even reading the same book. I don't think we're even browsing the same genre at this point. It's like I'm in fantasy and he's in non-fiction.

I walk quickly through the house looking for Kayla. I need her and I need to get out of here now. I need to go pick up my daughter and hold her.

I find Kayla standing outside with Bentley by the bonfire. She's laughing and touching his chest while he rubs his hand up and down her arm. Are they on the same page? They're both smiling and laughing but apparently that doesn't mean anything because Cooper and I were laughing and smiling and now my heart is breaking. At least he was honest with me and didn't lead me on, but maybe he should've told me all this before we had sex. At the same time, I'm glad I had this time with him. I refuse to regret it.

The truth is I'm not even mad, I'm just sad. I really just need to get out of here. Only a few more minutes. I need to hold it together for a few more minutes and then I can let go.

Bentley spots me coming over and nods my way. Kayla looks behind her and I know she can see the pained look in my face because she drops her hand from Bentley and runs over to me.

"What the hell happened, Liz? What did he do to you?"

"I can't talk about this here. Please. I need to leave. If you want to stay, it's fine. I don't want to ruin your..."

Kayla doesn't even let me finish the sentence before she cuts me off. "Stop! Stop it right now. You know damn well I have your back and there's no way I would *ever* stay at this party or anywhere else for that matter when you need me. Let's go."

She takes my hand and pulls me alongside of her to the car in silence.

As we're walking down the driveway, I hear Cooper scream my name once again. I attempt to run, but he catches up quickly. I get to the car and turn around to see him standing right in front of me. I can't say anything. I'm choking back the tears, and if I say a single word, the tears are going to release.

Cooper looks at me like I'm the one who just broke his heart as he lifts his hand up to my face to touch it. It's then I feel it, the wetness he's wiping off my cheek. *Damn traitor tears.* He wipes one on the other cheek away and chokes out, "I'm sorry." No sooner are the words out of his mouth, his back is turned to me as he walks away.

I want to scream at him, run up behind him and pound on his back. I want him to take back every word he said in the last ten minutes. I can handle him not wanting me. I can handle not having him. Yes, it hurts like hell, but I can handle it. I'm strong and know I can make it through anything, but the fact he doesn't want our daughter drives a sword right through my heart.

However, I don't go over to him, and I don't scream at him. I accept his decision because I would rather know now how he feels than take a chance of him hurting our daughter. It's for the best that it's over before it even began.

I get into the car and wait until Kayla is out of the driveway to cry. I cry for my little girl. I cry for the fact that she has a father who doesn't want her. I cry for my innocent, sweet angel who'll never know a father's love. For years, I wished to run into him so I could tell him he has a daughter. Well, you know what they say, *be careful what you wish for...*

While we're driving, Kayla tells me it's probably best to leave Bella with Ashley for the night. It's already after two in the morning and picking her up would mean waking everybody up in the house. As much as I want Bella in my arms, I agree with her, so we head to our apartment.

We get home and I'm surprised Kayla hasn't jumped on me to tell her what's happened yet. I get in the shower and let the hot water burn my skin. I grab my loofa and squirt some soap onto it, scrubbing down my body and wishing I could scrub away all the hurt I feel inside me right now.

When I can't take the pain in my chest anymore, I sink down to the floor of the shower, letting the water beat into the back of my skull. I close my eyes and let the tears fall as I make a new wish—to go back five hours and not see Cooper because then I can have it in my head that my daughter's father doesn't see her because he doesn't know about her, not because he doesn't want her. I make a deal with myself. When I get out of the shower, I'm going to start fresh. Looking back it's almost like I put my life on hold in hope one day Cooper would come back. Now that I know how he feels, it's time to move forward. I refuse to be some pathetic woman who wants a man who doesn't want her back.

Kayla knocks on the door and I realize the water's gone cold. I stand, turn the water off, and get out. I look in the mirror and promise myself I'll never cry over Cooper again.

Hearing the knocking still coming through the door, I yell out that I'll be out in a second, then grab a towel, dry myself off, and put on some comfy pajamas.

I take several deep breaths, then head out to the living room where I find my best friend sitting on the sofa with two pints of our favorite Sorbet ice cream and a bottle of sweet white wine. She hands me a spoon and pours us each a glass. Ice cream and white wine is our thing. For a second, the urge to cry again hits me, but when I look at Kayla, I remember that while Cooper may not want us, I'm surrounded by people who do.

We sit in comfortable silence, eating our ice cream and sipping our wine, when she finally brings the subject up. "So, what happened? You guys were practically dry humping in the living room before you went to the bedroom. You come out and it's like somebody just told you there's no Santa Claus."

I have to laugh at that, and then I look at her and scowl, which makes her laugh. When we were nine years old, I spent hours writing my letter to Santa. When Kayla came over to play one day, she saw it on my desk. I asked her if she wrote her letter yet and when she said no and she isn't going to, I asked her if she believed in Santa. Kayla told me flat out she didn't believe and that he was fake. It was the first and only fight we ever got into. I told her she was a liar and that I couldn't be friends with somebody who lies. Santa was real. She told me I was acting like a baby and kept insisting there wasn't a Santa. I went to my mom and demanded to know the truth. She admitted there was no Santa and I swear I cried for like three days.

"Remember after my mom admitted there was no Santa, what you said to me?"

She thinks for a minute. "Yeah, I told you I wish I would've lied and said Santa was real because I hated to see you cry."

"Well, right now I'm wishing I could've been lied to."

She waits for me to continue, but when I don't, she prompts me. "Lied to about what?"

I start from the beginning when we went into the room. I tell Kayla how he said he missed me and wished so many times he would've gotten my information. I tell her about us making love and how attentive and sweet he was the entire time. She laughs when I tell her how he pulled out and came in his hand because he said it wouldn't be gentlemanly of him to knock me up.

"Boy, if he only knew that ship has already sailed. Wait, does he know about Bella?"

I breathe in, and let out a cleansing breath, as I prepare to get to the hard part.

"I never got a chance to tell him. After we got cleaned up and dressed, he got all weird on me. It's like a switch flipped in him, and he went from sweet and flirty to depressed and sad. Before I could tell him about her, he flat out told me he can't...no, he told me he doesn't *want* to offer me any type of future. He said I deserve everything he can't give me. When I asked him why, he said he doesn't want to be a husband or a father. I didn't even know what to say. My heart just broke thinking about one day having to tell Bella her dad isn't around because he doesn't want her, so I decided not to tell him. At least then I can be honest and say he doesn't know about her. After he said all this, I got up and left, and that's when I found you and you know the rest."

"So, he doesn't know that Bella exists?"

"That's what I just said. What was I supposed to say? 'Oh, that sucks you don't want to ever get married or have kids because surprise, you have a daughter.' Um, no. I wasn't about to open myself or Bella up for him to tell me flat out he doesn't want our daughter."

Kayla stays silent for a minute thinking. "Maybe he only said that because he doesn't know he has a daughter. Sometimes we don't know what we want until it's right in front of us. Maybe if you tell him he has a daughter he'll change his mind. When he said all this to you, it was strictly hypothetical, right? He wasn't actually saying he doesn't want Bella. It's like when you send me to the grocery store with a list and I end up picking up a ton more junk food than you told me to. You don't even know you want it and you don't miss it because you don't have it, but once I get home and put those yummy brownies on the counter, you can't help but eat one. No, you didn't put the brownies on the list, but once it's right in front of you, you still want it, right? Maybe right now Cooper doesn't think he wants a kid, but once you show him Bella, I bet he'll totally want her."

I stare at her for a second thinking about what she just said then bellow out a laugh so hard, my stomach cramps up. "Did you seriously just compare my daughter to a brownie? We're talking about a living, breathing, innocent tiny human being. Not a piece of chocolate."

Kayla laughs and then gets serious. "Well, she is as sweet as a brownie, and once you get to know her, you're addicted."

And this is why Kayla's my best friend. She knows just what to say.

Twelve

COOPER

IT'S TWO IN THE AFTERNOON AND I'M PRETTY SURE DEATH is knocking on my door. After Liz left last night, I tried my hardest to forget about her, but I should've known by now, that girl is unforgettable. As proof, several hours and a bottle of Jack later, not only did I not forget about her, but I couldn't take my mind off her.

At one point my drunken ass wanted to go after her, but Bentley told me to leave it be until I was sober. Being drunk and trying to talk to her wouldn't help the matter. I finally passed out in Kaden's guestroom to the smell of Liz's sweet scent all over the bed.

Now I'm in the gym fighting against Bentley and I'm pretty sure I'm sweating out the entire bottle of Jack through my pores. My head is pounding and I'm close to throwing everything in my stomach up.

"So now that you're sober, what do you plan to do about Liz?" Bentley asks while throwing a punch to my stomach.

I dodge it, and sigh in relief, almost positive if he'd connected, I would've thrown up all over the ring. I stop fighting and bend over panting like I haven't worked out in years. He walks over and punches me in the arm, while chuckling at my pain. *Asshole.*

"There's nothing to do. For one, nothing has changed from last night to today. She deserves to be with a man who can one day marry her and gives her kids. I can't be that man. I would never want her to go through what my parents have gone through. And two, even if I wanted to take back what I said, it wouldn't matter because I didn't get any of her information. I wouldn't even know how to contact her."

Bentley looks like he's going to give me another one of his lectures but changes his mind. "You're aware her best friend works at this gym, right? And even if she didn't, I got Kayla's number last night."

I shoot my head up. *Shit, this is a game changer.* How will I ever be able to stay away from her knowing I have access to her? It was easier when I thought by not having her information, the choice was made for me. Now, knowing I can get ahold of her, makes me second-guess everything.

Of course, my dad decides to come over at this moment, and by the look on his face, I can tell he overheard our conversation.

"Bentley, if you want to stay training at this facility, I suggest you make choices that help Liam and not hurt him. I would recommend you throw that number away and both of you focus on what's important." First, he points to me. "You have a title fight in six months you need to be training for."

Then he points to Bentley. "And you need to stop fucking around and take this shit seriously. Any more losses and you're going to be removed from this team. I can't have you tainting my gym's reputation.

I signed you up to fight against Dante Cobalt. The fight is in two months. You need to win this. Understand me?"

Bentley looks like he's about to rip my dad's throat out, so I jump in and tell him we understand so he'll walk away. Bentley turns to me, fuming. "Bro, why the hell do you let him talk to you like that? If it wasn't for your reputation, this gym wouldn't be doing half as popular as it is. It's you that brings the people in. Fuck him."

I get what he's saying, but it's pointless to argue with either of them, so I just shrug my shoulders and head to the locker room to try and wash away some of this hangover. I need my mind clear if I'm going to figure out my next move.

Thirteen

LIZ

KAYLA AND I ENDED UP TALKING THROUGH THE NIGHT while enjoying our ice cream and wine. On my way to Ashley's to pick up Bella, I can't stop thinking about what Kayla said to me about Cooper. She's right in a sense. He doesn't know he has a daughter. I think I need to tell him about Bella and leave the ball in his court. If he still doesn't want anything to do with her then at least I can say I tried. I don't want Bella to grow up one day and think I purposely kept her father from her.

I pull up to Ashley's house and am barely out of the car, when Bella barrels out of the door, leaving it wide open. She throws herself into my arms, and I pick her up, holding her tight as she pulls her head back and gives me the most adorable toothy grin. "I missed you sooooo much, Mommy! Did you miss me?"

"You bet I did. I missed you to the farthest, brightest star and back."

Her eyes go wide before she starts to giggle. "Mommy, you're so silly. You can't miss me that much. The stars are like infinity miles away!"

"Well, that's how much I missed you. Did you have a good time with Tristan?"

"Yes! We played Uno like a gazillion times and I won more times than him." Her voice goes lower like she's telling me a secret. "But I saw he was getting sad, so I let him win so he would be happy again."

I look at my little girl and feel so proud to call myself her mother. She's so caring and has such a huge heart. I can't imagine not having this beautiful little miracle in my life. If Cooper doesn't want her in his life, he's the one losing out.

She hugs me again and thanks me for letting her spend the night here. I tell her she's welcome and decide for sure I'm going to tell Cooper about Bella. Whether he wants her in his life or not, he deserves the chance to make the decision.

Then it hits me...I left the party without getting his information again.

After having coffee and chatting with Ashley, we head back home to find Kayla passed out on the couch, limbs sprawled out, looking like she's barely breathing. This is what happens when she drinks too much.

Bella walks up to her slowly, placing her fingers under Kayla's nose, and smiles at me.

"Whew! Don't worry, Mommy, I can feel her tickling my finger. She's okay."

I try not to laugh at the fact that my daughter just confirmed Kayla's not dead.

"Bella, you're silly. Of course, she's okay. She just fell asleep on the couch watching TV. Why don't you bring your backpack to your room and empty it out and I'll make you some cereal?"

"Ooo-kay, Mom!" She drags her backpack full of toys and clothes she brought to Tristan's last night down the hallway to her bedroom.

"Hey sleepy-head, wake up!" I yell into Kayla's ear, causing her to jump a half a mile into the air and grab her chest like it's about to explode. She looks around and then glares at me.

"Was that necessary? After I stayed up all night comforting you with ice cream and wine, that's how you repay me?"

I ignore her question and ask the one that's been on my mind since I left Ashley's. "You don't by any chance have any of the guys' numbers from last night, do you? I made the decision to tell Cooper about Bella and then realized I, once again, didn't get his damn number."

"You're in luck. I just so happened to get Bentley's number last night."

"Oh, awesome. Wait a second, you, miss no commitment, miss one-night stand, miss no strings attached, miss never get a guy's number or give him yours, actually got a guy's number?"

"Trust me, I didn't ask for or want it. When I set my phone down on the counter to pour myself a drink, he stole my phone and wouldn't give it back without calling himself from my number so he could have mine. I was seriously pissed, but it looks like it was for the best, because now I can look in my call log and we can get Cooper's number from him."

She gets out her phone and pulls up the number from the recent calls list and hits call. She waits a beat and gets the voicemail. After a few seconds, she hangs up and starts typing on her phone.

"What are you doing?"

"I got his voicemail, so I'm texting Hayley to find out the name of the gym. Okay, here we go. She said it's called Cooper's Fight Club and it's only ten minutes from here. Here's the address. This should be something you do in person." She sends the address to my phone and it beeps with the text from her.

"Isn't it crazy that for the last few months Hayley has been working with these guys and we had no idea?"

"Seriously! To think Cooper was so close this whole time is mind blowing."

"Okay, just pull the address up on your GPS and head over there."

I don't think I can do this in person. It's one thing to tell him about Bella over the phone where I can't see his looks, but to tell him in person feels like I'm making myself too vulnerable to him.

Kayla must sense what I'm thinking because she doesn't give me a chance to protest. She is literally pushing me out the door as she yells for Bella to get her cute butt to the kitchen to help make pancakes.

"Go. Go tell Cooper about Bella and we'll be here when you get back. I got her. Everything's going to be fine." *I really hope she's right.*

I follow the directions on my GPS and pull up to what looks like a state of the art gym. The building is huge and looks like it is three stories high. It's all by itself in its' own complex. The entire front of the building is made of mirrored glass and there's a huge sign that reads:

COOPER'S FIGHT CLUB
HOME OF UFC'S OWN 'THE RAGE'

Directly underneath it, is a life size *Cooper* in a fighting stance in gym shorts and nothing else. He has his hands up in fists and he's glaring in the photo. It looks so real, it's scary. I would seriously hate to get on his bad side.

I stand outside of the door for a few minutes, staring at his picture and trying to muster up enough courage to tell the man who told me less than twenty-four hours ago he doesn't want a wife or kids that he does, in fact, have a kid.

Just when I finally decide to put on my imaginary big girl panties and go inside, the door swings open and almost smacks me in the face. I jump back, immediately recognizing the person holding the door open. It's the older guy from the other night, no wait, from last night. *Jeez has it only been less than a day since the fight? This has seriously been the longest twenty-four hours, ever.*

He clears his throat to get my attention and I smile at him. If I'm right, this man could be Bella's grandfather. He doesn't smile back, though. In fact, the glare Cooper has on that poster on the wall has nothing on the daggers this man is shooting me with right now. Instinctively, I back up a little and get control of myself.

"Hi, my name is—" I'm not even able to get out my name before this guy cuts me off.

"I know who you are and I know who you're looking for. You're wasting your time. He doesn't want anything to do with you."

Well, okay then. I try my best to keep a smile on my face. "That may be true, but I need to speak to him, nonetheless. It's very important."

"Well, he's not here, and even if he was, he made it clear he doesn't want to speak to you."

The way he says it leaves no room for argument, so I simply say okay and walk back to my car. I'm not about to get into a fight with this man. Something about him feels off.

Fourteen

LIZ

THE REST OF THE WEEKEND'S SPENT LAZILY LOUNGING ON the couch while watching movies with Bella. Of course, her latest favorite is Disney's *Maleficent* so we have to watch it twice.

The second time we're watching it, when the mom dies, Bella turns to me with a sad look on her adorable face. "Mommy, if you die, who will take care of me since I don't have a daddy?"

I look at Kayla and she gives me a small encouraging smile. I really need to tell Cooper about her. This isn't about anybody but Bella.

"Angel, first of all, I'm not going anywhere. However, if something did happen to me, Auntie Kayla would still be here and so would Grammy and Papa and Uncle Mattie even though they live in Florida. You would never be alone."

I hope this will satisfy her, but of course it doesn't. She's way too inquisitive to accept that answer.

"Okay, Mommy, but where's my daddy?"

I've always known this question was coming, but nothing prepared me for the pleading look in her eyes when she asks it. I'm her mother, which means it's my job to protect and love her. It's my job to make sure she always feels wanted and never hurts, especially when I can help it.

"Umm..." I'm totally stalling, having no clue how I'm going to explain any of this to her. Thank God for Kayla's quick thinking.

"Oh, my goodness! Bella, I just remembered I have all the ingredients to make a batch of fudge brownies. Want to help me?"

Bella's eyes light up and she jumps up and down cheering, "Yes. Yes. Yes," forgetting all about the Daddy question for now.

Of course, when Kayla blurted out that she has the ingredients what she really meant was she has no ingredients. So now we're on our way to the grocery store to pick up the stuff to make the brownies. I want to be annoyed, but I can't be because she totally saved me. I have no idea what I would've said to Bella about her daddy. There's so much going on in my head, but I know that the first thing I need to do is corner Cooper and tell him he has a daughter, even if he wants nothing to do with me. Once I know whether or not he wants Bella in his life, I can figure out my next move to ensure my daughter doesn't get hurt.

We walk up and down the baking aisle, gathering all the ingredients to make my mom's famous fudge brownies. Once we have everything we need, we're heading to the checkout line, when I hear, "Excuse me Miss, I think your daughter dropped this."

I turn around to the familiar voice and stare into the same beautiful green eyes my daughter has.

I'm stuck frozen in place as I catch the recognition in his eyes.

First, that it's me he's speaking to, then at the fact he just referred to Bella as my daughter. His eyes turn cold and hard, his body visibly tensing, as he places all the pieces together in his head.

Slowly, I take the raggedy pink stuffed flamingo from him. "Thank you."

Luckily, Bella breaks the uncomfortable moment with her sweet little self. "Mommy, my flamingo! I didn't even see it drop." She turns to Cooper. "Thank you. I love my flamingo. Mommy gave me it when I was a little, little, tiny baby, and she said it's very special to her because somebody special gave it to her. You know what else I love?" She doesn't even wait for him to answer. She just keeps on going in typical Bella fashion.

"I love *Maleficent*. It's my most favorite movie ever. And there's a dragon in the movie. I want the dragon so he can be friends with my flamingo. I asked my Mommy to buy me the dragon, but she said I have to ask Santa. Do you know how far away Christmas is? Like a gazillion trillion days away. I will die before I get my *Maleficent* dragon."

I laugh quietly at her ranting away to Cooper. It's her favorite movie right now, but by next month it'll be something entirely different. I must be smiling outwardly because Cooper cocks his head to the side like he's waiting for me to fill him in.

"She has a different favorite movie every month."

One of his brows quirks up, and I realize that's not what he was referring to. *Oh, shit.* He wants me to address the elephant in the room, or in our case the adorable four-year old standing next to me.

"Mommy, let's go! You promised we would make Grammy's

brownies. Auntie Kay is waiting for us."

She grabs my hand to pull me away, ignorant to the silent conversation currently taking place. When I don't move, she looks up at me with a questioning stare.

Of course, this is the moment when Kayla decides to end her phone call outside and comes walking over oblivious to what's happening. How she doesn't see Cooper standing there boggles my mind. The guy is like a damn wall. He takes up so much space, it's impossible not to notice him.

"Hey Liz, what's taking so long? I thought for sure you would be done before I got off the phone with my boss. Now I'm craving some vanilla ice cream to go with the brownies." She laughs but stops when she takes in the intense situation in front of her.

"Oh, fuck," she spouts out before covering her mouth, remembering there's a little person right here.

"Ooooohhhhh, Auntie Kay! You said a bad word." Bella starts wagging her finger at Kayla like I do to her when I'm upset with her. Even though she's so damn adorable, this does nothing to break the awkwardness surrounding us. Cooper is watching all of this probably thinking we're nuts.

"Yes, I did. I'm sorry. I shouldn't have said that. Bella, why don't you come help me find the vanilla ice cream to go with our yummy brownies?"

She doesn't wait for her answer as she grabs Bella's hand and drags her along, giving us both one last glance before disappearing down the aisle.

"Is she mine?" *Well, damn, I guess we're going to dive right in.* There's no reason to deny it at this point.

"Yes, she's yours."

"Did you plan to ever tell me about her?" Is this guy serious right now? Judging by the look on his face, I think he's dead serious. If looks could kill, I would be in a puddle of blood on the ground right now. Well screw that and screw him. He has no right to be mad at me. I didn't do anything wrong.

"When would you have liked me to tell you, Cooper? When I found out I was eighteen and pregnant with no way to contact you since you never gave me any information on you? Or how about the other night when you made it clear you wanted nothing to do with ever being a husband or father? Or maybe I should have screamed it from outside your gym when your asshole bodyguard told me that, according to you, I'm not welcome there, and you want nothing to do with me. When should I have told you that we have a daughter? Huh, Cooper?"

His face softens for a second and then goes hard again. "What fucking bodyguard? You came to the gym? When?"

"I showed up yesterday morning, determined to tell you about Bella, and before I could make it in, some asshole guy, who looks a lot like you, stopped me and said he knew who I was and that you want nothing to do with me, leaving me no choice but to leave. I was planning to try again, but I needed to figure it out in my head how to handle it. None of this is going how I spent the last five years imagining it would. I'd never keep your daughter away from you even if you don't want anything to do with either of us."

He looks so pissed I swear smoke is about to come out of his ears. That rage better not be aimed at me. "I can't believe him. I told him to mind his own business." I tilt my head to the side confused. Is he talking to me or to himself?

"That must have been my father. He makes it a point to get into my business when it can possibly take my full attention away from fighting. God forbid I do anything that messes with his potential income."

It's clear there's huge animosity between Cooper and his dad and that saddens me. I can't imagine not having my dad as part of my support system. It doesn't matter that he lives across the country. He's there for me in every way that matters, same as my mom. They've always been my two biggest cheerleaders supporting me, even from afar.

When I found out I was pregnant with Bella they begged me to move home so they could help me, but I knew if I did, I'd never graduate from college. Bella and I try to visit them a few times a year and they come up to Las Vegas to visit us as often as possible as well. Since we're long distance, Bella video chats with them on the computer often.

I hear Bella's excited voice coming back down the aisle and remember we're having this conversation in the middle of the grocery store.

"Look," I say quickly before she gets within hearing distance, "I tried to find you when I found out I was pregnant, but I had nothing to go on. When we had sex, I was on the pill. I just didn't know it wasn't effective yet. I've tried to tell you a few times since I found you, and I'm sorry it never actually came out, but I never intentionally kept this from you. When your dad insisted you wanted nothing to do with me, I thought you told him to say that. I was still going to find you to tell you, though. I get you don't want to be with me..."

He attempts to interrupt me, but I don't have time to argue, so I shake my head and continue talking faster.

"...but I would never keep a child from her father. If you want her in your life, we can figure it out, and if you don't then that's on you. I get you don't want kids and a wife and I respect that. I know I should be sorry I messed up with my birth control but I'm not because Bella is my beautiful little miracle. You need to decide what you want and either way I won't hold it against you. I just don't want her to know anything until you decide. It would break her heart if she knew you knew about her and didn't want her. So, think about what you want. None of this is Bella's fault."

I grab his phone and dial my number into it and hear the ringing on my phone.

"Here's my number. Call me when you decide. But Cooper, think hard because she deserves more than a guy to claim her as his just because he thinks it's what he is supposed to do, and then change his mind later because he doesn't really want her. You can hurt me all you want, but you will not hurt our daughter."

And with that, I hand him back his phone and head into the checkout line. He grabs me by my wrist, looks deep into my eyes, and says, "You gave her the flamingo I gave you." He doesn't ask. He states it. He remembers.

I nod my head quickly and then he nods back before walking away as Kayla and Bella walk over to join me.

"You okay?" Kayla whispers.

"Yeah, let's go make some yummy brownies and ice cream."

"Finally," Bella huffs out, and we laugh at her impatience.

Fifteen

COOPER

TOTAL. MIND. FUCK. THAT'S WHAT I FEEL RIGHT NOW AS I watch Liz walk out of the store holding hands with my daughter. *Our daughter. Liz and I have a daughter.* We created that precious little girl five years ago. I have a daughter that I had no idea about and it's my own fault for walking away that day and leaving her no way to contact me.

She looks like a perfect, beautiful mixture of Liz and me. She has my green eyes and light brown hair, but it is curly like Liz's. She has tanned skin just like the both of us, and when she smiles I can see a piece of my mom in her from her happier days.

For the last fifteen years, I've told myself a wife and kids will never be in my future. After watching my parents destroy each other and our home, I never want to put anyone I care for in that position, which means there has never been any room for love in my life. But looking at that precious little girl and her mother walk away from me makes me want to run after them. I can't believe my dad actually told her I wanted nothing to do with her. He and I are definitely going to get a few things straight.

I jump in my car and head back to the gym and go straight to his office. He's finishing up a phone call, so I wait. He looks up at me without a smile and I'm once again reminded of how miserable this guy really is. I don't think he's smiled in years. He has no real friends and he hasn't dated that I know of since my mom. I can't imagine living my life like this.

"To what do I owe this pleasure, Son? Are you planning on training at all today or are you taking a page from Bentley's book and are simply here to take up space?"

To think for a second I almost felt sorry for him. The truth is he's chosen to live this way. He's chosen to push everyone away, including his own son, and now, without even realizing it, he tried to push away the mother of his granddaughter. I've had enough.

"I'm so sick of the way you treat everyone around you. We all bust our ass at this gym yet nothing is ever good enough. You walk around here all high and mighty, putting everybody down. I get Mom cheated on you, but did that make it okay to destroy her? And what the fuck did I ever do to you? I have tried to love you and be a good son to you, but you don't want love and you sure as hell don't want me as a son."

He leans back in his chair, annoyed that I am ranting to him. "What's got your panties in a twist now, *Liam*? I don't have time for this. Get to the point, please." I hate when he calls me Liam. It's why all my friends call me Cooper. Since I was little, he would only use my first name when he was upset with me.

"All right, I'll get to the point. Did you tell Liz I want nothing to do with her and then send her away?"

"Yeah, I did. You don't need that distraction and she definitely doesn't need to be coming in this gym looking for you. Keep your pussy where it belongs, in the bedroom!"

It takes everything I have not to punch him in his face. I only refrain myself because I know if I do punch him I'll be falling into his trap. He's always looking for a fight.

I do and say the only thing I can, because at the end of the day the only person I can control is myself. "I'm done here. I'm done with you and this fucking gym and I doubt that you even care, but I'm done being your son. Find a new moneymaking machine for this gym. I. Am. Fucking. Done."

I turn to walk out the door and he calls my name. For a second, I hope he'll apologize, tell me to come back in, and want to make this right, but I know deep down that's not his style.

He lifts his chin and says, "Don't bother coming back when you destroy your entire career over a piece of trashy pussy. You're a disgrace to this gym and to the UFC. Close the door on your way out."

I don't even bother to respond. Instead, I simply shake my head and walk out. He'll never change and I'm done living my life like this. If his advice is to stay away from Liz, maybe I should do the opposite because I'll do anything to not end up like him.

I head to the locker room to gather my shit. Once I have it all and am about to leave, Bentley and Kaden come walking in. Seeing all my stuff in my hands, they look from me, to my now open, empty, locker, and back to me again.

"Are you seriously leaving? Where are you going to go?" Kaden asks. I know he's concerned because he's under contract with this gym. He can't train me if I'm not training here.

"I have no idea. I just found out my dad sent Liz away when she came here yesterday to tell me that...get this shit, I have a daughter."

"Oh, shit."

"What the fuck."

"Yeah, I ran into Liz and Bella—that's her name—at the grocery store. She looks just like me. It's crazy. Apparently, she was scared to tell me because I pushed her away by telling her I didn't want a wife or kids the other night. She got the guts to come here to tell me anyway, feeling I should know about my daughter, but my dad decided to be my personal secretary and tell her I didn't want to see her. He actually sent her away. I went to his office to confront him and not only did he admit to it but he defended his actions. I told him I'm done here. I just can't do this shit with him anymore."

Both of them are looking at me with sympathy in their eyes. They've seen the shit I've gone through with my parents for the last several years.

"So, what are you going to do?" Bentley finally asks.

"I don't know. I just need some time to think. I'm going to head home and take a few days to figure this all out. Liz told me I'm either all in or all out as far as our daughter goes, and I don't blame her. Bella deserves to have stability in her life. I need to think about all this. You guys should have seen her. She's so adorable and so freaking smart, and she has my attitude."

The guys laugh at that.

I take a deep breath, then release it and continue. "I just don't know if I can be the dad she deserves. Look at the example I had growing up. A dad barely home, who put his career above his family, then when his wife cheats on him, he lashes out and destroys her entire world, turning her into a drunk. And where does that leave Liz and me? She's been doing this on her own for four damn years because I walked away without giving her my number. She doesn't need this shit in her life. She had this image in her head of what it would be like when I found out and I fucked it all up before she could even tell me. I just need to wrap my head around all of this. I don't want to make their life worse."

Kaden and Bentley both nod in understanding. I'm sure they want to say something, but they can sense I just can't deal with it right now.

"I'm gonna head home. I'll let you guys know what I decide."

"Bro, you know I got your back. If you're sure about leaving this gym, I am too."

I nod and give Bentley a small smile to thank him.

Kaden adds, "You know I can't leave here, but whatever you need from me, I got you. We'll figure this out."

I pat him on this shoulder and thank him, then I walk out of the locker room and out of the gym for what I believe will be the last time.

Sixteen

COOPER

IT'S BEEN FIVE DAYS SINCE I WALKED OUT OF THE GYM. I haven't spoken to anybody during that time. I've started going for a run in the morning and in the evening down by the lake in my neighborhood. Years of training for hours a day keeps me from being able to just sit at home and do nothing. I've had some time to think about what I want to do now that I'm away from my dad and the gym. I'm thinking about joining another training center to get me through this title fight and then taking some time off.

Between all the wins I've had over the last ten years, my contract with the UFC, and the several endorsements and sponsorship deals I have, I have a nice cushion in the bank.

It sucks that Kaden won't be able to train me anymore, but I just can't be around my dad. His latest stunt was the last straw. I've been thinking a lot about Bella and Liz and where I want things to go with them. I need to spend some time getting to know my little girl and her mother. Now that I know I have a daughter, I need to step it up as a dad and make sure I'm nothing like mine. Then there's Liz and me...there was definitely a connection there between us both times we hooked up, but I don't know if I fucked it all up beyond repair when I said all that shit to her. When she was going on and on at the store she made a comment about me not wanting to be with her, but she never actually said she doesn't want to be with me, so maybe there's still a chance for us to get to know each other.

I glance at my phone ringing and check the caller ID hoping it's Liz, but it's just my mom. I send it to voicemail, having too much going on in my head to deal with her right now. I'm not surprised Liz hasn't reached out to me since the day at the grocery store, but I was still hoping she would. She obviously meant it when she said she was leaving the ball in my court so I'm going to need to call her soon so we can talk.

My phone rings again, and I see it's my mom, again. I haven't had a real conversation with her in almost two years. She calls and leaves voicemails occasionally, and I text her back that I'm busy. She doesn't usually call back to back, so I answer it in case it's important.

"Hey, Mom, sorry, I was just out running. Everything okay?"

I can hear her sniffling into the phone but she hasn't said anything yet.

"Mom, are you drunk?"

She starts crying harder. "No, I'm not drunk. If you could ever stand to speak to me for more than five seconds you would know that."

I cut her off, not having the patience to deal with her right now on top of everything.

"Okay, Mom. If you aren't drunk then what's going on? I'm kind of busy right now."

I can hear her sigh into the phone. "Liam, it's your father. He had a heart attack."

"Is he okay?"

"No, sweetie, he's not. I'm sorry but he didn't make it. I guess he never updated his emergency contact information, so they called me."

I sit in the grass and stare out at the lake. I don't know whether to be happy or sad about this. For years, I wished he would just disappear, but I never wished him dead. He was so damn unhappy all the time. I just wish he could've found a way to be happy before passing away. He never even knew he had a granddaughter. Shit, my mom doesn't even know she has a grandmother.

"How did it happen?"

"The doctor said he was feeling chest pains, so he went to the ER. While running tests he had a heart attack and they couldn't revive him. The tests they ran afterward said he showed signs of smoke inhalation, which is weird because he doesn't smoke. They said they found traces of soot in his lungs as well as fluid. They think he might've been in a fire and the fluid in his lungs most likely lead to the shortness of breath, which caused him to have respiratory failure. I'm here at the hospital now. Can you come down?"

"Yeah, I'm heading back to the house now. I'll be there as soon as I can."

"Okay, sweetie. I'll see you when you get here."

I hit end on the phone and begin jogging back to the house.

Respiratory failure from smoke inhalation? It doesn't make any sense. *Where the hell was he that he was inhaling smoke?*

Seventeen

LIZ

Three Hours Earlier

"BELLA, IF YOU DON'T GET OUT OF BED RIGHT THIS INSTANT I'm going to hide *Maleficent* from you!" I yell down the hall to my sleepyhead daughter as I finish getting dressed.

I have an interview at an accounting firm and, if we don't get moving, I'll never make it across town in time. I don't know what I was thinking agreeing to an interview so close to when I have to drop Bella off at school.

The first week of school went great. She was so excited to be going, she was up and ready before the crack of dawn. Now, the newness has worn off and she's back to wanting to sleep until noon. Not happening, especially not today. I finish putting on my heels and run back to her room to make sure she's up and getting ready. The fact that she didn't respond to my threat of taking away her favorite movie isn't a good sign.

I walk inside her room and sure enough she's still curled up in her sheets with her little head poking out softly snoring away.

"Bella Faith! You've got to get up. Did you hear me? I'm going to take away *Maleficent* for a week."

She pushes her covers down just enough, so I can see her attitude peeking through. "Oh, Mommy, you can have it because it's not my favorite no more. Dolphin Tale is my new favorite." See? Didn't I tell you? New movie every month!

She starts to contemplate something, and if I wasn't running so late, I might find it funny. Then she actually has the nerve to say, "Mommy, if I get out of bed, can we go buy a dolphin? I want a *Winter!* Pleeeease!"

And with those words, I draw the conclusion my daughter could be a professional hostage negotiator, and to be honest, at this point, I probably would buy her her own dolphin just to get her out of bed, but I'm definitely not going to tell her that. Parenting rule number one: You don't give in to the battle. You give in once and it's all downhill. At this rate, by next week, I'll have to buy her a car to get her out of bed.

"Bella Faith Browning." I'm trying hard to keep my composure because you can't let the enemy know you're sweating. "No, I will not buy you a dolphin, and I'm not negotiating with you. They belong in the ocean! Get up now."

She starts giggling. Yup, actual full-on giggling. I have no clue what she thinks is funny, but in a second I'm going to send her butt to the ocean to play with the dolphins!

"Bella what is so funny? Please get out of bed."

"Mom," she says between giggles. "I don't want to buy a real dolphin! I want to buy a cute squishy one at the toy store. One that is grey and smooth just like Winter the dolphin. Duh! Where would we even put a real dolphin? Wait a second, can it fit in the bathtub? How big is a real dolphin?"

Once again, Kayla, my savior, comes to the rescue.

"How about you go to your interview and I'll take Bella to school? I have the morning off. They're cutting back hours at the sports center." She's sporting a sad smile, which tells me her loss of hours is really upsetting her even though she doesn't want me to worry.

God, I'm such a crappy friend. Kayla works so hard and she's stressing out since she's the sole provider in this house. I really need to get this job. She's done so much for us over the years. I need to pull my weight around here as well.

"Okay, thank you," I say, as I glare at my darling daughter who's back to snuggling under the sheets. I'll deal with her later, hopefully after I'm gainfully employed.

"Wish me luck." I kiss Bella on the forehead and give Kayla a one-armed hug before I rush out the door, hoping I'll be coming home employed.

I'M AT THE INTERVIEW AND IT'S NOT GOING WELL. FIRST OF all, my phone keeps vibrating in my purse, which keeps distracting me. On top of that, the gentleman, Bernard, who's running the interview is speaking in a monotone voice and looks like he's bored out of his mind to be here. I know. I know. Do I really expect a job that involves crunching numbers to be fun? I guess not, but I think he should at least look somewhat happy to be here. If this is how I'm going to look if I get a job here... No, thank you.

My phone vibrates in my purse again, and he looks at me with a brow raised, daring me to answer it. What the hell, I'm not going to take this job anyway. What if it's an emergency?

I excuse myself for a moment to take the call. "Liz, thank God you answered." I glance at the screen, but it doesn't have a name on the caller ID.

"Um, yes, it's me. May I ask who's calling?"

"Liz, it's Bentley. Listen, there has been an accident. Kayla and Bella are both in the hospital. I was here getting my hand checked out and saw them come in the ambulance. You need to get here right away."

Without bothering to explain anything to Bernard, I grab my purse and, with the phone still to my ear, run out the door with a million horrible thoughts going through my head. "Okay, I'm on my way. Bentley, are they okay? What happened?"

"I don't know. I'm not family so they won't tell me anything. Apparently, you're Kayla and Bella's only emergency contact and they've been trying to reach you. I would get down here now."

After telling him once again, I'm on my way, we hang up.

As I drive down the highway, I feel like I'm having a panic attack. Not having any idea what's wrong causes me to consider every worst-case scenario possible, and as a mom, those scenarios are really freaking scary.

After going at least twenty over the speed limit, and running every light and stop sign on the way, I make it to the hospital and run up to the front desk in a panic.

"Hi, I need to find out what's happened to Kayla Peterson and Bella, I mean Isabella Browning. I was told they were brought in by ambulance. Do you know where I can find them?"

The nurse gives me a small smile and types on her computer. "Isabella Browning is the children's wing, room 245C, and...Kayla Peterson is in the patient recovery wing around the corner, room 156R. It says here they were brought in for smoke inhalation."

My heart starts beating even faster, my lungs feeling like they're having trouble working. It's suddenly hard to breathe. *Oh God, my poor baby and Kayla.* "Smoke inhalation? What happened? Are they okay?"

"I'm sorry, ma'am. Unfortunately, I can't answer either of those questions. It does say both are stable. If you want to head to the children's wing, the nurse there can fill you in."

I thank her and head to the children's wing first. I hate that I can't go to both of them, but I know Kayla would understand the need to get to my precious baby first.

When I reach the second floor, the sound of a child crying causes goose bumps to prickly my skin. Every mother knows her child's cries. Not only is it the sound of child's cry, but it's a cry of pain. I pick up my pace and rush into her room, and what I see, breaks my heart. There are what looks like two nurses and a doctor standing over Bella while trying to hold a mask over her face. She has an IV in her arm and she's thrashing around crying. The nurse is trying to soothe her, but isn't having any luck.

I make my way to her bed and lock eyes with my little angel. Her eyes are red and blotchy and filled with tears. Her cheeks are stained pink, telling me she's been crying for a while. The doctor and nurses try to speak to me, but the only thing I can focus on is getting to my baby and hugging her. I wrap her into my arms, holding her close, and attempt to inhale her shampoo, but it doesn't smell right. I can't think at the moment what it smells like, though. She's okay and that's all that matters right now. I can feel her pulse and her heart beating, and that means she's okay.

Bella sobs against my chest, her hot tears spilling onto my skin. I pull my face back a little, trying to kiss away those tears as I rock her back and forth the best I can from next to her bed, murmuring softly into her ear, "It's okay, baby. It's okay. Mommy's here."

She finally calms down and the doctor begins to explain what's going on. "I can't give you the specifics of what happened since the police and firemen haven't come in yet, but according to the EMT's that brought your daughter in, she was in a fire."

I gasp and look down at Bella to reassess her. She looks okay. I do a mental inventory of her body parts, looking for any indication she was in a fire. Her arms look okay and her face is perfect aside from the tearstains. I pull the bedding down to check her legs and everything looks okay. When I get a closer look, though, I notice she has soot all over her hair. I sniff her again, recognizing what I smelt is smoke, like what you smell when you sit around a campfire too long.

I bring my attention back to the doctor and he continues. "When she came in, she was coughing very badly. We hooked her up with a saline drip to make sure she's hydrated and when you walked in, we were trying to get her to put an oxygen mask on to help the oxygen flow. We did a scan and her lungs are clear. She's very lucky, ma'am. The man who saved her covered her face with a wet washcloth, which kept the smoke from entering her lungs."

I feel like I'm in a nightmare. I have no idea where Kayla and Bella were or why they were with a man who needed to save Bella. "Thank you, doctor..."

"Dr. Maven. Please let me know if you have any questions. I'd like for your daughter to breathe into the oxygen mask as much as possible and we're going to keep her overnight to monitor her to be on the safe side."

He gives me a smile, and I shake his hand. I sit next to Bella and thank God she's okay, and that's when I remember Kayla.

"Um, nurse..." I look at her nametag. "Nurse Holly. Is there any way you can stay with my daughter for a few minutes? My best friend was brought in with my daughter at the same time and I have no idea how she's doing."

"Absolutely. I'll be happy to keep Bella company while you go check on your friend." She turns to Bella and bribes her with an iPad to play with if she can put on her oxygen mask for a few minutes. Bella gives in, of course, because, really, what child would turn down the chance to play electronic games? I give Bella a kiss on her cheek and tell her I'll be back soon.

I head down the hall to the adult recovery wing and press the button on the elevator to go down. I need to call Bentley to thank him for getting ahold of me and to let him know where Kayla's room is. As I'm getting on the elevator, I'm staring down at my phone, and without realizing it, I run straight into the wall. Only, it's not actually a wall, but a beautifully fit man, and that man is Cooper standing in front of me. My breath catches and he looks just as confused to see me.

"Did you come here to see Bella?"

"Um, no. I came here to see my dad...well, not see him...Wait, Bella is here in the hospital? Is she okay?"

He visibly begins to panic, so I grab his hand to calm him down. "Yes, she's here, but she's okay. I don't really know what happened. I was actually just heading to see Kayla. This is all so crazy. Both of them were brought in by ambulance. Bella inhaled smoke, but the doctor said she's okay. However, they're keeping her overnight to be on the safe side. I haven't had a chance to see Kayla yet, so I don't know how she's doing or what the heck happened. I guess some guy was there and saved Bella. I really need to find out who he is and thank him. The doctor said he saved her life."

When I notice that Cooper has visibly paled, I stop rambling. "Cooper...are you okay?"

Eighteen

COOPER

I CAN FEEL MY HEART SHATTER. I MEAN, I CAN ACTUALLY feel the pieces falling apart as Liz tells me our daughter was brought to the hospital. I don't even know this little girl, but I can feel it in my heart and in my bones when she tells me about what happened. To think I could have lost her before I even got to know her. What was I thinking taking time to consider whether I should be in her life? I'm her father. It's not her damn fault I was raised in a shitty situation. That little girl deserves the world and she deserves for her father to be in her life. I have so much to make up for.

"...I guess some guy was there and saved Bella. I really need to find out who he is and thank him. The doctor said he saved her life."

I suddenly feel sick when I hear Liz speak these words. What are the odds that my dad's cause of death is the same reason my daughter was brought into the hospital? Something is definitely off. It's all way too much of a coincidence. She stops talking and looks at me closely, then asks if I'm okay.

I clear my throat. "Yeah. Yeah, I'm okay. If you're going to see Kayla, who's with Bella?"

Liz straightens up, and it hits me I just asked that too harshly. She probably thinks I'm judging her. I quickly back track before she flips out. "I'm just asking because I can go stay with her if you want. I mean, if it's okay...you know, while you go make sure Kayla's okay."

Her body relaxes and she gives me a small smile, but it isn't her usual happy one. It's got a sad tilt to it.

"I would like that Cooper, but..." She stops for a second to consider what she's going to say next and then sighs loudly. I can tell she's exhausted, so I don't give her a chance to explain. I get it. I might be Bella's dad, but she doesn't even know me.

"You don't have to finish your sentence. I completely get it. She doesn't know me and seeing me would only confuse her. It's okay. I'm really glad she's okay. I was actually meaning to call you. I've thought about everything the last few days and I'd really like to be a part of your and Bella's life, if it's still on the table, that is."

She gives me a soft smile and then wraps her arms around my waist. As she hugs me, her body shakes with soft sobs. I can't even begin to imagine how emotional she must be, and I have no words to comfort her, so I put my arms around her back and rub circles to try to soothe her, just letting her cry it out.

After a few minutes, she calms down, then backs up and gives me a shy smile. "I'm sorry. I don't know what came over me. I'm glad you want to be a part of our life. That makes me very happy. I better go check on Kayla."

Her phone rings from her back pocket, and after looking to see who it is, she answers the call. "Hey, Hayley, I'm so glad you called… Yes, we're at the hospital now, but Bella and Kayla are in different wards…Great, thank you so much…Okay, bye."

She turns to me and looks a little calmer. "That was Hayley. Bentley called her and told her we're here. She's going to come and stay with Kayla tonight, so I can be with Bella."

"That's good. I've only known Hayley for a few months from the gym, but she seems really nice. She's a good asset to the gym."

"I can't believe she's been working with you the last few months and I had no idea you were working with her." She laughs softly.

"Yeah, it's crazy. Do you mind if I join you in visiting Kayla? I think Bentley is in there with her."

I need to get to the bottom of all this, and since Kayla was there, I'm hoping she'll help me get some answers. Luckily, Liz agrees to me joining.

We get to Kayla's room and Bentley's sitting by the side of her bed, holding her hand. Kayla's eyes are closed, and I can't help but think the worst. She must hear us approach because she opens her eyes and starts crying, and although she looks devastated, at least she's alive and okay enough to cry. Liz runs over to Kayla and gives her a hug. They both cry for a few minutes and then calm down.

"Oh, God, Liz. I'm so sorry. I don't even know what happened. After you left, Bella asked for ten minutes more in bed so of course I gave in because I'm a softy. I went back to my room to browse the online classifieds to see if there's anybody looking to hire a physical therapist. I must have dozed off because the next thing I know the fire alarm was going off. I immediately ran to Bella's room to check on her and to see what was going on, but when I stepped into the hallway the whole apartment was filled with smoke. I ran to Bella's room, but it was empty. I started freaking out. I checked her closet, under her bed. I screamed her name several times.

"That was when I started to choke on the smoke, but I swear to you, I kept looking. I went to the bathroom to see if she was in there and I couldn't find her anywhere. By then I heard the fire sirens so I knew they would be there soon, but I kept looking." At this point, Kayla is crying hysterically, tears pouring down her cheeks.

"I started to panic and ran to the kitchen. The smoke was just too much and I blacked out. She could've died and it would've been my fault. I'll completely understand if you hate me. I hate myself. I just don't know what happened. Nothing was on. It doesn't make any sense. Anyway, the next thing I knew I was in the ambulance and they were giving me oxygen. I told them there was a little girl in there and they said she was already out. I thought maybe she got herself out, but the EMT said some guy got her out. I don't know who, though, maybe a neighbor. I'm just so thankful she got out."

"It's okay," Liz says. "I could never be mad at you. Yes, things could've ended badly, but thankfully they didn't. I know you would give your life for Bella. I'm just so glad you're both okay."

As they're talking, there's a knock on the door and in walks a police officer with two firemen. Hopefully we'll get some answers from them because right now I have some crazy thoughts going through my head.

"Hello, ma'am. I'm officer Jim Kelley and these two gentlemen are the ones who showed up to your home to put out the fire. This gentleman, here"—he points to the guy on the right—"pulled you from the fire." They both give a small nod and smile. "I'm glad to see you're okay. Is it okay to speak to you in front of everyone?"

Kayla says yes and informs the officer that Liz is Bella's mom and they all live together.

"Unfortunately, everything in the home was destroyed from the fire. After assessing the situation, we've determined the cause of the fire was intentionally started from arson. We were able to pull up the footage of the security cameras and we have a shot of a guy entering your apartment and leaving, and then entering again. The first time he enters he's carrying a small can of gasoline. What's odd, though, is that he's also the man who saved your daughter."

As he says this, he glances over at Liz, hoping she can help him figure out the confusion. He hands her a grainy-looking picture and she gasps loudly, dropping to her knees. She looks up at me with such confusion in her eyes and I already know who she's looking at in that photo. I can feel it in my bones.

She puts her hand out and I take the photo, looking at it closely. I can tell right away it's my father, and there's no reason for him to be anywhere near where Liz lives.

"The man in this photo is Marc Cooper. This is my father."

The police officer must know what Liz, Kayla, and Bentley don't know yet, that my dad is dead, because he looks at me with a look of sympathy and simply nods his head.

Liz stands and I can see the fire in her eyes. Mama bear is pulling out her claws. The problem is the man she plans to go after for answers is in the morgue.

"Cooper," she spits out. "Where is your dad at? I want to know what the hell happened. Why was he at my apartment? Why did he torch it and then save my daughter? I don't even know what to think right now. I need to find him."

She takes a deep breath before she continues. "If you don't want to tell me, fine! You want to save the man who could've killed Kayla and *our* daughter? Fine! I'll find him my damn self."

As she goes to leave, I grab her arm and spin her around to face me.

"He's dead, Liz. My dad is dead."

Nineteen

LIZ

DEAD. HIS DAD IS DEAD. THE MAN WHO TORCHED MY HOME, destroyed everything in it, and nearly killed my daughter and best friend, only to turn around and save my daughter, is dead.

I back up against the bed and sit on the edge in shock. I don't even know what to think or how to feel at this point. This is just one big cluster-fuck. He looks at me with tears in his eyes and I don't know whether they're in mourning over his father or the fact that his father almost killed his daughter.

"Did your dad know about Bella?"

He shakes his head. "After I found out you came to see me, I confronted him and we got into a huge fight. I told him I was disowning him and I quit the gym. He blamed you for me leaving the gym. The only thing I can think of is when you left to go to your interview he went in to torch your place. He must not have known you lived with Kayla and have a daughter. Once he realized somebody was in there he must have gone back to save her. Only he didn't realize Kayla was in there or maybe he couldn't make it back in. He died from a heart attack caused by smoke inhalation. I'm so sorry, Liz. This is exactly why I didn't want to be in a relationship or create a family. My life is so fucked up. This is why I told you that you deserve more."

Bentley walks over to Cooper and gives him a hug, telling him he's sorry for his loss. "I know you two didn't get along, but I never thought he was capable of this."

Cooper doesn't say anything. I can't even imagine how he feels right now knowing his father is the one who put our daughter in danger and then saved her.

I walk over, wanting to comfort him. I place my hands on his forearms, but he flinches at my touch. "I'm sorry for your loss. Your father shouldn't have done what he did, but I'm grateful he made the right choice in the end to save Bella."

He takes a step back and looks at me with a resigned face. "It's probably for the best we didn't tell Bella I'm her father. Neither of you need this in your life. I'm not good for you. I'm sorry."

As he walks out the door without looking back, I repeat the words he said in my head.

I'm not good for you. I'm sorry.

Those words hit me like a dagger to my heart. I've waited for five years for this man, hoping to one day find him, and without even discussing it with me, he makes the decision for both of us to walk out of my life once again. I clutch my hands to my heart in a pointless attempt to ease the pain as I close my eyes, trying to keep the tears that are threatening to release at bay.

The police officer and firemen let us know the report will be available later today to pick up for the renter's insurance and then excuse themselves.

I look over at Kayla and Bentley and start to cry. Kayla waves me over, and I climb into bed with her. I cry for Cooper and the loss of his father. For Kayla and what she went through, worried sick about my daughter and almost dying while trying to save her. I cry for my daughter who was almost killed by her grandfather, who she'll never meet. I cry for the man I care about, who doesn't think he's worthy of love. When I'm all cried out, I wipe my eyes and sit up, moving back to the bottom of the bed.

"Now what?" I ask Kayla.

She sighs heavily. "It'll be okay, Liz. We'll figure it out. We always do." And I know deep down, she's right. With Kayla by my side, we can get through anything.

Bentley clears his throat, and we both look over at him. I completely forgot he was even in the room. He gives us a small smile and says, "Why don't you go back to Bella, and I'll stay here with Kayla. When they're both ready to be discharged tomorrow, you girls can come stay at my place. You've met Caleb. He lives there with me, but he's usually working or at the gym. We have a guest bedroom and, although it isn't huge, we can get a small bed for Bella and it'll give you a place to sleep until you figure things out."

I'm so choked up by his generosity, I just nod.

Luckily, Kayla speaks up and thanks Bentley for the both of us. I give Kayla and Bentley a hug and then head back to Bella's room for the night. I run into Hayley on my way out, but I have a feeling she won't be needed after all.

WHEN BELLA AND KAYLA ARE DISCHARGED THE FOLLOWING morning, we head over to Bentley and Caleb's place. It's a decent sized condo in the heart of downtown Las Vegas.

We walk in and I'm thankful Bella's old enough to know better than to touch stuff because this apartment is definitely not kid friendly. Bella goes to the couch to find the controller while pouting that there probably won't be anything good to watch, when Bentley points her in the direction of a stack of movies that's almost as tall as she is. She squeals in delight as she starts naming every Disney movie known to man. I smile at Bentley and thank him.

"Don't thank me. Coop came by last night after you left. When he found out you guys were going to be staying here, he went out and bought all that. There are also clothes for you, Kayla, and Bella in the room. He wasn't sure of your sizes, so he had to guess. He said the receipts are in the bags in case you have to exchange anything. There are some toiletries in the bathroom, and he also bought toys and a bed and sheets for Bella. It's all in the guest room as well. He bought all types of groceries, which are in the fridge and pantry, since all we had was water and beer. He said if you need anything else to let me know and he'll make sure to handle it."

I'm awestruck. For him to go out of his way to make sure we're taken care of is so thoughtful, yet it's also saddening because he's made it clear he doesn't want to be part of our lives. He most likely bought all this stuff out of guilt for what his father did even though it's not his fault.

"How is Cooper doing?"

"Not good. He and his mom decided to just hold a small funeral instead of something big. He told his mom that his dad didn't deserve a funeral after what he did, but she insisted they needed to do something. She probably wants Cooper to have some kind of closure. The funeral is in a couple of days. I despise his old man, but I'm gonna go to support Coop. If you need anything, just let me know. I'll have keys made up while I'm out tomorrow. If you hear somebody coming in late at night it's probably Caleb. He works security at a club and casino on the strip, so he gets in late."

With that, he pats Kayla on the shoulder and kisses her cheek then excuses himself to his room.

I know Cooper made it clear he doesn't want to be part of our lives, but I can't just let him bury his father and not be there for him. I decide then that I'll be at that funeral. Not for his dad, but for Cooper. He needs to see that his father's choices aren't his own. I don't blame him, and he shouldn't blame himself either.

Twenty

COOPER

AFTER GETTING EVERYTHING SITUATED WITH THE FUNERAL director, my mom asks me to go to dinner with her. We head out in my vehicle to the local steakhouse I know she loves. Once we're seated, she looks at me softly and says, "We need to talk." I nod, indicating for her to go first.

"When I met your father, I fell in love immediately. Things progressed so quickly that he soon became my entire world. We were inseparable and within a year we were married and a year after that you were born. At first, your dad was so sweet. He was completely devoted to us. He was boxing, but he never allowed it to take over his life. Once he started winning and felt that sense of accomplishment, he clung to it. I was home with you and we were close. In some ways, I think your father resented that my world no longer revolved around his. He would go away for boxing matches, and where I would've gone with him before, I chose to stay home with you. Please understand I'm not in any way blaming you. I just think we had different priorities and we grew apart. There were times when he would be gone for weeks and I became very lonely. Sure, I had you, but it's not the same thing as being with another adult. I tried to fix us, but when I realized we were just going through the motions, I sought comfort elsewhere.

"I know I was wrong. I just felt like he didn't even notice we were there anymore. I didn't want to disrupt our house. My affair went on for five years. When you were twelve, he threw out his back while training and had to come home. He was so miserable, abusing the drugs, and drinking. He missed fighting. I told him I wanted a divorce and when he refused, I admitted to having an affair. He threatened to take me to court if I didn't give him primary custody. Losing you was the worst thing that ever happened to me. I didn't care about him. You cried several times that you wanted to stay with me, but every time, he would tell me that he would destroy me if I tried to get custody. Then, when I had to watch him put all his effort into training you because he wasn't able to fight, I just lost it. I started to drink. But here's the thing. I stopped drinking five years ago."

I open my mouth to say something, but she holds up her hand, motioning to let her finish.

"It's true, I have not had a sip of alcohol in five years. I wanted to be a part of your life so badly, but when you told me you were moving back to Vegas to work with your dad, I knew the best thing I could do was keep my distance. Your father was a miserable, spiteful person, and if he knew you and I were close, I was afraid he was going to take it out on you and your career. I just couldn't do that to you. I don't know if it's too late, but I'd really like to be in your life."

I feel like everything I thought I knew is wrong and I don't really know anything. My parents weren't fucked up. My dad was. My mom made choices she felt were best to save me from him, just as he made choices that led to the life he lived.

I reach over and take my mom's hand. "Of course you can be a part of my life and there's something you should know. I recently found out that I have a daughter, which means you are a grandmother. It's a long story, but her name is Bella and she's four years old. She is the most perfect little princess I've ever seen."

She cups her hands over her mouth and silent tears pour down her face. "Oh, sweetheart, I can't wait to meet her. Thank you!"

"It's time for a fresh start, Mom."

And it really is. I need to get through this funeral tomorrow and then I need to go over to Bentley's to get my family. They don't belong with him. They belong with me. Hopefully I can convince Liz to give me a second chance.

THE FUNERAL IS FILLED WITH PEOPLE WHO'VE ASSOCIATED with my dad in some way the last several years. He may not have been liked, but I have to hand it to everyone who showed up to pay his or her respects.

I feel a hand on my shoulder and when I turn around I see Liz. "What are you doing here?"

"I came to support you. Whether you like it or not, you're the father of my daughter and he was her grandfather."

This woman's selflessness knows no bounds. I pull her into a hug and thank her. As we're breaking apart, my mom comes walking over and introduces herself to Liz.

"Mom, this is Liz. She's Bella's mother."

Liz looks at me bewildered. The last she heard I wanted nothing to do with our daughter or her.

"Oh, sweetie! It's a pleasure to meet you. My son told me all about Bella. I'd love to meet her."

"Of course. She's at home with my friend Kayla right now, but I'm sure we can arrange something soon."

My mom gives her a hug and excuses herself to speak to other people who are here to pay their respects. When she leaves, I look at Liz and give her a soft smile. "I know you just settled in at Bentley's, but I would really like for you and Bella to come and stay with me."

She looks dumbstruck for a second, but it quickly morphs into anger. She pulls me by my hand into a private room away from everyone else and closes the door behind us.

"What changed from the other day to today? You do remember telling me you wanted nothing to do with our daughter or me, right? And that was after you said you did. You are giving me whiplash, Cooper. You've changed your mind like five times. How do I know you won't change your mind, again? Sorry, but Bella and I are just fine where we are. As soon as I find a job, we'll move out. If you want to get to know your daughter, fine, I won't stop you, but you can't expect us to just move in with you after you've played ping-pong with my emotions. I already gave you one chance and you threw it out the window the second shit got rough."

I know she's right, but shit, I've lost enough time with them. I need to take a step back and take things slow, so she doesn't freak out on me anymore.

"Okay, I understand," I say, as I close the space between us.

Needing to touch her in some way, I run the back of my hand down her cheeks. She freezes, unsure of what my motives are, and I hate that I've created this awkwardness between. Leaning down, I kiss the side of her mouth and whisper into her ear, "For now, I understand. I get I have to earn your trust, and I will. And once I do, you'll be in my bed, and in my arms, that's a promise." I leave her to think about everything I just said because I'm not playing around. I'm going to get my family back.

Now, I just need to get this damn funeral over with.

A FEW DAYS AFTER THE FUNERAL, MY MOM AND I MEET with the attorney who's in charge of my dad's will. The attorney lets me know I've inherited all the training centers, as well as his life insurance policy, his house, and cars. Of course he didn't leave shit to my mom, but since I have more than enough money, I insist that she gets the money I make off the house when it sells. I make the decision to take the insurance money and put it away in an account for Bella. After what he did, she deserves the money. There's enough that she'll be able to go to any college of her choosing and have a nice nest egg when she decides to start a family or pursue whatever dream she wants.

After our meeting, I go to the gym to let everyone know I'm the new owner. I ask for everyone who works here to join me quickly in the office, and once it looks like most people are here, I begin informing everybody of the change in ownership. Thankfully everyone seems okay with it. Some of the guys give their condolences, but most of them know my dad was a prick, and instead congratulate me on the inheritance.

After they all file out, Kaden lets me know that right before my dad died, the physical therapist on staff quit to move across the country to be closer to family, and that sparks the perfect idea. I just need a little time to form a plan.

I show up to Bentley's place around ten o'clock, hoping to talk to Kayla and Liz, and walk in like I always do without knocking. I have a key and I've never knocked before.

Bentley and Kayla are at each other's throats arguing about something. They stop when they see me and Kayla looks pissed while Bentley looks exhausted.

"What's going on?"

Kayla is the first to respond. "Oh, you know, Bentley thought it would be okay to bring some whore around here last night, and when she went to leave after he was done with her, she walked out half-naked and Bella saw!"

"Look, I said I was sorry fifty damn times! Liz is being understanding about this. I forgot there's a child here. You act like I purposely brought her here and told her to leave, knowing Bella was out there. Damn it, woman! We both know you're just mad because you said you wanted nothing to do with me, so I went out and found someone who does."

Kayla huffs, and as she's about to start in on him again, Liz comes walking down the hall and gives me a smile that turns into a frown. I chuckle at that. She must've forgotten for a second that she's mad at me. Figuring now is the perfect time to throw my plan into motion, I say, "Okay, well, first of all. Before we get into all that, Kayla, I have a job opening at the training facility and was wondering if you'd like to come work there. You would be working with Hayley and the fighters—"

I don't even finish my sentence before she runs over to give me a hug as she chants, "Yes, yes, yes. You are a life saver!"

"You don't even know the specifics. Don't you want to know your hours and pay?"

"Yes, of course, but the job I am at now just let me go today, so whatever you're offering I'll take. The sooner I have an income, the sooner we'll be out of here," she says while glaring at Bentley.

I move on to the next part of my plan directing myself to Kayla still. "Also, about the living arrangements...After what I just walked into, I'm thinking that while you guys start saving for a new place, you girls can come stay with me. I have three extra bedrooms and I promise I won't bring any other women home." I look over at Liz and give her a wink. She just rolls her eyes and crosses her arms over her chest. She looks so damn cute when she's mad.

Kayla looks between Liz and me, then smirks. "Actually, I think all of us there would be too much. How about Liz and Bella stay with you, that way you can spend time with Bella, and I can stay here. It's just temporary. I can handle the whorehouse." Bentley scoffs under his breath at that.

I look over at Liz and she's shooting daggers at Kayla. I also notice Kayla is making it a point not to look at Liz. I already like this woman. Bentley jumps in and says he agrees it's a good idea, and I know Liz can't say no, not when everybody else is saying yes.

She throws her arms in the air, huffs, and says, "Fine. We'll move in with you tomorrow after Bella gets home from school." Then she moves toward me and gets right into my face. She's so close I can smell the vanilla on her, and it's taking every ounce of restraint I have not to grab her and kiss her right now.

She leans in close and says, "But know this, Cooper. I'm only there temporarily, and I'm only there for my daughter, so she's not traumatized from the half-naked women wandering around this place. You and me, not happening. My mom taught me a long time ago that if you share your toy with someone and they break it, it's their fault. If you share it with them again, and they break it again, it's your fault. You have already broke my heart once, Liam Cooper, and you aren't going to get the chance to play with and break it again."

She turns to make a grand exit, but she's crazy if she thinks I'm going to let her have the last word. I trail down the hallway after her, until we get just outside her door. Of course she turns around, raising her eyebrows, daring me to continue this fight.

But I don't need to say shit. I just need to show her. So, I take her face in my hands and kiss her. She tries to pull away, but I hold on to her. When I finish kissing her, I trace my lips to the corner of her mouth and give her another soft kiss, then I move to the spot just under her ear and kiss her again. I know she's affected. I can feel her trembling under my touch, trying to remain calm. I give her one more kiss on her collarbone, and then I turn and walk away. Before I get to the end of the hallway, I look back and see she's staring at me, so I give her that wink that drives her crazy.

"See you tomorrow, baby girl.

Twenty-One

LIZ

WE DON'T HAVE MUCH STUFF SINCE WE LOST EVERYTHING in the fire. The only items we have are the ones Cooper purchased for us the other night, so it's easy to pack everything up quickly. I drop Bella off at preschool and then attempt to scour the classifieds for a job. Living with Cooper is not a good idea. Sure, it's the lesser of the two evils, but at least living with Bentley meant my heart was safe. I seriously need to find a job so we can move out as soon as possible.

And what the heck was Kayla thinking? Staying with Bentley instead of coming with Bella and me? What ever happened to bros before hoes or I guess for us it would be hoes before bros? Okay, that doesn't exactly work in our favor either, but you get what I mean.

I know she has a thing for Bentley but I didn't think it was enough to make her stay living with him, especially since he's clearly hooking up with other chicks. She and I will definitely be sharing some words.

My phone pings with a text from Cooper. What more could he possibly want?

Cooper: What time does Bella get out of school?

Me: 2 p.m. Why?

Cooper: So, I know what time to get you guys.

Me: I have my own car, and we only have the stuff you bought. Just give me your address and we'll head over after she gets out of school.

After a few minutes, he sends me a text with his address. I go back to looking for jobs, copying down the information of a few possible leads.

After picking up Bella, we head back to the apartment to get our stuff. Before heading over to Cooper's, I need to explain to her what's happening. I'm sure she's confused about moving so many times.

"Angel, do you have any questions about what's going on with us moving?"

"No. I'm just sad all my stuff is gone away and I can't get any of it back," she says with the most heartbreaking look on her face. I make a promise to myself that as soon as I'm gainfully employed, I'm going to buy her as many new toys as I can.

"Do you remember the gentleman we ran into at the grocery store a while back? You dropped your flamingo and he picked it up?" Her eyes go bright at this and then dim down.

"Yes, he was so nice to find my flamingo. My poor flamingo didn't make it in the fire."

"I know, and I'm so sorry." I give her a hug. "But you're right, he was nice. His name is Cooper, and we're going to live with him until we can get a new home. Kayla is going to stay here, though."

Bella takes a minute to think about what I'm saying. "Can he be my daddy since I don't have one? Tristan said Daddies live with you."

This would be the perfect opportunity to tell her that he is in fact already her daddy, but I think it would be best to talk to Cooper first, just to make sure we're on the same page. Then we can tell her together if that's what he wants.

"That is true. Daddy's do live with kids, but how about we focus on moving there first, and then we'll figure it all out." Thankfully, she accepts this answer and starts to gather up the few toys Cooper had purchased for her.

When we finish packing all our stuff, we head to Cooper's house. For some reason, this feels like a new chapter of our life is starting, and I'm not sure how I feel about it.

We arrive at Cooper's neighborhood and I press the button on the call box, so he can let us in. He hits the buzzer and I drive until I see the address he gave me. This neighborhood is absolutely gorgeous. I would never imagine somebody like him living here. I shouldn't be surprised because Bentley and Caleb's place is really nice, but looking around, their complex has nothing on this one.

I pull up into the driveway and park next to his slick, black Range Rover, which puts my old Nissan to shame. We get out and look up at the townhouse in front of us, if you can even call it that.

"Mommy, is this my new house?" Bella asks, awestruck.

"Yes, baby. For a little bit."

We both stand there checking out the home. She's standing by my side, and in one hand, she's holding the replica of the flamingo she lost in the fire that Cooper replaced. She reaches up and grabs my hand with her other one.

The house might be called a townhouse, but it's really more like a miniature mansion. It's got to be three stories high. The only difference between a mansion and this place is that all the homes are connected and all are identical. It looks like there's four homes connected in each set. The outside of each home is white with cute black shutters and a set of stairs that lead to a dark red front door. Directly under the stairs appears to be a garage door. The garage must be the first floor and the next two floors are the home.

I'm no stranger to a nice home. The home I grew up in was very nice but modest, built in the 1960s. It was a typical family-style home. For the last five years, Kayla and I have lived in an apartment made for college students. It did what it needed to do and allowed us to live close to campus and gave Bella her own room, but I think my entire apartment could fit in Cooper's driveway.

We must be admiring his home for a while because he walks out of the red door with a quizzical look on his face and says, "It's not going to bite you. Get in here you two." I nod quickly and go back to the trunk to grab our stuff as Bella runs up to the door. Cooper meets me at the trunk and helps me grab everything.

"This car isn't suitable for driving Bella around. We need to do something about that soon."

He says this so nonchalantly I almost think he's just thinking out loud, until he looks at me and raises one brow.

"Let's just focus on one issue at a time. I can't afford a new car, and once I find a job, my money needs to go toward a new place for Bella and me, and hopefully Kayla, too."

His jaw ticks like he wants to protest, but he decides to let it go. Good thinking on his part, that's for sure. We get inside and the first thing I do is introduce Cooper to Bella. Although she's seen him a couple times, they haven't formally met.

"Bella, this is Cooper. We're going to be staying here in his home for a little bit. Cooper, this is Bella."

They both suddenly look so shy. "Hi, I'm Bella. You found my flamingo when it fell at the store. I have a new one now because it went away in the fire."

"Actually, Bella, Cooper is the one who bought you the new one and...he's the one who bought me the one you had before."

Bella's eyes bug out with this new information. "You're the special person who gave my mom the flamingo?"

Cooper nods. "Yes, I gave it to your mom five years ago when I met her. She said she liked to count animals when she couldn't sleep."

Bella laughs. "She still does! When I can't sleep, she always counts the flamingos for me until I fall asleep." Cooper appears to be so overcome with emotions, I quickly change the subject before it gets too deep.

"Yep, I count flamingos. Anyway, how about you give us a quick tour of this beautiful house and show us to our rooms?"

I hope Bella's room is near mine since I've never been too far from her. Bella must just now notice the stairs because she starts squealing and jumping up and down. "Yay! Stairs! I love stairs. Is my room up the stairs? Huh, is it? Please? I will be so happy and I promise to walk so slowly up and down the stairs. Please!"

Cooper starts chuckling at her rambling, and I can already see the love in his eyes. Bella is easy to love. I just hope it's enough to keep him around, for her sake.

"There are four bedrooms. The master is on this floor with its own bathroom, along with the library-slash-office and a half bath in the laundry room. Upstairs are two more bedrooms. One is your bedroom."

He stops for a second because she starts jumping up and down again, saying, "Thank you" over and over.

Once she calms down, he continues. "There's a bathroom connected to your bedroom and the third bedroom was converted into a small gym. There's another guest bathroom up there as well."

Bella doesn't even wait for him to tell her it's okay to head upstairs before she's flying up the stairs. *So much for taking them slow.*

We both follow her up and when we catch up, she's standing outside her room with her hands over her mouth. "Is this my room?" she whispers with such hope in her voice.

I walk closer to see what the big deal is, and when I look inside, I see the most beautiful little girl's room I've ever laid my eyes on. The room is light pink with a white chair rail running along the length of the walls. On the walls are huge hangings of all the different Disney princess characters including a huge hanging of Cinderella's Castle.

In the center is a huge bed fit for a princess with pink and white polka dotted bedding and in front of the pillows is the dragon from

Maleficent she's been asking for. Bella spots it and hugs it to her chest then continues to look around the room.

There's a delicate, light pink, silk canopy spread out over the top of the bed. White wood dresser and nightstands are placed against the walls, and since the floors are all hardwood, there's a cute pink princess rug spread out in the center of the room. Near the bathroom, there's a sitting room that's about half the size of the bedroom. Against one wall is the most adorable pink chair that looks like it's from Pottery Barn kids, and on the other wall is a flat screen television with a DVD player. I walk into the bathroom and the princess theme continues. I look back at Cooper and he looks uneasy like he's suddenly unsure of himself. He's staring down, and his feet are shifting from one to the other.

Bella run around the room, checking it all out, and then stops right in front of Cooper, making him look up. "Is this all mine? Like really mine? Like black-black no trade back, mine?"

"Um, I'm not sure what black-black no trade back means, but yes, this is your room. I hope you like it. I wasn't really sure what you're into," he says, his lips curling into a slight frown.

He's second-guessing all of this, and he shouldn't be. He just made Bella's entire year and he doesn't even know it. "What you did here is amazing," I tell him. "I don't even know how to thank you. Any chance my room looks half as good as this?" I ask jokingly to lighten up the mood.

He starts laughing, and I get to see his beautiful smile return. I can't help but smile back.

"Well, I haven't done anything to the master bedroom since I moved in, but you're welcome to add or change anything you like," he says with a huge knowing smirk across his face.

It takes a second, but then I remember when he named all the rooms he didn't mention a room for me. *Motherfucker. He thinks he's slick. Two can play this game.*

"Oh, that's okay. I'm sure this bed is big enough for Bella and me to share."

Liz: 1 Cooper: 0

Bella glances back and forth from the bed to me, and with hands on her hips, says, "Mommy, I'm almost five years old. I don't want to share a bed with you. Remember when I tried to sneak in your bed and you told me big girls sleep in their own beds." *Well damn it, she has me there.*

I swivel around to give Cooper the evil eye and almost run right into his chest. He must've moved closer to me while Bella was giving me her mom speech.

His eyes are dancing with laughter as he sucks in his bottom lip to keep from laughing. When my eyes lock with his, he says, "Don't worry, baby girl. My bed is big enough for both of us." Then the cocky bastard winks. He actually winks. He's so lucky our daughter is in the room or I'd choke him with my bare hands.

Cooper: 1 Liz: 1

I rub my hands over my face in frustration then walk out of the room. I walk toward the room he said holds the gym and open the door to see if I can put a bed in here. Unfortunately, the room is filled with tons of gym equipment, and a bed, no matter the size, would never fit. I continue down the stairs opening each door along the way. I open the door to the master bedroom and close it immediately. I can feel Cooper on my heels. but I ignore him.

When I open the door to the library-slash-office, I notice there's a comfy oversized reading chair in one corner and a chaise lounge in the other. *Well, this will have to do.*

"I'll just sleep in here. Hopefully, I'll find a job soon and then we'll be out of your hair. Until then I can just sleep on this couch. It looks super comfy." *Ha! Another point for me.*

Cooper walks up to me slowly like he's afraid I might attack him, and I almost laugh at how nervous he looks. He grips the curves of my hips, and before I realize what he's doing, he kisses me softly. I can't help the sigh that escapes my lips as I get lost in his touch. When the kiss ends, I assume he's going to pull back, so I'm shocked when he places another kiss to the corner of my mouth. When nipples tighten and my lady parts tingle, I back up before I completely embarrass myself.

"Look, I know I've messed up," Cooper says. "But I'm here now and I'm fighting. Just give me a second chance to fight for us. Let me at least have one more shot. I have a proposition for you, if you'll hear me out."

There's now a huge lump in my throat. This is all I ever wanted, all I ever prayed and wished and hoped for. I nod my head for him to continue.

"I have a job opening at the gym. My dad ran all the books. I have no clue what I'm doing and I'm too busy training to focus on the money aspect of the business. Come to work for me and live here. Give me this last chance to fight for my family. If, after a while you don't want this, you can move out and we can figure out the custody arrangement for Bella. But I really hope it doesn't come to that. I want both of you. Please."

I want to say no because I feel like he's offering me a job I didn't earn, but I need the money and it would be great to work in the same place as Hayley and Kayla, plus Cooper would be there often. The problem is, can I give him another chance? He's already broken my heart once, and I honestly don't think I would survive a second time.

He takes my chin between his fingers and kisses me once again, letting it linger for a few seconds, when we both hear little feet padding into the room and a shriek coming from Bella.

"Ewww, you guys are kissing like Cinderella and the Prince! Does this mean Cooper can be my daddy? He gave me the most bestest room ever and I love him now."

I laugh at that. It clearly doesn't take much to win over my daughter. Cooper looks scared shitless and that makes me nervous, so I elbow him and tilt my head to the side, silently asking if he's okay.

He snaps out of it and whispers, "She wants me to be her daddy and she loves me." It must all be hitting him at once.

"Bella, why don't you go pick a movie for us to watch in your new room." Yep! Parent of the year award goes to me for once again ignoring her daddy question. She says okay and runs out to pick a movie. I wait until I hear her feet thumping up the stairs, then I turn and look at Cooper, who's sporting a mixture of emotions on his face.

He backs up and sits in the reading chair. Without saying a word, he scrubs his hands up and down his stubble. Figuring he just needs a moment to catch up, I stay where I am.

Finally, after a good minute, he glances up at me and says, "I never thought anybody would ever call me Daddy. And when she asked if I could be her daddy, I thought it would scare me to death, but it didn't. I just wanted to grab her and hug her and never let her go. I barely even know her and I already love her more than life itself. I felt it in the hospital when you said she was brought in, but hearing her calling me Daddy, my heart feels like it just grew ten times bigger. I just want to give her the world."

"I know what you mean. When she was born, I held her in my arms and stared at her, refusing to believe she was mine. I guess it's a parent's love. You don't have to know everything about her to feel that connection."

His gaze locks with mine, and a single tear falls down his cheek. "I missed it all. I missed you being pregnant. I bet you were so beautiful carrying our little girl. I missed her birth, her first steps, and her first words. Damn it, Liz. I missed everything. All because I was a fucking idiot who thought I didn't deserve any of this so I pushed you away. For four years, I had a daughter who had no father all because of the choices I made. I will never be able to get any of that back."

I move closer to Cooper and put my hands into his. "You didn't know, Coop. It wasn't your fault. You had a crappy childhood and you made the choices you thought were best at the time. I was just going off to college. I didn't try to give you my number either."

"Yeah, that was cute the way you got into a twenty-one and older club and acted like you just graduated college," he says with a smirk. "Any younger and you'd have been jail-bait."

I smile big and stick my tongue out at him. Wait until he hears the other half of it. "Oh, well, you also didn't realize that I was a virgin when we hooked up."

His eyes bug out and he goes serious. "Liz, what the fuck. I took you in the shower our first time. Why didn't you tell me? I would have been gentler or caring..."

"No." I shake my head. "You were perfect. My first time, and second time, and third time were all perfect. I don't regret anything we did. I wasn't lying when I said I was on the pill. The problem was I had only just started it a couple days before. I didn't plan to have sex so I didn't look into when it becomes effective. I had no clue birth control pills take a week to work. I was eighteen and stupid. I got to Las Vegas and four weeks later, after throwing up for days, went to the doctor where she confirmed I was pregnant."

"I can't even imagine how scared you were. I wish I could've been there for you. I'm so sorry, Liz."

"It's okay," I say honestly. "Kayla was there every step of the way. We worked part time and took classes and graduated together. It wasn't easy, but we did it."

He lets out a loud sigh, shaking his head. Before he can respond, Bella comes running back into the room. "I got the movie!" She waves it in the air.

"Perfect! Go pick out a couple of stuffed animals and we'll be there in two minutes to watch it." She nods excitedly and runs back out.

"You're the strongest woman I know," Cooper says once she's gone. "You're raising a beautiful, sweet, little girl. Thank you for taking such good care of her. But I'm here now. Please give me the chance to take care of you."

"I want to, Coop. I want to so badly. But you're the one who told me several times you don't want to be a father or a husband. I know I owe it to you to let you get to know Bella, but I'm scared for her and for me. I don't know if I can handle you breaking my heart again. What if you wake up one day and decide you don't really want a family after all? Then what? What would I say to Bella? How would I explain to her that her daddy doesn't want her? You heard her. She's been on this daddy kick for weeks. She hears at school from all the kids who have a daddy. In her movies and shows there's a mommy and daddy, or in many cases like the Disney movies, there's only a dad and no mom. She wants one so badly. What if I tell her you're her daddy and then you change your mind...it'll devastate her. And I'll be left to pick up the pieces."

I wipe away a traitor tear and Cooper frowns. "Baby girl, I know my words don't hold any weight and I've confused the shit out of you with everything I've said. But I promise you, I'm not going anywhere. The fact is, you don't owe me anything, but please just give me a chance to prove I'm in this for the long haul with you and Bella."

It suddenly occurs to me that he isn't playing a game. He isn't keeping points and it doesn't do any good for me to play games. Bella deserves for us to try. We deserve for us to try. This is what I wanted for so long and I'll always regret it, if I don't give us a shot. Sure, there's a chance Bella and I end up hurt, but I want so badly for the other option, the one where we end up together as a family.

So, I give in and say, "Okay, one more chance. We'll see how good of a fighter you really are."

Cooper leans forward and, grabbing my waist, pulls me up into his lap so I'm straddling him, one leg on either side of him. "Thank you, baby," he whispers. Then he kisses me like I just told him he's won the lottery, his lips attacking mine. His hands roam all over my body—up my arms, over my breasts, down my back. I can feel him getting excited between my legs.

Instinctively, I grind against his hardness while lacing my fingers into his hair that's just long enough to grab ahold of. We continue to kiss and his fingers tweak my nipples over my clothes. I need him. I need his body on mine without any clothes...and then suddenly I'm flying through the air, my butt hitting the couch. *What the heck?*

I shoot him a look that conveys he's damn near lost his mind, but he shakes his head, quickly looking toward the doorway, and in the next second, in walks Bella. *Holy. Shit. What kind of mother forgets her daughter is in the other damn room while trying to get laid?*

"C'mon! Movie time!" Bella bounces up and down and then grabs one of my hands to pull me up.

Cooper starts to chuckle. Guessing what's going on in my head, he leans over and whispers, "Tonight, baby girl. You're all mine tonight." And with that, my panties dampen.

Damn this man and his way with words.

Twenty-Two

COOPER

AFTER BELLA DETERMINES HER BED ISN'T BIG ENOUGH FOR all of us, we get situated in the living room, instead, to watch some movie called *Frozen* as Bella explains why she wants to watch this movie even though it came out a long time ago. It's so hard to keep a straight face listening to my four-year-old explain why it's okay to watch an old movie even though she has a lot of new ones.

"It's not that I don't want to watch Dolphin Tale. It's still my favoritest ever. It's just that I love Anna and Elsa and I want to be Elsa for Halloween. I can't be a dolphin for Halloween because that would be so silly!" She says all this as she explodes into a fit of giggles at her own comment. I have no idea what she's talking about, but she's the cutest damn thing.

Liz obviously understands completely as they go back and forth about her Halloween costume.

"Mom, it's so important to get my costume now. If I wait too long and they have no Elsa, I will die." Holy shit. Apparently, costume shopping is a life or death situation to a kid.

"Bella, why don't you wait to decide what you want to be for Halloween? We still have six weeks and you might change your mind."

Bella huffs, clearly not happy with her mother's answer, but chooses not to argue either. *Oh man, I haven't lived with a woman in years, and now I'm living with two. This should be interesting.*

After popping some popcorn and ordering a pizza, we all get comfortable. Liz is snuggled up to me with her head resting just under my chin and Bella is spread out on the floor using the pillows from the couches as a makeshift bed. She looks so adorable lying on her belly with her hands under her chin. I should probably be focusing on the movie, but I can't stop watching my girls. *My girls.* I had no idea I even wanted any of this, and now, sitting here with them, my heart feels so full.

The pizza arrives and we eat in front of the television still watching the movie. Bella gets up every time a song comes on and dances across the room belting out all the words. She has an awesome personality. When the guy kisses the girl, Bella looks back and gives her mom and me a knowing look. I laugh softly at that and give Liz a kiss on her forehead. She looks up at me and smiles contently.

The movie ends and Liz announces to Bella it's time for bed. She groans and begs for ten more minutes, but Liz isn't having it. I wonder if she's thinking about what I mentioned earlier.

Bella says, "Fine," then stomps up the stairs to her room, Liz following behind her. I'm not sure what my role in all this is, since we still haven't told her I'm her dad, so I hang back and wait to see what

Liz wants me to do. A few minutes later I hear Bella scream my name from upstairs and I head up there to make sure everything is okay.

"Hey princess, you okay?" I ask as I walk into her room. She's wearing one of the nightgowns I picked out. It's pink with ruffles and has a picture of a princess on the front. She's rummaging through her bag, until she finds what she's looking for.

"A-ha! Got it. I found my favorite book. Will you read it to me?" She hands me the book and climbs into bed.

I look at Liz to make sure it's okay and she nods her head that it is. I walk over to the bed unsure of where to sit when Bella looks up at me smiling and pats her hand on the bed next to her. *Damn, this little girl has officially stolen my heart.*

Sitting awkwardly on the bed next to her, I read the title. "The Giving Tree by Shel Silverstein." I open to the first page and begin reading. At first, Bella is sitting up, her body not touching mine, but eventually she snuggles up next to me to see the pictures while I continue to read. The pages and images are in black and white but that doesn't stop her from enjoying this book. Several times I hear her recite the words along with me. I don't think she can read yet, but she must have heard this book so many times she has the words memorized.

About fifteen minutes later I hear a light snore and glance down to find her fast asleep. I look over at Liz smiling. "She sounds just like you the nights we spent together five years ago. You snore the same."

She narrows her eyes at me, clearly not taking my comment as a compliment. I laugh as I set the book down and gently move Bella's head off my side, slowly moving off the bed.

Liz kisses Bella on her forehead, then turns the light off. The night-light spreads a soft glow over the room, and I take a moment to watch my little girl sleep.

"C'mon, Coop," Liz whispers. "It's bedtime."

Once we're in my room, I jump in the shower to wash the day off me. Definitely not expecting her to join, I'm pleasantly surprised when she enters the bathroom right after me.

Twenty-Three

LIZ

I SWEAR MY OVARIES JUST ABOUT BURST AS I WATCHED Cooper read our daughter a bedtime story. After she falls asleep and we head to our room. He goes straight to the bathroom and a few minutes later the water turns on. Flashbacks of our first time at the resort in Miami, up against the shower wall, surface, sending shivers down my spine.

I don't know what's come over me, but without even thinking, I brazenly enter the bathroom, remove my clothes, and join him in the shower. He turns around, his eyes slowly running down my body, assessing me. Feeling suddenly shy, I cast my eyes down, only to find his erection growing.

He grabs my hand and tugs me into him, putting us both under the water. His hands come up to my face, and with a soft smile, he wipes the wet tendrils of hair out of my eyes. "Baby girl, I want you so bad," he says, his voice thick with emotion. "If you aren't ready, you need to tell me now because having you in this shower, naked and wet...you're making it hard as hell to control myself."

I don't respond. Instead, I squat down so that I'm face to face with his hard erection. Glancing up at him, I find his chest is rising and falling heavily, and his eyes are hooded over with lust. I love that I haven't even touched him, yet he's already completely turned on. He doesn't say anything, so I take his dick in my hand and start stroking it from the root to tip. It's thick with a few veins popping out as it points straight at me, only centimeters from my mouth. I can't be this close to it and not taste it, so placing my hands on his thighs, I steady myself then take his full length into my mouth until it hits the back of my throat.

"Oh, fuck. Liz, that feels incredible," he groans.

His words spur me on as I continue to lick and suck his dick like it's a lollipop, before going deeper and taking more of him. I gaze upward and notice his back is against the wall and his fists are tightened at his sides. I don't want him controlled, though. I want him to let go.

Steadying myself by putting my hands on his thighs, my head bobs up and down sucking his dick forcefully, swirling my tongue around the head every time my head comes up. This seems to do him in and, a few seconds later, his legs are trembling and he's warning me that he's about to come. I don't stop, though. I want to taste him. I want him to come undone because of me.

If I'm honest with myself, remembering all those girls shouting his name at the UFC fight makes me feel like I need to remind him why he wants me and not them.

A few seconds later, his dick swells and he lets out a loud grunt.

Then he's coming down my throat. I taste his seed on my tongue before it coats the back of my throat. I take it all, every drop, until his dick starts to go soft in my mouth. His lips lazily stretch into a smile as he looks at me with awe and maybe something else. Could it be love? No, he's just received good head, that's all it is. But I can't deny that it makes me happy I'm the one to put that look on his face.

We finish showering and make our way back into the bedroom to get dressed in comfortable silence. Before I can grab my clothes from the luggage, Cooper pulls me against him, my back hitting his front. Every time he touches me, I swear my body comes alive.

I glance up and can see him in the dresser mirror staring at me with lust-filled eyes. Taking both my breasts in his hands, he begins to massage them. I should be embarrassed that we're both watching him touch me like this, but I'm not. Instead, I simply feel wanted...and seriously turned on. I squeeze my thighs together, failing to quell the ache, needing more.

He continues to palm my breast with one hand, but moves the other straight down to the area between my legs. *Thank God!*

"Spread your legs, baby," he murmurs, and I do. He separates my pussy lips with his two fingers and then push one deep inside me. Simultaneously, he leans down and starts planting kisses along my neck, trailing his way up to the sensitive spot below my ear. He moves his lips up to my ear and gently bites down on my lobe, causing my body to shudder and tighten from sensory overload.

"Oh my God, Cooper. Please." I can see him through his reflection in the mirror, silently laughing at my neediness, but my body is wound too tight to focus on anything but him giving me an orgasm.

"Please what, baby girl? What do you need?"

"I need you. Now. More. Now." I know I'm not making any sense, but surely, he gets the damn point. Of course, his ass laughs at my incoherence, but at least while he's laughing, he obeys by sticking another digit into me. He stops palming my breast and instead begins to tweak the nipple between his fingers. My head goes back against his chest, my eyes closing, as the pleasure from his fingers and mouth shoot straight to my core causing me to moan embarrassingly loud.

And then the feeling stops. My eyes fly open in time to see Cooper walk around to face me until he's sandwiched between me and the dresser. Before I can ask what the heck he's doing, he places my hands against the dresser on either side of him then drops to his knees. I have no idea where he's going with this, but I'll trust he knows.

With him no longer standing in front of me, I see my reflection in the mirror. My hair is a mess and my cheeks are a light pink from being worked up and turned on. I look crazy, but at the same time, happy, carefree.

Something soft and wet hits my clit, and I jump slightly. Looking down, I have a bird's eye view of Cooper's tongue lapping at my pussy. *Holy. Shit. That feels good.* He taps my thigh to spread them wider, then puts two fingers back inside me while he gives my clit plenty of attention. Hot damn, this guy is an amazing multitasker.

While fucking me with his fingers, his mouth is feasting on my pussy. At first, he licks his way up my slit, then he sucks on my clit before he bits down on it, only to lick away the pain. I can hear the slurping sound coming from my pussy while he drinks up all my juices. I can't stop watching him. I've never witnessed something so intimate and erotic in my life.

He continues to suck and lick while fingering me deep. His fingers start to hit that spot, the one that will have me coming in no time. Then his tongue hits my clit in just the right way and I know I'm about to experience the biggest orgasm to date.

He takes his mouth off me just long enough to say, "Look in the mirror. Watch yourself as you come all over my tongue and fingers." And then his mouth is back on my clit. My body, wound up too tight, begins to spasm and shake, as waves of pleasure course through my body as I ride out my orgasm. His tongue and fingers never stop until I've completely come down from what I can only imagine heaven on earth feels like.

"Damn, baby, that was fucking hot, the way you just came all over my tongue. You taste damn good." He stands and licks his fingers clean, leaving me wanting him all over again.

We both clean up in the bathroom then get dressed. As much as I want to lay naked with him, I can't chance our four-year old running in here in the middle of the night or in the morning and seeing us without clothes on. He flicks the light off on the nightstand and spoons me from behind.

No words are spoken for a few minutes, so I assume he's fallen asleep, when he says, "I want Bella to know I'm her dad, Liz."

I know it's only been a few hours, but I'm all in. Watching him tonight with her, I can't deny him this chance. All I can do is hope and pray he doesn't break either of our hearts.

"I know, Coop. We'll tell her tomorrow. I promise."

I feel him relax against me as we both allow sleep to overtake us.

Twenty-Four

COOPER

I WAKE UP TO THE SMELL OF VANILLA AND IT MAKES ME smile. I look down and my beautiful girl is next to me, wrapped up in our blankets. I can't help but laugh at the fact she's still a damn sheet-hogger. I don't know how I got this lucky to be given this second chance, but I'm going to do everything in my power to make sure Liz never regrets it. I start to stretch and remember today is Sunday, which is my day off from training. I'm hoping we can tell Bella about me being her dad and do something as a family. *What do families do?*

Not knowing the answer to that simple question reminds me that my parents never did any family stuff. My dad was either traveling for fights or at the gym training. My mom was always home with me, but we didn't really go anywhere as a family. She always seemed upset that my dad was gone. Eventually she'd leave me with a sitter and go out by herself.

And those thoughts start to make me panic. I'm home right now, but soon I'm going to have to be away from home training long hours.

I'll have to start traveling again to promote the upcoming title fight. There'll be press releases and conferences and then the fight itself. Bella is in school, so Liz will have to stay home. Will she regret giving me this chance? Will she turn to someone else who can give her more attention? I feel my anxiety rising, my chest tightening at the image of another man comforting Liz. I need to calm myself down. Liz is not my mom and I am not my dad. We will get through this.

"Mommy, Cooper, can I come in?"

Lifting my head, I see my little princess poking her head around the corner. I look back at Liz and she's still sleeping, so I place my fingers over my lips so Bella doesn't wake her mom up.

Carefully, I get out of bed, making sure not to jostle Liz. Then, taking Bella's small hand, I give her a smile and whisper, "Why don't we make your mom breakfast in bed?"

She lights up at the idea and starts skipping down the hallway, pulling me along.

"Yes, please! Can we make chocolate chip pancakes? Oh! And bacon? And can we make cupcakes and cookies, too. Mommy loves all that."

"Bella, you sure it's your mom who loves cupcakes and cookies for breakfast?" I ask, chuckling. The fact my daughter is already trying to get one over on me has me grinning like a Cheshire cat. This girl already has me wrapped around her cute little finger and I'm absolutely okay with that.

"Maybe it's me that likes all that stuff, but I bet my mom would eat it all. She likes junk food too. Her and Auntie Kay always buy it and say junk food makes every woman happy."

"I'm sure they're right. Why don't we start with pancakes and bacon, and we'll see about maybe going out for lunch and dessert later."

"Okay." She stops abruptly and turns around, pointing her crooked pinky out at me. *Damn, kids still do this shit?* I give her my pinky and we hook them together for a good ol' pinky promise. I hope Liz is okay with going out later because there's no way I'm breaking our first pinky promise.

We get to the kitchen and I'm glad I bought groceries once Liz agreed to move in. I grab the griddle and plug it in, then set about grabbing all the ingredients to make pancakes. Bella grabs a chair and drags it to the counter to stand on. Even on a chair she's still so tiny.

"Can I put all the stuff in and mix it all up, please?" She looks at me while batting her eyelashes.

Fuck! Are all women born with the ability to make a man do whatever they want through their damn eyelashes?

"Of course, you can, Princess."

I place all the stuff within her reach, and she begins pouring it all into the bowl carefully, then mixes it all together. While she's doing that, I throw the bacon in the oven. I have to wonder if all kids are this cute and helpful. One thing is for sure, Liz has done a damn good job raising her. At eighteen, I was fighting and fucking. Liz was going to college and taking care of a baby. I wish I could do something to show her how amazing she is, but I can't think of anything that's anywhere near equivalent to this amazing woman caring for our daughter for the last four years.

I spoon the pancake mix onto the hot griddle as I listen to Bella rattle on about preschool and the mean boys who have cooties.

"...And then I told Tristan if he touches me one more time and gives me the cooties, I'll punch him in the face." Hmm...I don't like this Tristan. I'll have to ask Liz about this kid. I can't have some little shit giving my princess any cooties.

"Good for you, Princess. Don't take anyone's crap."

"Ahem. I don't think it's a good idea to encourage our daughter to punch anybody."

Bella and I both turn around to find Liz standing against the island giving us what I imagine is the *mom look.*

"Mom, you're supposed to be in bed. I can't bring you food in bed if you aren't in bed." Bella's standing there looking all cute and mad with her hands on her hips just like her mom does, when she switches gears.

"Wait, Mommy. I'm Cooper's daughter too?"

Liz's eyes open as wide as saucers when she realizes what she just implied, and I grin. Now's the perfect time to tell Bella she is in fact my daughter.

I take the pancakes off the griddle and pull the bacon out of the oven, setting it all on the center of the table. I pour everyone some orange juice and we all sit at the table, Bella and I both looking at Liz.

"Bella, how would you feel if Cooper was your daddy?"

I tense up, waiting for her answer, as Bella nonchalantly grabs a pancake from the platter and says, "I would feel happy. Duh!"

And...my entire body relaxes.

"Well, yes. Cooper is your daddy," Liz says.

I'm wondering if she's going to go into all the specifics. I mean, how do you explain to a four-year-old a *thirty-hour stand*? Yep, I'm still sticking to that. Liz was so much more than a one-night stand.

Apparently, that's all the explanation she needs, though. "Cooper, can I call you Daddy?"

And there goes half my heart...gone. It's now been handed over to the four-year-old sitting across from me, and I pray she never gives it back.

I have to take a second to control my breathing. I'm suddenly choked up and there's a lump in my throat. I'm afraid if I speak, I'll start to cry. Bella's looking at me shyly and I know I need to answer her before she thinks I don't want that. Screw it. *If I cry, I cry.* If that makes me a pussy then so be it.

Sure, enough as the words come out so do the tears. I get up and walk around the table to kneel next to Bella, turning her little legs to face me.

"Oh, Princess. I would love it more than anything in the world if you would call me Daddy."

Bella reaches her hand out and swipes at my face to get rid of the tears.

"Then why are you crying?" she asks in a sad voice.

"These are happy tears. I know it doesn't make much sense, but I promise you, I am so happy right now."

I pull her into a tight hug, never wanting to let her go. She's mine. This precious little girl is mine.

"Daddy, you're squeezing me so tightly my head is going to pop off!"

I let go of her and we all laugh. I go back to my seat, looking around, as we all grab our food and begin to eat. This is my family and I'm the luckiest damn guy in the world.

Twenty-Five

LIZ

AFTER BREAKFAST COOPER ANNOUNCES TODAY IS SUNDAY-Funday Family Day. What that entails I have no clue. When Bella and I ask him, he tells us to go get dressed and be ready to head out in fifteen minutes. *Ha! That's funny.* He clearly hasn't spent enough time with women to know we don't get ready in fifteen minutes. That's okay, though. He'll learn.

An hour later we're piling into his Range Rover to head out. I go to grab Bella's booster seat from my car, but he tells me he already has one. *Is there anything this man hasn't thought of?*

The entire drive Bella keeps guessing where we're going. Cooper keeps laughing and saying he's not telling her. About twenty minutes later we pull up to a grocery store, where he insists we wait in the vehicle for him. When he gets back, he's carrying several bags and a wicker picnic basket. He loads the shopping bags and the basket into the trunk and then we're back on the road.

A few minutes later we pull up to the Town Square. Bella is trying to figure out where we are, but she can't see beyond the parking lot.

"We've never been here. What's there to do?" I ask as we get out.

"You'll see." He grabs the basket, which must be filled with the stuff from the bags, slams the trunk closed, and we all head toward the buildings. As we walk down the sidewalk, in the distance, it looks like there are a bunch of playhouses. Bella starts walking faster, wanting to see what's going on. When we get closer, sure enough there's a huge park filled with sidewalks and playhouses everywhere. To one side, there's a huge Oak tree, and connected to it is a tree house with a rock wall and a fort. Just past that there, is a cool fountain that's shooting water up in the air. On the other side, is the most adorable princess tower playhouse with slides coming out of the sides.

"Oh, my God! Mommy. Daddy. Can I go play?" Bella squeals in delight. She's looking every which way, not even sure where to begin. I see a couple benches nearby and Cooper must notice them too because he heads straight for them. I think he's going to sit and watch her play, but he shocks me once again when he sets the basket down on the bench and says to Bella, "C'mon, Princess! Let's go play."

She's so excited he's joining her, she jumps up and down, grabs his hand, and then pulls him along. *Mom who?*

We follow Bella through the playground. She runs from playhouse to playhouse and Cooper keeps up with her every step of the way. It's hilarious to watch this six-foot-three man try to go where the barely three-foot little girl goes. I have to give him credit, though. Cooper can barely fit in some of the tunnels and slides, but it doesn't stop him from trying. Where Bella goes, Cooper goes.

I pull out my phone and snap a bunch of pictures of them running around, climbing up the rock wall, and going down the slides. I'm sure he'll love to see these later.

After a while of playing, Bella spots the water fountains from earlier and asks if she can go play in them even though she didn't bring a suit.

"Um, Bella, we don't have a change of clothes. You can't get back in the car wet."

Of course she pouts and looks right at Cooper. *Little girl is smart.* Cooper gives her pout one glance and of course comes up with a solution.

"Sure, Princess. You go play and when you're done, we'll buy you a towel and a new outfit at a store."

After squealing her thanks, she takes off like a bat out of hell, racing toward the fountains while we sit on the bench and watch her.

"Coop, you can't just give in to everything she wants. I can't afford to just buy her a new outfit whenever she wants. I'm going to take the job you're offering, but I need to save for a place."

Cooper's jaw begins to tick and then his face softens. "I'm glad you're taking the job because I know you want to work, but Bella and you aren't going anywhere. I make more than enough money to support both of you, and I have four years of her life to make up for that I missed out on, on top of four years of making up to do with all the time you and I missed. You don't want to work, you don't have to. You want to stay home and take care of Bella, I'm more than fine with that. Whatever money you make is yours. I don't care what you do as long as you both are under the same roof as me."

I want to get angry with him because I don't appreciate him going all alpha-male on me, but I can see it in his eyes. *Guilt.* He thinks he owes us because he wasn't there.

While still watching Bella, I tell Cooper, "This whole situation, you not getting to see Bella, wasn't either of our faults. It was a crappy situation, but we're here now and you don't need to make up for anything. I don't want you to take care of us. I want us to be equal."

He looks over at me and takes my hand in his. "Baby girl, I own several training facilities left to me by my dad. I have endorsements and contracts, and I make decent money fighting. I make more than enough to take care of you, and that's my job. Your job is to take care of our princess. My dad's life insurance policy was several hundred thousand dollars and I didn't even touch it. I put it in a trust account for Bella. She can use it to go to college, get a car, buy a house, whatever she needs or wants to make sure all her dreams in life are within her reach. If we have more kids one day, we'll make sure they have one as well. Please, just let me do this. Let me take care of my girls." I glance over at him and see the need in his eyes. It's obvious this is important to him.

"Okay, but don't spoil her, Coop. She needs to learn that getting handed everything isn't reality. You, of all people, know it takes hard work to accomplish your dreams."

"Okay, I'll try my best," he says, and for some reason, I think he's full of it, but I let it go for now.

We sit and watch Bella for a while until Cooper gets up and walks over to a woman and gives her a big hug. She turns to face me and I see it's his mom. What a nice surprise.

He calls Bella over to make introductions. "Mom, this is my daughter, Bella Faith. Bella, this is my mom, your grandma."

"Oh, Liam! She is absolutely beautiful! And she looks so much like you."

Bella looks confused and asks, "Are you my grandma like my mom's mom? I call her Grammy, and who's Liam?"

Ms. Cooper laughs. "Liam is your daddy's real name. All his friends call him by his last name, which is Cooper. And yes, I'm your daddy's mom, so that makes me your grandma as well. You can call me Grandma if you like."

"Okay! Cool! Now I have two grandmas! Do I get another grandpa, too? I call mommy's daddy Papa. I can call daddy's daddy...uhhh... Grandpa."

Everybody goes quiet, clearly at a loss on how to handle this, so I step in and explain the situation to Bella the best I can. Fortunately, we haven't had any deaths in our family, so I haven't had to explain death to her.

"Angel, remember the fire that happened in our apartment?"

"Yes, all my toys and clothes and bed went away."

I hear Cooper suck in a loud breath at the same time his mom puts her hand to her heart. They can't possibly think I would tell my daughter the whole story of that day. I rush out the words before they freak out on me.

"That's right. Well, your grandpa was the one who saved you that day."

"Wow, that was really nice of him. Can I say thank you? I was really scared and the smoke was choking my throat really badly."

"He knows you're thankful, but he had to go to heaven. Heaven is where people go when they die."

Bella's bottom lip juts out. "Like Carl in the movie *Up*? When he takes the balloons, and goes into the sky?"

Leave it to my daughter to compare her grandfather's death to a Disney Movie, but she's nailed it right on the head. "Yes, Angel, like Carl. Grandpa went to heaven so we can't see him or thank him, but he knows we're thankful he saved you."

"Okay, I'm hungry. Can we eat?"

Cooper and his mother release an audible sigh, most likely thankful the conversation is over.

Cooper jumps in and says yes, but first we have to get Bella a dry outfit. In and out of a small children's clothing store and Bella's dry and starving.

We find a spot in the grass and Cooper pulls out a large blanket, shaking it open and laying it across the ground. We all find a place to sit and he dishes out the food. Subs, cookies, some fruit, and bottles of water for everybody.

"Ms. Cooper, I'm so glad you were able to join us today," I tell her, trying to make conversation.

"Oh dear, please call me Lauren. We're family."

"Okay." I feel so blessed that Bella and I have another family member close by. I always miss my parents and brother since they live so far away.

After we have lunch, Bella is rearing to go once again. We spend the rest of the afternoon checking out a cool hedge maze, and then head to a sweet little bakery that looks like one of the playhouses. Cooper let's Bella pick out a treat and then we walk around some of the shops until Bella is so exhausted she has Cooper carry her while she sleeps with her head resting on his shoulder.

I can't help but snap another photo. It's just too darn precious not to. His mom sees me snap the picture and gives me a wink in agreement.

We walk back to the car and say bye to his mom, promising to have her over for dinner soon. Cooper puts Bella in her booster seat and she doesn't even attempt to stir. Precious little thing is knocked out from all that playing.

We drive home in a comfortable silence and as we're getting out, Cooper comes around to my side of the vehicle and blocks me in before I can get out.

"Thank you."

I have no idea what I even did. "For what?"

"For today. It was one of the most amazing days of my life."

"Um, Coop. I didn't do or pay for anything. I was just along for the ride."

"No, Liz. You aren't just along for the ride. You gave me a second chance, even though I didn't deserve it. You gave me that miracle sleeping in the back seat. You helped create priceless memories today. You gave me a family. Thank you."

Damn this man. I frame his face with my hands and give him a soft kiss on his mouth. "I love you," I say without meaning to.

Cooper's entire body stills and I want to back track. I want to take it back before he shuts me out. It's not that I don't mean it. I do. I love Cooper. I think I always have. I know realistically people don't fall in love when they first meet, but between the time we shared years ago, watching Bella grow up with his beautiful features, and listening to and watching him these past few days, I can feel it. I love this man.

Just when I think he's going to leave me hanging, he kisses me. It's not a soft kiss like the one I gave him, but it's not rough either. It's a beautiful, sensual combination of both. His lips move over mine with ease, his tongue smoothly slipping in, and I swear this man is making love to me with his mouth. When he ends the kiss, he pulls back and smiles at me with a big cheesy grin.

"Baby girl, I love you, too. I love you so damn much."

I can't see myself, but I'm almost positive I'm mirroring the same cheesy-ass grin on my face that he's still sporting on his.

After Bella's nap, we spend the rest of the afternoon lounging around, playing Uno. Bella beats us every game. We order Chinese for dinner, and then I give Bella a bath while Cooper excuses himself back downstairs.

After Bella's in bed, Cooper tells me to get changed into my pajamas and then meet him in the living room. When I ask him why, he tells me he has a surprise for me.

After getting changed I enter the living room to find a ton of candy, popcorn, and drinks spread out across the coffee table.

"What's all this?" I ask.

"It's an adult movie night," he says as he grabs a DVD from inside the entertainment center, puts it in, and comes to sit next to me. I grab the throw blanket from the back of the couch and spread it across our laps as I snuggle into his side.

After skipping through the previews, the title screen comes on and I squeal in excitement like my daughter. "You remembered?" I slap him on the chest, and he laughs.

"*Love and Basketball* is my favorite movie!"

"I know! I remember everything you tell me, Liz. You and that girl upstairs are my world. You mean everything to me." *And swoon...*

"We might be now, but I wasn't five years ago. I told you this was my favorite back when it was just a one-night stand."

Looking anger at what I just said, he says, "First of all, it wasn't a one-night stand. It was a thirty-hour stand." *He is so damn adorable.*

"Second of all, I knew you were my world back then. I was just too stupid to do anything about it. I've never even spent the night with another woman. You were the first and you will be the last. Got it?"

"Yeah, I got it," I say as he presses play on the movie. He may not know it yet, but he's quickly becoming my entire world as well.

Twenty-Six

COOPER

I'M AT THE GYM TRAINING WITH KADEN, BUT INSTEAD OF training it's more like I'm getting the shit kicked out of me. I can't focus and it's not my fault.

"Coop! Put your fucking hands up. How are you supposed to beat this guy if you can't even remember how to block a simple punch?" I hate to admit it but Kaden is right. I'm off my game and I blame the sexy woman who's invading my every thought. My mind goes back to that first Sunday we spent together as a family when we got home from the Town Square, after we both declared our love for each other.

After Bella went to sleep, we watched *Love and Basketball* while cuddling on the couch, and when it was over, I had to make a few calls for the gym, so Liz went to take a shower and then read one of her trashy novels on her iPad she loves so much.

Once I was done with my calls, I went into the room to shower as well, but when I walked in, I found Liz lying on the bed in a black silk negligee looking sexy as fuck. Her legs were spread wide open and

I could see her bare pussy peeking out through the silk crotch-less panties.

I walked over to the bed and crawled across it, until I was nose to nose with my woman, with a hand on either side of her head, kneeling between her sexy thighs. Leaning on my forearms, I began to kiss her neck as I trailed my lips down her collarbone, stopping at each breast. I sucked on each nipple through the silk material leaving wet spots where my tongue was. She arched her back, begging for me.

I moved down to her stomach and lifted up the silk top with only my teeth. Liz froze and tried to move my mouth away, but I wasn't having it. I knocked her hand away with my head and continued on. I could feel her tense as her stomach became exposed. "Relax, baby."

That's when I saw what she was trying to hide—stretch marks. They were left over from her pregnancy with Bella and for some crazy reason she was ashamed for me to see them. Shaking my head, I thought to myself, *This beautiful woman has nothing to be ashamed of.* She has a banging body and a few stretch marks aren't going to turn me off. Plus, these aren't just stretch marks. These are proof this beautiful woman carried our baby in her belly for nine months, keeping her safe. She should get a fucking medal for that. However, I knew if I said that to her, she'd just shoo me off. So, instead, I showed her exactly what her stretch marks did to me.

As I trailed my tongue down her stomach, I stopped at the first stretch mark and gave it a soft kiss, causing her to tense up. I moved to the next stretch mark and once again gave it a kiss. This time she didn't tense. I continued kissing every stretch mark, until I had kissed them all. From there, I moved lower, stopping at the scar from when they had to take our baby out of her. Starting on the left side, I trailed kisses from one side to the other. Her body started squirming, her legs tightening, trying to seek relief, and I knew she was starting to get turned on.

It was time to take care of my girl. I moved my mouth lower and placed a wet kiss on the top of her pussy. She jerked her hips upward in response, and I chuckled at her impatience as I took one finger and pushed it inside her.

"Fuck, Liz, you're soaked." And she was...dripping fucking wet.

"I know. Please. I need you inside me. Now."

"I will, baby, but first I want to make you come with my fingers."

I pushed my fingers back inside her, pumping them in and out. With my other hand, I massaged her clit with my thumb. She continued to writhe all over the bed until finally her body began to shake and I knew she was about to orgasm. Moving my thumb off her clit, I latched onto it with my teeth and tongue, sucking hard. She completely lost it, calling out my name as she came all over my mouth and fingers.

That will never get old.

When she came down from her orgasm, I crawled up her body and kissed her on her mouth.

"Can you taste me on you, baby? You taste so fucking good."

She whimpered and attempted to reach for my cock, but before she could, I took both her hands in mine and lifted them up over her head, holding them there. My cock was hard as steel and she was slick to the touch as I slid my cock right into her warm, wet pussy and almost came right then and there. We'd had sex a few time, but tonight was different because we didn't just have sex, we made love. Slowly, never breaking our kiss, Liz and I became one with each other until we both found our release.

And every night since then, I've been inside my woman making sweet, sweet love to her, confirming over and over again, there'll never be another woman for me. Liz, is it.

"Cooper! Earth to Cooper! You gonna focus or do you want to just call Griffin and let him know he can keep the title because you forfeit?"

"Yeah, sorry. Give me a few minutes. I'm just going to go check on Liz before she heads out to get Bella."

"C'mon, man. We all know that's code for you going to get a quickie in the office on the damn desk."

Okay, so maybe I've been inside her during the day as well. Hey, like I said, I blame my sexy-as-sin woman. This isn't my fault. I repeat this is *not* my fault. Her sexual appetite is insane. She's clearly trying to make up for lost time and I'm just trying to be the dutiful boyfriend and make sure she's satisfied.

Boyfriend. The word sounds so insignificant compared to how we feel about each other. She's the mother of my child, the love of my life. I wonder what she would say if I proposed. I could become her fiancé and eventually her husband. Fuck, what the hell am I thinking? It's only been a few weeks. She'd probably freak the hell out.

Kaden calls my name, but I ignore him as I make my way out of the ring and head to check on Liz in the office. We originally agreed we would keep our personal life separate from our professional one while at the gym, but so far I've yet to keep to that agreement and it won't be happening today either.

"Knock, knock," I say as I walk into what was once my dad's office. The feeling I get when I enter now, is warmth compared to the coolness I used to feel. Liz hasn't changed much in the office except adding a few pictures on the walls and a couple on the desk. She even blew up a few from our family day at the park. The truth is, she could've made zero changes and the vibe would still be completely different because wherever Liz is, she emits a warm feeling into those around her. You can't help but gravitate toward her—she's just good. Even guys who come in to pay their monthly dues can't help but hang around her. I swear I'm going to have to kick some ass soon to remind them whose woman she is.

I frown when I see, sitting at the desk with Liz, is Hayley and Kayla, and they all appear to be having lunch together. Liz glances over at me and gives me a knowing smirk, while I pout at her like a child. So much for getting into her sweet pussy today. Looks like I'll have to wait until tonight.

She mouths, *"I'm sorry"* as the other girls turn to say hi.

"Hello, ladies. How's everyone doing today?"

All of them answer various responses of good, then Kayla adds, "I was just telling Liz, how Hayley and I are traveling with you and the other guys to Boulder at the end of October since you and Caleb will be training while shooting promo photos for the fight in February, and

Bentley is fighting at UFC Fight Night. I told her she should join us, but she isn't having it. Tell her she should go."

*Oh, hell...*I haven't discussed this trip with Liz yet. I'll be gone for four days at the end of October doing some press shit for the title fight that's taking place in February, and I need to be there to support Bentley at his fight. Ever since I took over the gym, he's been working hard to get ready for this fight.

"Kayla, I can't just up and leave. Bella's in school and she needs stability, plus it's going to be around Halloween and she will die if she can't wear her Elsa costume and go trick-or-treating in the same neighborhood we take her to every year."

Kayla pouts when she hears this. "Oh, no! I forgot about Halloween. I've never missed a single one of Bella's Halloweens. This seriously sucks."

Damn it, it does suck. My first holiday with my daughter and I won't even be here with her.

Liz gives Kayla a sad smile. "Things have changed." She shrugs. "Jobs have changed, living arrangements have changed, nothing can stay the same forever. I'm sad that you guys won't be here, but I need to stay here and make sure Bella's schedule is stable. I don't want her to get confused. It'll suck going trick-or-treating without you guys, but I'll send pictures. I promise."

Of course she won't drop everything, take Bella out of school, and travel to Boulder with us. Why not? It's simple. Liz is a damn good mother and puts our daughter first, always. Just like my mom tried to do every time my dad traveled, but look how that ended. The question is, how long will she put up with me being gone and missing important family moments like taking our daughter trick-or-treating? How long until she feels lonely like my mom did and she seeks comfort in another guy who can be at all those events?

Twenty-Seven

LIZ

I CAN TELL SOMETHING IS BOTHERING COOPER, BUT I DON'T want to ask him in front of Kayla and Hayley, so I let it go for now. I check the time, seeing I need to leave soon to pick up Bella from school. I promised her we'd go get her costume today, so, we'll find out soon if she sticks to the Elsa one.

"All right everyone, I need to go pick up my daughter and take her costume shopping. I just spoke with my mom and they're about to board their flight, and should be in tonight around dinner, so don't forget about the barbeque Sunday." I walk over to Cooper and give him a quick kiss. "And I will see you tonight."

He grabs me by my arm, looking conflicted. Something is clearly bothering him and I need to make sure we get time alone later to talk about it after Bella's sleeping, so I can find out what's going on.

"Can I go with you to get Bella? It's bad enough I'm going to miss her trick-or-treating. I'd like to at least be there to help her pick out her costume."

Oh, this man. My heart swells every time he says stuff like this.

"Well, I don't know how much helping you're going to be doing since our sweet child has a mind of her own when it comes to all important decisions such as which costume to get, but you can always join us, Cooper. You never have to ask."

I run my hand down his cheek and a hint of a smile graces his face. "Give me a few minutes to shower and change."

"Sure."

After he exits I notice both my friends are staring at me.

"What?"

Hayley is the first to comment. "Nothing, he's just so sweet. I want a man like that."

Kayla nods. "I don't want a man like that because we both know I don't want a man at all, but I'm glad you have a man like that. You deserve to be happy."

I debate on how to reply to Kayla's comment because it drives me nuts that she never wants to be in a relationship just because her parents' marriage isn't one based on love.

"Hayley, you'll find your man. I didn't think it would ever happen to me, but I'm glad I waited, and you"—I mock glare at Kayla—"need to stop. Just because your parents chose to have a marriage of convenience doesn't mean all couples choose that. If you never let a guy in, you'll never see how different it can be, and trust me, it can be amazing."

Both girls wave me off and we all exit the office and head to the front. Hayley goes to her office and Kayla stands with me in the front as we discuss our plans for the weekend. I'd like to take my parents and brother out to dinner tomorrow night. I hate they are only here for a short time, but I'm so excited to just see them. Kayla mentions us going to get manis and pedis in the morning with my mom.

Cooper and Bentley walk up, overhearing our conversation. "Why don't you guys schedule a full spa day and I'll watch Bella and hang out with your dad and brother? Bentley can even come over and chill. We can invite Caleb and Kaden as well."

Kayla gets excited at the mention of a full day at the spa, but there's no way I'm spending that kind of money. Yes, I'm working and I'm pretty sure Cooper is paying me more than he should be, and yes, I do have a home to live in and I don't plan to move out, but I need to start saving just in case. I'm never going to be in the position I was in when our apartment caught fire with no money in the bank and nowhere to go.

But before I can say anything, Cooper gives me a raised brow indicating he isn't going to let me argue. "And it's all on me. I've been meaning to add your name to the account so I'll do that today when we get done at the costume store. Kayla, I know Liz, and I'm willing to bet she won't book it. So, you're going to need to book it. Make sure you include whatever you ladies want and I got it covered."

And with that, he grabs my hand and stalks off, dragging me behind him and not leaving any room for argument, as the sounds of Bentley and Kayla's laughter ring through the building. *Damn this man. This is just another example of why I can't help but love him.*

We leave my car at the gym and take Cooper's Rover. He refuses to take my car anywhere we don't have to and he keeps complaining my car needs to be thrown into a junkyard, but I continue to ignore him. I'm hoping to save up enough in the next year to buy a newer used car.

We get to Bella's preschool, and when she sees her dad, she comes running over to him, jumping straight into his arms. After she shows him her cubby and desk, we say good-bye to her teacher and head out.

"Daddy! Are you here to go with Mommy and me to pick out my costume?"

Cooper smiles wide and gives her a big kiss on her cheek. "You betcha, Princess."

"Mommy never gets a costume. Do you want to get a costume so you can go trick-or-treating with me?"

Cooper's smile fades instantly, and I think I'm starting to understand why he was upset earlier. He's going to be missing his first holiday because of work. It's part of his job and I won't let him feel guilty over something out of his control. He works hard and without even blinking an eye has offered everything he has to Bella and me, and the last thing he needs is to feel like he's done something wrong by making a living.

"Bella, unfortunately, Daddy is going to be working on Halloween. He has to go away for a few days and one of the days he'll be gone will be on Halloween. But we'll take a lot of pictures and I'll text them all to him, and when he gets home, we can show him all the candy you got. Does that sound good?"

Bella's look of disappointment mirrors her father's, both of them looking adorable with matching pouting faces. "No, that doesn't sound good. That doesn't sound good at all. That sounds bad, really bad."

Whoa! I knew she was disappointed, but I didn't expect her to get so angry over him not going trick-or-treating with her. I take her out of her father's arms and set her on her feet, then I kneel down so I can make eye contact with her.

"Well, I'm sorry that doesn't sound good, but that's the way it has to be. I'll be with you and you'll have lots of fun."

She pouts some more. "Will Auntie Kay be with us?"

Oh Lord, this conversation is going downhill fast. "No, you know how Mommy and Auntie Kay work with daddy now? Well, when Daddy travels, sometimes Auntie Kay has to travel too, so she'll be gone with Daddy. It will just be us this year."

Bella stomps her foot and crosses her arms over her chest in full-blown temper tantrum mode. "Then I don't want to go trick-or-treating. This is stupid. Can we go with Daddy and Auntie Kay where they're going?"

"First of all, Bella," I say in my mom voice that seems to just make her even more mad. "We don't say stupid. That isn't nice, and no, we can't go away with them. They're working and you have school. I'm sorry you're upset, but that's the answer. Would you like to go get your costume, or go home and take a nap? Because if you keep up this attitude, you will not be going trick-or-treating."

She huffs and puffs but finally relents. "Okay, I guess I'll go get my costume." My poor baby looks so defeated, it breaks my heart.

I look over at Cooper and he looks just as defeated as our little girl. These two are going to be the death of me. I can't have them ganging up on me.

When we get home from the costume shop, Bella takes her costume up to her room to put in her closet. Luckily once we got there her mood improved and after almost an hour of debating, she decided on the Elsa costume. Of course, Cooper bought her every matching accessory to go with the costume, most likely out of guilt, but I didn't stop him. He tried to be upbeat for Bella, but I could still see the sadness in his eyes.

Glancing at the clock and seeing it's almost time for my parents and brother to arrive, I do a sweep through of the house, making sure everything is clean. Because we don't have any guestrooms, they'll be staying at a hotel nearby, but they'll be coming here after they check-in to have dinner with us and meet Cooper.

I look around for Cooper and notice he's disappeared. I search the house for him and find him in the office.

"Hey, handsome. What are you up to?"

He looks up and with sadness in his eyes. "Nothing, just looking at a couple of work emails. What time will your family be here?"

Wanting to speak to him about his sour mood, but knowing we don't have time since my family is due to arrive any minute, I move in front of him to sit on the desk, wrapping my legs around his body and my arms around his neck. I pull his face toward mine. He knows what I'm after, and as always, he doesn't disappoint.

His lips meet mine in a punishing kiss as his hands move to my ass. He pulls me closer to him until my body is almost one with his. We kiss for several minutes, our tongues swirling around one another until Cooper backs up.

"Fuck, baby girl, I needed that. I'm sorry I'm being a cranky ass. I'll try to shake it off before your parents get here. I don't want them to think I'm an ogre."

Laughing at his comment, I lean in for another kiss, my tongue swiping across his lips, seeking entrance. When my tongue enters, he sucks on it before backing away leaving me unsatisfied and frowning.

"Hey, now who's the one pouting? We both can't be cranky." He runs his thumb along my lips to straighten out the frown on my face.

"Cooper, there's no reason to feel guilty. You have to work. There'll be plenty of holidays in the future. Don't let this get to you and ruin your day."

"Liz, did you see how upset Bella was? Of course I'm going to be upset and feel guilty. I don't want to miss important shit in her life. This is exactly why I said..."

I cut him off, knowing exactly where he is going, refusing to let him go there.

"Oh no, you don't. Don't start. Missing a holiday doesn't make you a crappy dad or boyfriend and it doesn't mean you don't deserve to have us in your life. So just get those thoughts out of your head. You hear me?"

"Yeah, baby," he says, the sad undertone still residing in his voice. I'm going to need to come up with a way to make this right. I can't have him beating himself up every time he has to go away for work.

I hear a knock on the front door as Bella starts yelling my parents are here.

Letting her open the door, she squeals in glee as my mom and dad both take her in their arms for a hug and then move on to me. My brother lifts Bella into his arms and gives her a huge hug as he carries her into the living room.

"Mom, Dad, Mathew, this is my boyfriend, Cooper. Cooper, this is my mom, Macy, my dad, Randy, and my brother, Mathew."

Cooper shakes everyone's hands and says it's nice to meet them. Bella watches the entire exchange and then has to join in the conversation.

"Umm, you forgot to tell them the best news ever. Cooper is also my daddy! And the bestest daddy ever."

Everybody laughs. My family might live long distance, but we talk almost every day and they know all about Cooper. Bella runs right into Cooper and latches on to his legs, giving him the cutest leg hug.

My mom looks at me, her eyes glossy like she's about to cry from the sweet exchange. I understand completely. We agree on Chinese food to keep it easy, and Bella drags everyone upstairs to show off her room. She spends the entire time explaining every toy and movie her dad has bought her until the food arrives.

I nudge Cooper and nod toward our daughter. "See, one holiday isn't going to change how she feels about you. She loves you."

The weekend passes by way too fast. On Saturday, Kayla, Hayley, my mom, and I all spend a wonderfully relaxing day at the spa. I invite Ashley to go as well, but she's heading out with Tristan to visit her parents. When we get there, it's clear Kayla has booked us for everything. An hour massage, facial, mud wrap, and of course manis and pedis. I didn't realize how much I really needed this kind of pampering. Saturday night we all go out to dinner at a yummy Italian place, and Sunday everybody comes over for a backyard barbeque. I've noticed that while Bentley joins us for dinner and the barbeque, he and Kayla are completely avoiding each other. I really need to ask her how her living arrangements are working out.

Now it's Monday, and Cooper is dropping Bella off at school on his way to the gym, so I can see my parents and brother off on their flight back home.

I pull my parents into a loving embrace, sad their trip is already over. I love where I live, but I also wish I could be close to my family. "Oh, Mom, Dad. I'm so glad you guys came. I miss you so much."

"Sweetheart, I'm going to miss you, too. But I'm so happy for the love that Bella and you have found. Cooper is a great man and father, and I feel so much better leaving, knowing he's here taking care of my girls," my dad says through glossy eyes.

Next, I give Mathew a hug goodbye. "Don't be a stranger."

"You never know. Maybe after I finish my two years, I'll decide to transfer to ULV," he says with a wink.

"Don't even tease me!" I shout, and people walking by stare at me. We get to the security entrance, and since I don't have a ticket, I can't go any further. We exchange a few more hugs and then they're gone.

Twenty-Eight

LIZ

AFTER SEEING MY FAMILY OFF, I HEAD STRAIGHT TO THE gym to get caught up on some bookkeeping. Cooper is already there, training with Kaden, and when he catches my eye, he gives me a wink. *God, I love that man.*

I'm not even in my chair yet when Kayla comes bounding into my office, her face red and hands in the air.

"Aghhh!!! I swear that man is trying to drive me insane!"

I have a feeling I am about to hear all about Bentley. "Who?"

"Oh, give me a break, Liz. You know who I'm talking about... Bentley!"

And as if she's beckoned him over, the man of the hour comes walking into my office. *So much for getting any work done.*

"Hey, Liz." Bentley addresses me when he walks in, and it doesn't go unnoticed he just completely ignored Kayla. I look over at her and she's shooting daggers at the poor man.

"Hey Bentley, what can I do for you?"

Kayla huffs, and when nobody acknowledges her, she does it again louder.

"I just wanted to see if there's anything else I need to do before the fight next week." I do everything in my power to contain my laughter. It's blatantly obvious he's going out of his way to ignore Kayla, yet he looks so uneasy doing it. I just want to hide him under my desk to get him out of her line of attack. It's only a matter of time until Kayla boils over, burning everyone in her line of sight.

"Let me check for you." I pull up his file, but before I can get another word in, Kayla loses her shit.

"Excuse me, mister. I know you think the world revolves around you, but Liz and I were talking first. So, you're going to need to get in line. As a matter of fact, you can go wait outside." She's practically shouting by the time she makes it to the end of her sentence, and then she's up, out of her seat, and pushing him out the door.

Bentley looks terrified. Seriously? This is a grown ass man and a fighter. What the hell is he afraid of Kayla for? She weighs like one twenty dripping wet.

Before the door shuts, I yell, "It's all covered, Bentley. I handled everything."

And he may have responded, but the door slams shut, blocking out all outside noise. Kayla sits back down and takes a few deep breaths, trying to calm herself.

"Care to explain why you just lost it on your roommate?"

"Liz, he is so maddening. I seriously need to find a new place to live. The problem is I actually like living there. Caleb is awesome. He's barely home and when he is, he's totally chill. Bentley on the other hand is driving me up a damn wall."

"Driving you up a wall because you like him?"

Kayla sputters out a, "No!" But her face turns a deep shade of pink, telling me she's full of crap.

"Anyway," she continues. I'm here, not to talk about Bentley, but to tell you we were supposed to go get our shot almost two weeks ago. You always make the appointment. Can you make it for us, please?"

"Yeah, I'll call tomorrow. I completely forgot. Ever since the fire, it's been crazy."

"Yes, it's definitely been crazy lately. I better get back to work. Don't want the boss to fire me," she says with laughter in her voice as she gets up and walks to the door.

"You know, eventually, you'll talk to me about Bentley."

"Yeah, yeah." She waves me off before leaving my office.

Two o'clock rolls around and I head out to get Bella. Cooper texts me he'll be working late at the gym and to please save him dinner. I smile at that. Before I moved in with Cooper, I didn't do a whole lot of cooking and it definitely wasn't healthy. Because Cooper's a fighter, he's a health freak and has to eat a certain way. He's been teaching me about eating healthy and we've been cooking together. With him at the gym so often, I've started to find recipes and surprise him with dinner when he gets home. He seems to really love my cooking and it makes me want to cook for him more often. It also doesn't hurt that I'm shedding the few pounds left after having Bella.

Eight o'clock comes around and I'm tucking Bella in bed after I finish up reading her a bedtime story. She's eaten, completed her daily reading, watched some television, and is freshly bathed, in her pajamas.

"Mommy, can I please stay up and wait for Daddy? Please!" She begs like she does most nights when Cooper isn't here to tuck her in. We're lucky he has a flexible schedule, so if needed, he can be home any time. With the fight coming up and him the owner of the gym, he's been staying late to help with Bentley's training and such. Bella and I both miss him, but I try to bring her by the gym as much as possible to see him if I know he'll be working late.

However, today Bella had a playdate so we weren't able to stop by. I want to let her stay up, knowing it's important to her to say goodnight to him, but Cooper can be there extremely late and she needs to get her rest. Plus, if I say yes once, she'll continue to ask, so I never let her wait up. The problem is my consistency doesn't deter her from continuing to ask every single time Cooper isn't home on time. I make it a point not to tell Cooper since he has this crazy notion he must spend every waking moment making up for lost time or he'll receive the award for worst father of the year. If he knew Bella begs for him on the nights he's not here he'd feel even worse.

"No, Angel. We're not going to discuss this again. When Daddy isn't home you go to bed on time. You'll see him in the morning."

And cue my four-year-old's tantrum. Tears pour down her face instantly—I swear they're crocodile tears because really? How does one produce real tears that quickly? But she still looks absolutely heartbroken and pitiful, and as a mother, that's hard to deal with, especially when it's because of how much she adores her father and not over something materialistic.

"Mommy, it's not fair! I miss him when he's not home and he misses me. I have to go to school all day. I want to drop out of school and be a fighter like Daddy."

And now I'm about to cry right along with her.

Twenty-Nine

COOPER

I TRY SO HARD TO GET HOME BY EIGHT ON THE NIGHTS I don't see Bella at the gym, never wanting to go a day without spending time with my little princess. Our time together is so precious and I never want to take it for granted.

Tonight, Bentley and I were working on some grappling techniques for his upcoming fight and I completely lost track of time. When I realized how late it was, I ran out the door without even showering and rushed home determined to kiss my sweet little girl goodnight.

Growing up, my dad barely ever made it home, nor did he care to. My mom was the only one who tucked me in at night and the unhappier she became, and the more she went out, the more often a babysitter tucked me in. I don't ever want to become my dad and I never want to drive Liz to become my mom.

There are moments in life when one small thing happens that shouldn't be a big deal but it is, and it changes everything. It changes the way you see yourself, it changes the way you see those around you, and it changes the way you view the situation. I would define this moment as just that, a life-changing moment.

I run up the stairs to Bella's room, hoping to catch her still awake, and hear my princess sobbing. I'm about to enter the room when I hear her hiccup out, "Mommy, it's not fair! I miss him when he's not home and he misses me. I have to go to school all day. I want to drop out of school and be a fighter like Daddy."

Remember when I said my heart shattered the day she was in the hospital for smoke inhalation? I take that back. It must have been a mere fracture. What's the difference? A fracture isn't broken. It hurts like a bitch, but it's still intact. A shatter on the other hand is a full-on break. Pieces are everywhere and there's no way they're ever being put back together again. I clutch my chest and try to stop the pain from radiating inside of me. If I never hear my daughter sobbing and crying out like that again, it'll be too soon.

And what's worse is that I'm the cause. I listen for a second to hear Liz's reply. "Bella Faith, you need to calm down. I can't continue to do this with you several times a week. I understand you miss Daddy, and I miss him too, but you are not dropping out of preschool. If you want to work with Daddy one day then you'll go to school and graduate and get a job when you're older. Your job right now is to go to school. Becoming a fighter like your dad is a great goal, but you still have to go to school."

Liz sounds completely exhausted and aggravated. Judging by her response, this isn't the first or even third time Bella has thrown a fit about missing me at night. If Bella is upset then there's a good chance so is Liz. She gave me this second chance and I can't screw it up. If she isn't happy, she'll leave, which means Bella and Liz won't be living under my roof anymore. I can't imagine having to live without these two girls. They've turned this house into a home with just their presence alone.

I've heard guys complain about the messes their kids leave all over the house, or that their wife or girlfriend bought new furniture that's too girly. I don't know why they're complaining. Seeing the pictures Liz has put up, or the new pillows she bought to add color to the living room, or when I walk in and almost trip on Bella's cute princess shoes, it all makes my day. It's evidence that I'm living with the two most precious girls, and the day I don't see any of that is the day my life will no longer have meaning.

I hear Bella sobbing still, but she doesn't respond, which means she must be giving up. When she knows she's going to lose the battle, she shuts down. I absolutely love how bright her passion burns, and I hope it never burns out.

I knock softly on the door to let them know of my arrival then walk in. Bella tries to quickly wipe her tears and Liz freezes in place, probably wondering how much I heard.

I pretend like I didn't hear anything and ignore Bella's tears. "Hey princess, I was hoping you weren't asleep. Has Mommy read you a book yet?" I can see it in her eyes that her mom already read her a book and she doesn't want to lie, but she wants this time with me, shit, she *needs* this time with me, and I need it with her.

"I read her *The Giving Tree*," Liz replies softly, trying to gage my reaction to Bella's tears, but I make sure not to give anything away.

"Nice. Is it too late to pick one more book to read to Bella before she goes to bed?" I direct the question to Liz to make sure it's okay. I know it's after Bella's bedtime, so I don't want to step on her toes, but I really don't want her to tell me no. Bella waits for Liz's answer and when she says okay, Bella jumps out of bed to grab a book.

I mouth *"thank you"* to Liz and she gives me a small smile before walking out to give Bella and me some alone time.

"How's it going, Princess?" My daughter is a smart girl so she knows exactly what I'm asking, but she just lifts her shoulders up like she's not sure what I'm asking about.

"Are you giving your mom a hard time?"

The tears well back up in her eyes and she leans over to hug me tightly, sniffling back the cry that's threatening to breaking out. "I just wanted to see you before I went to bed, but she said I had to go to sleep. I just miss you so much sometimes. I'm sorry. It's just not fair. Bedtimes are dumb."

"I know it's not fair, Princess. Sometimes we have to do things we don't want to do because it's what's best for us. Your mommy loves you so much and she has you go to bed at eight o'clock because you need your sleep. You want to be a fighter, right?" She nods.

"Well, if you want to be a fighter, you have to get plenty of sleep so you can grow. Did you know we grow in our sleep? So, you need your sleep."

I know she gets it, but she wouldn't be my Bella if she didn't still state her case. That's where her passion comes in. When she believes in something, she fights for it. I can't even imagine what she'll be like when she hits her teenage years.

"Okay, Daddy, but I still miss you and want to say good night to you."

It hits me then that we have technology, and as annoying as it can be, it can also be very convenient. "How about we compromise? Any time I'm not home by bedtime, you can use your mom's phone to Face Time me on my phone so we can see each other and say good night?"

Her entire face lights up and she sits up straighter like I just gave her free reign at a toy store. "Okay, deal! Just make sure you answer."

I give her a kiss on her forehead and say with absolute conviction, "I will always answer your phone calls. No matter where I am or what I'm doing, I will also make sure I'm here for you, I promise. Now, let's read you that book."

When I finish reading the book, Bella is passed out, holding onto my arm like she needs it to breathe. It doesn't matter what I have going on, I need to make sure the only time I'm not here to tuck her into bed is if I'm away. Fuck, I can't believe in a couple weeks I have to leave. It'll be the first time I've been away from Bella and Liz since they moved in here. Sometimes it feels like I need them to breathe.

I walk downstairs to the living room to find Liz curled up on the couch reading, and I almost feel bad taking her away from her book but I need some quality time with my woman. She sees me coming toward her and puts the iPad away.

"Hey baby, I thought you were going to be gone longer. Is everything okay?"

I sit next to Liz's feet, dragging her body to me until she's sitting on my lap. Then I wrap my arms around her body and drink in her scent. This right here is home, yet looking at this woman, I feel like I barely know her. Yes, I know the person she was when we met five years ago and the person she is today. She was and still is fun, and sexy, and so damn smart. She's an amazing mother and friend, and she has the biggest, kindest heart. I mean, what woman goes to the man's funeral who almost killed her daughter?

She cooks dinner for us every night even though I know it isn't her cup of tea, and she works hard at the gym even though she knows how much money I have. Liz could easily stay home all day and let me take care of her, but she wants to earn her own way and be equal. What I don't know is the person I missed out on for the last five years, the woman who was forced to grow up at eighteen because she was pregnant so young but still determined to make it through college. I want to know all about that woman.

"Tell me about the last five years."

She seems a bit confused at my request. "What do you want to know?"

"I want to know everything. I want to know all about your pregnancy and Bella, every age, every milestone, and every detail. I hate that I missed out on so much, and I feel like no matter how much I try to catch up, I'm too damn far behind."

"Um, okay. Well, after I found out I was pregnant, Kayla started coming with me to all my appointments. From the minute she found out, she never missed one. We would make sure they were on a day neither of us had school. I think the nurses and doctors thought we were lesbians. I had morning sickness for the first trimester, which totally sucked, but then it went away and the rest of my pregnancy was smooth sailing, thank God. At twenty weeks, I could've found out the sex, but Kayla wanted to know so badly I decided to wait. It was so much fun driving her crazy. She couldn't even shop like she wanted to because everything had to be in neutral colors."

She laughs through all of this and I'm glad she had Kayla and has good memories, but I hate those memories don't include me. I cuddle her harder, needing her closer to me. "I wish I could have been there. I would've held your hair back when you were sick, and we definitely would've found out the sex of the baby. I would've gone crazy not knowing how to prepare. I know Kayla was there, but I hate that it wasn't me."

"I know, baby, but you can't think like that or you will go crazy from guilt about something you can't change. Okay, let's see...At forty-two weeks pregnant, they induced me because Bella didn't want to come out, and after forty-seven hours in labor they had to do an emergency caesarean because her heart rate dropped. When they took her out, at first, I couldn't hear her crying. I kept asking Kayla if she was okay and I could tell by Kayla's answers something was wrong, but they had a sheet put up, so I couldn't see.

"When Bella came out she wasn't breathing so they had to pump oxygen into her lungs. Finally, she took her first breath and started to cry, and it felt like my world was complete. They brought her over to me and announced she was a girl. After a few days, we both went home and then the fun began."

I know she's trying to make light of the situation by joking, but I can't even imagine how hard it was for her and Kayla to raise a baby on their own at eighteen. I don't say anything though, because I like listening to her talk. Instead I give her a kiss and she continues.

"The first year was exhausting. Bella had Colic, which is like acid reflux, kind of. So, she had to get put on a special formula, and I wanted to breastfeed, but I couldn't pump, and I had to go back to school. I had her in the middle of the semester, so I only took off the days I was in the hospital. I couldn't afford daycare and I didn't want her to be with strangers so Kayla and I made sure our schedules were opposite, so one of us was always home with Bella.

"My mom came to visit for a few weeks after Bella came home. She slept in my room, and I slept in the third bedroom with Bella." She smiles absently like she is reliving those memories. What I would give to be in her head and heart, and see all of her memories firsthand.

She pulls out her phone and opens a photo app. "I lost all our photos and such in the fire, but luckily, I have all Bella's pictures saved digitally."

She begins flipping through them showing me Bella as a newborn, Bella at one, two, three years old, Halloweens, Christmases, and birthdays. Most are of just Bella, but once in a while I see a picture of Kayla and Liz as well—it's like watching them all grow up together. When she gets to the last one, she has silent tears falling down her face.

I swipe them away and turn her to face me. "Why the tears, baby girl?"

"I love looking at pictures of Bella, but looking at them with you feels bittersweet. I have such mixed emotions because I feel like I should feel bad I messed up with the birth control but at the same time I don't want to feel bad because my screw up got me Bella and I would never wish to not have her. Then I feel bad that you didn't get to experience any of those memories, but at the same time I wouldn't trade those memories for the world because I created them with Bella. Does that make sense?"

"Yes, it makes perfect sense, and I'm thankful for your screw up. I can't imagine not having Bella in our lives." I kiss her forehead and we sit together for a few minutes just enjoying each other's company. I don't know what comes over me but suddenly I blurt out, "I want to have a baby."

She looks at me like I'm crazy so I continue. "I missed so much with Bella and she's already almost five years old. I want to experience all of that with you. I know we aren't married, but we're living together and we'll be together for the rest of our lives. I'm an only child and would have loved to have a sibling. I bet Bella would love having a little brother or sister, plus we have plenty of rooms here. I can move the gym to the garage or we can move. We can buy a bigger house with a bigger yard..."

"Whoa, whoa. Slow down, there. Are you sure, Cooper? I mean... you went from not wanting a family to having an insta-family. Are you sure you want to add another baby to the mix?"

My heart sinks. "You don't want to have another baby with me?"

"Of course, I do! I just want you to be sure. With Bella, you didn't have a choice. You've accepted her from day one and you two have an amazing relationship already. I know you'll be an amazing father to any other babies we have. I just want you to be sure. I actually have to go get my shot this week because I forgot after the whole fire situation. If this is what you really want I can skip the shot, or I can get it and we can think more about it."

"No, don't get the shot. Let's let nature take its course."

She smiles and turns to straddle my lap, wrapping her arms around my neck. "Okay, baby. We'll let nature take its course."

I lift her up by her ass and begin walking her to our bedroom. "I say we go practice baby-making right now."

"I agree," she says through her giggles as I slam the door behind us.

Thirty

LIZ

IT'S MONDAY MORNING AND EVERYBODY LEAVES tomorrow night to go to Boulder. Well, everybody besides me that is. I'll be here running the gym even though it pretty much runs itself. I walk into my office and see a huge bouquet of pink roses. The note on the front reads:

Pack an overnight bag and be ready to go at 6 p.m.
—Coop

Hmm...Well, okay then. The rest of the day I attempt to crunch numbers, pay bills, and print receipts, but I can't focus because I'm too intrigued about tonight. At one thirty, just as I'm about to give up and head out to get Bella, Kayla comes walking in shaking her head.

"Where do you think you're going? Home I hope, to get ready for your romantic night with Cooper."

"How did you know about that? I'm going to get Bella and then going home."

"Nope, not happening. I already have her stuff Cooper packed and snuck out this morning. She's coming to my place for a sleepover. I'm getting her from school and you're going home to get ready. I'll see you tomorrow." And with an over-exaggerated wink that reminds me of Marilyn Monroe, she exits as quickly as she came in.

Cooper gets home around five o'clock and runs up to jump in the shower while I finish getting ready. When he's done, we walk outside and waiting for us is a cab.

When I go to ask him a question, he raises two fingers to my mouth to shush me. We get in and he gives the driver an address to go to. When we pull up to a BMW dealership I'm confused. "I know you weren't big on relationships, but surely you know that a car dealership isn't considered romantic."

He laughs and shakes his head, while grabbing my hand, kissing it, and then pulling me along.

The gentleman manning the door asks how he can help us and Cooper tells him he's picking up a purchase. He gives him his name and the gentleman directs us to the pick-up area. Cooper signs a few papers and then is handed the keys and pointed in the direction we need to go.

When we get to the vehicle, it's a beautiful midnight blue SUV. I'm not sure why he's getting another SUV, but it's his money so who am I to judge. I go to get in the passenger seat, but he cuts me off before I can get in.

"Would you mind driving?"

Okay, I never drive. I mean, I *can* drive, but Cooper is one of those guys who insists the man drives everywhere.

"Sure," I say, taking the keys. We get in and I inhale the new car scent.

"Do you like it?" he asks, sounding almost nervous like whether I like it's important to him. I look around taking the vehicle in. It has pretty grey leather seats and touch screen everything. It has a built-in DVD player and TV in the back seat. It's a dream car. What's not to like?

"Yeah, it's a beautiful car. Are you getting rid of the Rover?"

He bites his bottom lip then pulls it out from between his teeth slowly. I'm kind of worried he's going to draw blood.

"No...this car is for you."

"What? For me? Cooper. No, you didn't." I should have seen this coming!

Damn, this thoughtful man.

"I did, but hear me out. I have to go away and I get you're okay with your car, but I'm not. I let it go because I've been around and if I'm not, one of the other guys usually are. So, if your piece-of-shit car breaks down we can handle it. However, we're all leaving and I need to know my girls are safe. It even has roadside assistance so you can get a tow truck or with one press of a button call someone to come fix your flat tire for you. You can even call to get gas delivered in case you run out."

I want to be upset, but when he looks at me with those cute puppy dog eyes begging me to understand, I don't have the heart to hurt him. I know his heart is in the right place and he genuinely cares about our safety.

I take his hand in mine, bringing it up to my lips, and kiss his knuckles. "Thank you, Coop. This was very sweet of you. I love the car and I love you."

I think I just put him in shock. He was obviously gearing up for a fight, because he doesn't even know how to respond.

"Well, good. I'm glad you like it. I love you, too."

He gives me directions to where we're going and we end up at the Venetian hotel on the strip. We pull up and valet park. Is it weird that I totally don't want to hand over my new baby to this stranger? Cooper sees my reluctance and whispers, "It's insured." *Whatever.*

We enjoy a great Mexican dinner at the restaurant and then we stroll over to one of the bakeries and share my favorite dessert, Crème brûlée. When we're both stuffed, we make our way to the counter where Cooper checks us into a room.

"You didn't have to do this. We could have gone home. Bella is at Kayla's you know."

"Please don't argue about this, baby girl. I'm leaving for four days and I want to give my woman a romantic night away from the house." *How can I argue with that?*

Once we're in the room, the door barely shuts before he's on me. He pushes me against the wall and begins to kiss me. God, I will never get tired of how remarkable this man can kiss. His hand lifts my chin and then his mouth is on me. He sucks lightly on my bottom lip and then on my top, asking for access. I open up for him and his tongue swirls in my mouth, his kisses feeling like the most potent drug. I honestly think it's possible to get high off Cooper's touch.

He moves his body closer, if that's even possible, and within seconds I'm shamelessly writhing against him, begging for him. He grinds his erection into me, and I moan loudly into his mouth. The need gets stronger, and suddenly we're all mouths and teeth and hands, and it's just too much.

I pull his shirt up and he yanks it off the rest of the way. He pulls down my dress and I kick it off. His hands grip my panties and I feel him rip them off me. I grab his belt to unbuckle it and his jeans fall to his feet, exposing his incredible erection.

The growing need for each other exceeds our ability to make it to the bed. I wrap my leg around his waist and he lifts me up, wrapping my legs around either side of him. Once he has me steady, he thrusts his hard cock up into me. There's no foreplay. There's no need. I'm wet, he's hard, and I need this man more than air.

My back hits the wall hard as he continues to pump into me. I lower my head to kiss and suck on the side of his neck and he tastes delectable, better than any dessert.

He hits deep inside me over and over again, the pleasure inside me increasing with every thrust. "Fucking hell, Coop. Right there. Don't stop," I pant. My pussy is clenching tight and I know I'm getting close.

A few more thrusts and I'm flying high, my orgasm exploding around his cock. Cooper picks up the pace and with a grunt he comes inside me. As he comes to a stop, both of us breathing heavy, he looks at me, beaming, and I melt inside. This man is my entire world.

We shower together and then get into bed with him spooning me from behind. He plays with my hair for a few minutes, combing it with his fingers, then stops. I think he's asleep until he lets out a heavy sigh. "I hate leaving you guys tomorrow."

"Cooper, it's going to be fine."

"I hope so, baby girl. I hope so." A few minutes later, I hear his soft snores, but I can't sleep. I just don't understand why he's so worried about leaving us. I have a feeling this all stems back to his parents, with his dad being away often and his mom cheating. At some point, he's going to have to believe in us, that we're not his parents and we aren't going to go down the road they did. I guess all I can do until he does, is believe in us enough for the both of us.

Thirty-One

COOPER

I WAKE UP IN THE MIDDLE OF THE NIGHT TO FEEL LIZ'S BODY rubbing up against mine as she moves a bit in her sleep. I don't know why it is, but I have this incessant need to show her she's mine and ruin her for any other man. No, that's a lie, I know why it is. I have it in my head that if I ruin her for other man she'll never leave me. My goal is to leave her with her feeling me between her legs for the next four days so she won't forget about me and seek comfort elsewhere.

Gently moving the sheets off her body, I move my hand to her pussy and slide one finger in and then another. She's still half asleep, but she's starting to move. I spread open her lips just enough to wrap my mine around her clit and pull it. Her body begins to writhe against my fingers and mouth, wanting more.

"Fuck, baby, you taste so good," I whisper as I go back for more. With my fingers still pumping slowly deep inside her warmth, I start to suck hard on her clit then soothe it with my tongue. Her legs tense, telling me it's going to be a quick but strong orgasm. Her body shakes and then her legs tremble around me as she softly moans my name.

"Well, that's one way to wake up," she says, and even though, it's dark and I can't see her, I can hear the laughter in her words. I give the top of her pussy one last kiss then I drag my body up hers until I'm face-to-face with her. I give her a kiss that begins soft, but quickly turns rough, all my emotions trying to convey what my words can't say, begging her to love me enough, to want me enough—for me to be enough— so she'll never leave me.

When I end the kiss, she licks her lips, tasting herself. "Does that taste good?"

She nods shyly and I laugh. Even with her own pussy juices on her mouth, she's still adorably shy.

We wake up around nine and order room service. I feel like the clock is counting down and it's making me sick. I want to beg her to come with me, but I know it would be for the wrong reasons. Of course, I'm going to miss her and Bella, but the real issue is, I'm scared shitless she's going to stray away from me. I know it's crazy because she loves me, and I know, deep down, she wouldn't cheat, but if you saw what I saw growing up you would understand. *Fuck, maybe I need to see a therapist.*

After breakfast, we pack up and head home to meet Kayla and Bella. As soon as she's through the door, she's in my arms. "Daddy, I missed you so much. I had so much fun with Auntie Kay and Uncle Bentley."

She started to call Bentley, Uncle Bentley, a few days ago and I swear the man almost handed over his life savings to her when he heard her say it for the first time.

"I'm happy to hear that, Princess. Why don't you go get dressed and we'll go out for the day before I leave tonight?"

Bella smiles wide at going out, but as soon as she hears that I'm leaving tonight her sadness mutes her smile. She says okay and runs upstairs to get ready.

The three of us spend the day at the park. Bella insists I push her on the swings even though she can do it herself, we make castles in the sand area, and we watch her play tag with other kids. I find myself mentally soaking it all in before I leave.

Eight o'clock comes around and we're all gathered in my house ready to go. Liz and Bella wanted to say goodbye at the airport, but with so many people going, we decided to take one vehicle to the airport. Plus, there's no reason for her to drive all the way there and have to drive back late at night with Bella.

"I love you so much," I tell Liz. "I'll call and text you. Please send me pictures of Bella on Halloween." I give her a chaste kiss because anything more and I just might not leave her.

"I love you, too, and I promise I will. Have a safe flight." She peppers several kisses on my face and neck before she hugs me goodbye.

We're taking a chartered jet over to Boulder because it's easier than dealing with a public flight. Bentley, Kaden, Caleb, and I are sitting in the chairs bullshitting while Hayley and Kayla are sleeping in the one bedroom the plane has.

I know my phone doesn't have service up here, but it doesn't stop me from checking it every five minutes.

"Bro, you're seriously pussy whipped. Chill out." Bentley laughs, nodding at my phone burning a hole in my hand.

"Yeah, whatever. I will gladly accept that name if it means I can be inside my woman's pussy for the rest of our lives."

Kaden jumps in. "Well, shit. Those are some big words. Are we talking marriage here?"

"Well for starters, I told her I want another baby, and she said okay. So, I would say marriage is definitely coming soon."

All the guys look at me like I've grown a third head and I chuckle, changing the subject. "So, Bent, what's going on with you and Kayla? Bella said she had a great time with both of you last night. I'm pretty sure we only asked Kayla to watch our daughter."

Caleb, who barely ever speaks, cuts in. "He's just as pussy whipped as you are except he isn't getting any of Kayla's pussy."

"Shut the hell up, man," Bentley retorts. "She wants me, but she wants it to just be all fucking and I'm not having it. She's either all in or not at all. She'll come around, it's just a matter of time. I told her the next time we fuck, she's mine."

Kaden throws his head back with a laugh. "So now you guys aren't fucking at all. How's that working out for you?"

Caleb adds, "It sounds like Bentley has the pussy in this relationship."

We all start laughing and the girls come out. Kayla looks around and asks, "What's so funny?" We all go quiet and both girls are glaring at us. Hayley says, "Hmm...Sounds like the guys were just caught gossiping like a bunch of chicks."

She's definitely not off base with that observation.

253

Thirty-Two

COOPER

IT'S THURSDAY NIGHT AND IT'S BEEN TWO DAYS WITHOUT my girls. I've been busy with interviews, press conferences, and photo ops. Between my title fight coming up in February, Caleb fighting that night as well, and Bentley fighting in two days, it's been crazy. People don't realize how much more goes into being a part of the UFC aside from the fight they see on the television. And now with me being the owner of several of the training facilities, I have even more responsibility.

It's nine o'clock here in Boulder, so it's eight o'clock where we live. Knowing Bella will be going to bed soon, I break away from the craziness and call my girls to say good night. Liz's phone rings but goes to voicemail. I try again and it does it again, so I send her a text asking her to please call me as soon as she can.

I spoke with Liz and Bella a couple times yesterday and was able to say good night to Bella. I would like to say good night to her tonight as well, so I can keep my promise to her. I hate that I'll be missing

Halloween with her, so I take a look at the schedule to see if I can find a way to fly home tomorrow to be there for the trick-or-treating and be back by Saturday morning. It would mean a lot of flying but getting to see my princess in her Elsa costume trick-or-treating would be worth it. I find a large enough gap in my schedule, only having to reschedule one meeting, so I pull up the flights to book one.

A few hours later, there's still no call back from Liz, and we're finishing up at the training center. Everybody agrees to grab dinner at a local pub on the way back to the hotel. I'm nursing my second beer when I see Caleb and Bentley looking down at one of their phones, looking nervous. I don't know why, but I get a bad feeling deep in my gut.

"What the hell are you guys looking at? Don't be rude. Share."

This gets Kayla's attention. "It's probably one of the whores Bentley brought home. Did she let you take pictures?"

His eyes turn murderous and he growls out, "That was one time! One time, woman! I didn't even sleep with her! I haven't brought anyone else home since then, and I said I was sorry a million damn times. I don't know why you even care because you sure as hell don't want me. And for your information, the picture we're looking at is of a woman, of your best friend actually, who appears to be cheating on my best friend. So, before you talk shit, get your facts straight."

He turns to look at me, realizing he just threw up at the mouth. "I'm sorry, man. It's probably nothing. Alex is at club Surrender. He just sent me a picture of Liz and some other guy there...together."

Kayla and Hayley both yell, "Bullshit," and stalk over to Bentley, yanking his phone out of his hand. It must not be good because one look at the photo and both women are trying to make excuses. "It has to be a mistake because Liz would never cheat. For God sakes, you are the only guy she's ever been with."

Hayley chimes in her opinion. "Yeah, plus, she went five years without getting any. There's no way she would cheat now, so there has to be a reason for this."

I get up and slowly take the phone from Kayla. Staring at me is my woman and she's absolutely stunning in a dark purple strapless dress with black fuck-me heels on. Her hair is down and curly, and I want to touch her through the screen. The issue isn't her, though. The issue is that with her, is a guy probably in his late twenties, with his arms around my woman, his front to her back, while she throws her head back against him. And it looks like they're fucking through their clothes.

I throw the phone on the table and stalk out. I can hear everybody around me shouting my name but I need to be alone. This is what I get for thinking for even a second I could have a career and a family. My dad warned me over and over again. He said I couldn't have both, but I thought he was wrong. I thought if I just tried harder, gave more, loved them enough, I would be able to prove him wrong. The man might have been a complete asshole, but according to that picture, it seems he knew what he was talking about. I guess the joke's on me.

Thirty-Three

LIZ

Four Hours Ago

"BELLA, GO HELP TRISTAN CLEAN UP THE TOYS AND GAMES you guys took out and played with, please. We need to go soon."

I'm sitting in Ashley's kitchen, having a glass of wine while gossiping over my sex life and her nonexistent one. We spent the afternoon shopping with the kids, and then took them to a cute trunk-or-treat event at the local church. They got a bunch of candy and are currently running around completely hopped up on sugar. I have no idea how I'm going to get Bella to sleep, but I'm glad her mind is off her daddy being gone. It was a rough night last night. After she spoke to Cooper, she threw another one of her tantrums and I ended up letting her sleep with me. I know, shitty parenting move, but I was exhausted and, to be honest, I hated the thought of sleeping in my bed alone.

"You know, my parents are coming over to watch Tristan tonight so a few friends of mine and I can go to Club Surrender. They wouldn't mind watching Bella as well. They would actually love it because Bella would keep Tristan busy."

"Oh, I don't know. I know Bella would be fine here but going out to a club without Cooper feels wrong."

"Sweetie, you are going out for some drinks and maybe some dancing. That's it."

I remember the first and last time I was at a club. It was the night I met Cooper. I fell in love with the music and ambiance. It would be fun to have a drink and let loose a little.

"Okay, I'm in. Drinking and dancing."

"Yay! Okay, let's find us something to wear."

Four hours later and I'm at the club, on my sixth, maybe seventh shot of tequila...I'm not exactly sure, but what I do know is Ashley's friends are drinkers. It's a good thing we cabbed it here because I'm definitely not fit to drive anywhere on my own.

I down another shot and it goes down my throat like water. I know I'm definitely drunk when I no longer feel the burn of the alcohol in my throat. I hear *Talk Dirty* by Jason Derulo come on and Ashley shouts this is her jam, so we make our way to the dance floor. We're having a blast, grinding up against each other and laughing at some of our drunken moves, when the room begins to spin. I tell myself after this song I'm done for the night. *2 Chainz* pops on the surround sound and I can't help but lower my ass and pop it out to his solo. Dancing can be so freeing. I should ask Cooper to come out with me to the club, again.

Out of nowhere, I feel a strong pair of hands wrap around my waist and it's like Déjà vu to the night in the club with Cooper. In my drunken state, I tilt my head back, but when I see the horrific look in Ashley's eyes, I jump forward, realizing it can't be Cooper because Cooper is in Boulder. *Shit.*

I make my way back to Ashley, a bit shaken up at the thought of another man's hands on my body. I know it isn't his fault. He didn't do anything inappropriate. I stopped it immediately, but I still feel guilty.

"I'm going to head back to your place," I tell Ashley when I get over to her.

"No way, I'm ready to go as well. What happened with that guy over there?"

"He came up behind me the same way Cooper did all those years ago at the club when I first met him, and for a second I thought it was Cooper. It wasn't until I saw your face I remembered Cooper's out of the damn state."

Ashley laughs and says, "Yup! We're definitely drunk. It is time to go home. Our rugrats will be up before we know it."

We make it back to Ashley's place and both pass out in her bed. Tomorrow is going to seriously suck. Hangover plus trick-or-treating equals...I don't even know what the hell it equals, but it sure as hell can't be anything good.

We wake up to the kids running around and playing. I grab my phone to see what time it is and it's dead. *Shit.* "Hey, Ash, I'm going to head out with Bella. My phone is dead, so I need to charge it." She mumbles what I think is a reply and goes back to sleep. Luckily for her, her parents spent the night and are hanging out all day with Tristan.

We get home and I jump in the shower to rinse off last night then swallow a few pain relievers hoping to get rid of this massive headache I have going on. Once my phone charges enough to turn it on, I check it and see my phone is overflowing with what looks like a million texts.

Coop: Hey baby girl. I tried to call you to say good night to you guys. Call me. Love you.

Coop: Baby, everything okay? You haven't called me back.

Coop: Bella must be in bed by now. I tried to call to keep my promise to her. Just let me know you guys are okay.

Coop: Liz, are you mad at me?

Damn, I should have told him I was going out, but I didn't even think to. I've spent so many years coming and going as I please, I didn't even think about that fact that Cooper would be worried if I didn't answer his calls or texts, and on top of that, he didn't get a chance to say good night to Bella. I keep scrolling through my texts.

This is where it gets weird...

Kayla: Liz, you need to call me ASAP

Hayley: Where are you?

Hayley: Liz, please call someone as soon as you get this.

Kayla: Liz, I know you wouldn't cheat on Cooper. Please just call so we can get this whole thing figured out.

Cheat. On. Cooper. What the fuck?

I immediately try to call Cooper, but his phone goes straight to voicemail. I try again and again and nothing. I feel sick to my stomach with worry. Why would they think I was cheating on Cooper? I try his phone a few more times and just as I'm about to try Kayla, I hear the front door open and close, and then Bella screams, "Daddy!"

I walk into the living room and see Cooper standing in the doorway with Bella in his arms holding her tight to his chest. His gaze turns to me, and my stomach drops when I see the exhausted and defeated look in his eyes.

He swallows loudly, composes himself, and gives his attention back to Bella. "Hey, sweetie. Did I make it in time to go trick-or-treating with you?"

"Yes! Yes! Yes, you did. Thank you, Daddy!" Bella gives him a huge wet kiss on his cheek.

"Good. Why don't you run upstairs and get your costume ready and then we'll all go to lunch and trick-or-treating."

"Okay, Daddy!"

Cooper waits until Bella is upstairs before he turns his attention to me. I open my mouth to say something but close it again. I'm not sure what happened, but for him to be here when he should be in Boulder says a lot. It should be a good thing that he's here, but after reading the texts Kayla and Hayley sent me, I have a feeling he's here for another reason.

"What's the matter? Not sure how to explain what happened last night? If you want, you can call up my mom and ask her how it's done. I'm sure she can help you explain and justify what happened."

I flinch at his words, like I was just slapped in the face. I don't know what's going on, but it must be bad because Cooper doesn't speak to me like this, ever.

He moves a step closer, and I finally speak up. "I don't know what you think I did, but you're wrong."

He moves a bit closer. "You didn't go to Club Surrender last night?"

"Yes, I did. Ashley and I went with a couple of her friends."

He moves closer with his eyes never leaving mine. "Did you dance with anyone?"

What. The. Fuck! "Yeah, Coop. I did. I danced with Ashley and a few other people. What's going on?"

He takes one more step and he's right in my face. If I didn't know Cooper would never hurt me, I would be terrified of the expression on his face. I can see why other fighters fear this man. When he's pissed, he's not someone you want to mess with.

He pulls out his phone and lifts it up to my face. It's so close I have to pull my head back a bit and squint to see what he's showing me. My stomach drops when I see the grainy photo of me and some guy, who isn't Cooper, extremely close to each another. I'm sweaty from all the dancing and shots, and I have my head thrown back up against the guy's chest while his hands are around my waist. *Fuck. Not good.*

"How did you get that?" I spit out more harshly than intended. I should feel bad about the picture but the truth is nothing happened, and I'm pissed that someone is sending photos to him. I'm even more pissed that he doesn't trust me.

"Does it matter how I got it? What fucking matters is why *my* woman is grinding all over another man's dick while he has his hands wrapped around her."

Wow, it's not even a question, just straight up accusation. Apparently, I'm guilty without even a trial.

"So, let me get this straight? You get some picture, taken by God knows who, and you jump on a plane, not to take my daughter trick-or-treating, but to accuse me of cheating on you."

He lets it sink in for a second before he responds. "No, I was already coming here to take *our* daughter trick-or-treating. I just figured while I was here I would find out why I was only gone for less than two days and the woman who supposedly loves me is already all over another man.

Taking a closer look at Cooper, I notice his eyes are dark with black circles under them like he hasn't had a decent night's sleep in a few days, his shoulders are slumped over a little, and while his words sound so sure, I can see he's sad and scared and confused. I could argue with him. I could scream and curse and be pissed about his accusations, but it wouldn't do any good. Cooper needs to feel secure about us and arguing isn't going to help anything. He might be a badass fighter on the outside, but on the inside, he's an insecure little boy who's been traumatized by the choices his parents made.

So, I wrap my arms around his torso and look up at him. He tenses under my touch, so I bring my hand to the back of his head to lower it, giving him a small kiss, and after a few seconds, I feel him melt into me. The kiss goes deeper and he sighs into my mouth. We kiss for a short time and when we separate he closes his arms around my body tightly, nuzzling his head into my hair. I hear a sob, so soft I almost wouldn't have caught it if it wasn't so quiet, and when he looks up, there's a tear falling down his cheek. I stand on my tip-toes and gently kiss it away.

"I love you, Cooper, and I'd never cheat on you. What you saw was a shitty picture and I'm sorry you saw that. While I was dancing, a guy came up behind me, and for a second I thought it was you. I was drunk and it reminded me of our time together five years ago, but as soon as I realized it wasn't you, I freaked out and decided to go home. Ashley was there and saw the whole thing play out."

He squeezes his eyes closed and then opens them again. "I'm sorry, baby girl. I know you'd never cheat. I just freaked out. I saw the picture and I lost it."

"It's okay." I give him another kiss to calm him down.

"Kayla said I'm the only guy you have ever been with. Is that true?"

"Yeah, it is. I just couldn't stop hoping that maybe one day you'd come back to me. I focused on school and Bella, and I just had no desire to be with anybody but you."

Just then Bella comes prancing down the steps looking like a princess in her Elsa costume.

"I'm ready to go!" she squeals.

We head out to eat lunch and then take Bella trick-or-treating around the neighborhood Kayla and I take her every year. We've never lived in this neighborhood, but we found it years ago. It has nice houses that are close together and the people who live there all sit outside at the end of their driveways giving out candy.

After going up and down several streets, Bella is candied out and Cooper is carrying her back to the car. Every time she asked for a piece with her cute little voice while batting her eyelashes, he would give in. The day started off rough, but it ended up being an amazing Halloween.

We get back home and after Cooper takes Bella to bed he finds me in our room. I'm changing into my pajamas when he comes up behind me and wraps his strong arms around my torso. Remembering this is why he accused me of cheating, I freeze. He must sense what happened, because while nuzzling my neck he says, "I'm sorry, baby. I just want to be the only man to ever touch you like this. Please forgive me."

I turn around to face him. "And you are the only man who will ever touch me this way. You own me, Cooper, Mind, body, heart, and soul. There's nothing to forgive. I love you."

We make love several times throughout the night before we pass out with our bodies entangled in one another.

Thirty-Four

LIZ

IT'S BEEN ALMOST A MONTH SINCE COOPER WENT AWAY and received that stupid picture. Thankfully we've moved passed it, for the most part. There are times when I still see Cooper's insecurities come out, like when he texts me and I don't answer or if I go somewhere and don't mention it. He isn't an asshole about it. He doesn't yell or get mad. It's more like he gets sad and worried like I'm going to leave one day and never come back.

He's been busy at the gym training for his fight. Bentley won his fight in Boulder, so he's been helping Caleb and Cooper train for theirs. Cooper has been insisting Bella visit every day and is home by her bedtime every night.

Thanksgiving is almost here and we've decided to fly to Florida to have Thanksgiving with my parents and brother. Kayla is flying with us, but will be spending the day with her family. Cooper's mom has decided to join us tomorrow as well so it will be nice.

I've been feeling kind of queasy lately so I'm hoping I'm not catching something before Thanksgiving. That will surely ruin our trip to Florida.

We arrive at the Palm Beach Airport on Wednesday afternoon to find my brother waiting for us.

"Hey you! We could have taken a cab."

He just scoffs at me and gives Bella a big hug, then shakes Cooper's hand. We grab our luggage and head home. I'm excited to show Cooper where I grew up. Kayla catches a ride with us since she only lives down the street. Matt drops her off first and then we head to our house. Bella spots the beach across the street and asks if we can go swimming.

"It might be a little chilly, Angel, but we can head down later to at least walk along the sand."

When we pull up, my mom and dad come out to give us all hugs and kisses before we make our way inside. As soon as I walk in, the smell of pumpkin and stuffing makes me stumble back. I put my hand over my nose and excuse myself to the bathroom. After throwing up everything in my stomach, it hits me that I've been feeling queasy a lot lately. I have also been extremely exhausted, and now I'm throwing up. I thought maybe I was catching the flu, but when I was pregnant with Bella certain smells made me feel the same way. *Could I be pregnant?* Before I tell Cooper, I want to get it confirmed. I don't want to get his hopes up if it's just a coincidence.

I give Cooper a tour around my house, including my bedroom where he laughs at the fact my parents have kept it the same since I left, and wants to know if I still have my cheerleading uniform from high school. *Damn perv.* Needing to get away from the smells that are making my stomach churn, I suggest we take Bella for a walk on the beach.

It's beautiful outside here in the fall. Florida doesn't really have different seasons and it barely even gets cold, but it drops enough in the fall and winter occasionally for it to feel nice. Today, it's in the low seventies so it's too chilly to go swimming but perfect for walking along the beach.

Cooper is walking between Bella and me, holding our hands, as Bella stops every couple feet to pick up a new shell. They all look the same but Cooper shows the same amount of excitement every time she shows him a new one. It makes me sad to think this time last year we were here without Cooper. This Thanksgiving I'm so thankful for Kayla making me go to that UFC fight. I can't imagine Cooper not being part of our lives.

We decide to sit in the sand while Bella plays at the edge of the water. Cooper sits first then pulls me down in between his legs, wrapping his arms around my waist.

"Thank you, baby girl," he says, giving me a soft kiss on my cheek.

I twist my neck to look at him. "For what?"

"For everything...for giving me a second chance, giving me Bella, turning my house into a home. I've never felt so at peace."

I don't say anything. I feel the same way, but I'm suddenly so emotional. *Pregnancy hormones?*

"I've been thinking...After this title fight, win or lose, I'm going to take time off from fighting."

"Cooper, you love fighting. Why would you do that?"

"I'm still going to run the gym, but I just want to focus on Bella and you. I've spent the last fifteen years fighting, and I want to take a break and spend some time with my girls."

I want to ask if it's because of the picture, but I'm afraid it'll upset him. So, I just say, "Well, if that's what you really want to do I'm not going to complain. But make sure it's for the right reasons. Are you actually retiring?"

"I'm not saying I'll never go back, but it won't be any time in the near future."

THANKSGIVING IS AMAZING. COOPER'S MOM GOT IN EARLY this morning, and Kayla ended up getting into a fight with her parents so she's here as well. Bella is chowing down on cookies and biscuits in the living room sitting on Cooper's lap while the guys all watch football.

"Dinner's ready," my mom announces. Everybody makes their way through the lines of food spread out across the countertops and gather around the table. Sadly, my plate is a bit bare. Food I'd normally eat doesn't seem to be appetizing at all, and I'm struggling not to throw up.

"Liz, don't you want some sweet potatoes? They're your favorite," my mom asks innocently. I haven't told anybody I suspect I might be pregnant so it doesn't make sense why I'm not grabbing all my favorites. I take a scoop of sweet potatoes and plop them onto my plate, making sure they don't touch my other food. *Please Lord, don't let me throw up all over my plate of food.*

Before we dig in, it's a tradition for everyone to say what he or she is thankful for. Bella begs to begin, so of course we let her.

"I am soooooo thankful for my mommy because I love her because she gave me my daddy." Everybody *oohs* and *ahhs* around her, but she keeps going naming everybody around the table. "I'm thankful for my auntie Kay because she is the best at painting my nails. I'm thankful for all my grandmas because they let me eat cookies. I'm thankful for my grandpa because he gives me a dollar every time he sees me. I'm thankful for my uncle Matty because he always sneaks me bubblegum even though my mommy says I'm too little to eat bubble gum."

Matt laughs out loud and says, "Kid, you aren't supposed to tell people that!" She looks genuinely confused, not realizing she's telling on everyone around her while saying thank you. Finally, she gets around the table to Cooper and says, "And I'm thankful for my daddy because he is the bestest daddy ever because he's going to get me a puppy and a baby brother or sister. I really want a sister, but a brother will still be good."

Cooper turns white as the entire table goes quiet, looking at him, and then we all burst out laughing.

"I squeeze his hand and whisper loudly, "Sounds like someone has been making secret promises to our daughter."

He just nervously laughs. Everyone takes turns going around the table, saying what they're thankful for, and after the final person goes, it's time to eat. Of course, within twenty minutes, the food is completely gone.

Friday morning Cooper offers to keep Bella with him and the guys while the women check out the crazy Black Friday sales. While I'm out, I put a call into my doctor so I can make an appointment for next week to confirm if I'm pregnant. Nobody is in the office, so I leave a message with the answering service for someone to call me back with an appointment.

Thirty-Five

COOPER

WE HAD A GREAT WEEKEND WITH LIZ'S PARENTS IN FLORIDA. We'll definitely need to plan another trip back soon, especially once it's warmer and we can take Bella swimming in the ocean. It's Monday morning and we're at the airport with Kayla and my mom since we're all flying back together. Liz's phone rings and she glances at it nervously. Before it goes to the voicemail, she answers the call and excuses herself to speak to whoever it is on the other end away from us. Kayla raises her brows at me, telling me to chill out. Fuck, I'm not that guy. I don't do jealousy and I sure as fuck don't monitor who my girlfriend talks to.

Liz comes back over and doesn't say who it was, but she looks guilty as hell. I know I have my issues, but I'm not seeing shit. My woman looks like she needs to tell me something but decides not to, so I let it go because I need to trust her and trust us.

We make it home and we're all completely jet-lagged. The five-hour flight to and from Florida was no joke. On top of that, add an energetic four-year-old to the mix, and a three-hour time difference, and we're done for.

Liz and I cuddle up in our bed with Bella between us and sleep for hours. I'm sure we'll regret this tonight when Bella is wide-awake, but right now it feels damn good.

I groggily wake up and reach for Liz when I feel Bella beside me laughing softly to something on her iPad. I look over her to see if Liz is in bed, but she's not.

"Hey, Princess, where's your mommy?"

"She said she had to run out."

"Do you know where she went?"

"Nope, she just kissed me goodbye and left."

I grab my phone off the nightstand and see we've only been asleep for a couple hours. I look to see if there are any texts from Liz, but there isn't, so I shoot her a text asking what time she'll be back and what she wants to do for lunch.

She replies back almost instantly letting me know she'll be home soon and we can order something in. I repeat the mantra in my head, *I will not assume shit.* I trust her and we're not my parents.

She gets back a couple hours later and joins Bella and me on the couch. We're watching some crazy movie where everything is made out of Legos and they run around singing some weird ass song about everything being awesome.

"Hey baby," Liz says. "I was thinking we could take Bella to see Santa today since he's at the mall."

Bella jumps up like she wasn't just in a trance watching these weird fuckers building and tearing shit down Lego-style. "Yes, please! I want to go see Santa. I know what I want for Christmas."

She runs to her room to get dressed, leaving Liz and me alone. "Everything okay?"

"Yeah." She gives me nothing more except a kiss on the cheek, before she heads upstairs to help Bella get dressed. *I will not assume shit.*

We get to the mall and you can tell Christmas is around the corner. The mall is packed with people and Christmas music is playing through the speakers. We head straight for Santa, and once we get through the line, Bella sits right on his lap, telling him exactly what she wants. "My daddy already said he's going to give me a baby and a puppy, so from you, all I want is a swing set for the back yard. I would like for it to be pink and purple please. I would also like for it to have benches with a table where I can have tea and cookies with my daddy and mommy and my dolls. I've been really good, well...except for when I don't want to go to bed, but I'm trying really, really hard."

Damn, this girl is so sweet, and honest to a fault. She'll be getting that swing-set and puppy. Now, the baby on the other hand, that's going to take a little bit of work. I smirk at Liz and she hits my arm. "Are you thinking about sex?" she whisper-yells.

"What? No! I was thinking we needed to work on Bella's Christmas gifts." She laughs at me and when she's done, her smile still lingers. I love her smile and will do anything in my power to keep it there.

"And what do you want for Christmas?" she teases.

"Not a damn thing. I have everything I could want right here." Her smile widens and I can't help but kiss it.

We join Bella for pictures with Santa and I insist on buying them all, including the frames, so we can put them out around the house. We decide to do a little shopping, but when Bella sees the giant Christmas tree in the department store she begs for us to go get ours.

After picking one out for the living room and a mini tree for Bella's bedroom, we head to Target to get the decorations. Liz lost all hers in the fire, and I've never had a tree since living on my own, so we're buying all new stuff. I think the last time my mom got us a tree I was twelve and it was right before my parents split up.

"I think this one is perfect." Bella holds up a cute pink princess crown ornament. When I nod my okay, she places it into the basket.

"How about this one?" Liz holds up an ornament that reads *First Family Christmas.*

"That one is absolutely perfect."

This goes on for the next hour. The girls pick out ornaments, while I push the cart through the store. We eventually move on to lights, and while we're in that section they convince me to get lights for the outside along with some huge blowup snowman. I don't know why they even ask. We all know I have a problem with saying no to anything they ask for.

On our way home, I call my mom to join us for dinner and to help decorate the tree. Liz insists on getting break-n-bake cookies and eggnog on the way home as well.

And that's how we spend the night. Sipping eggnog, eating cookies, listening to Christmas music, and decorating our first family tree. Today will definitely go down as one of the best days of my life.

Thirty-Six

LIZ

IT'S BEEN TWO WEEKS SINCE FINDING OUT I AM INDEED pregnant. Hiding it from Cooper is killing me, but I decided since Christmas is so close I could give him—and Bella—the gift of a new baby. The first couple days I felt like I was betraying him by not telling him right away. I think he even noticed how guilty I felt, but since then it's been smooth sailing.

Christmas is in two weeks and I need to think of a cool way to tell him. Simply putting a box under a tree and saying, *Surprise you're going to be a daddy again* isn't fun enough. So, I've gathered my girls together to help me figure it out. I know, I admit them knowing first probably isn't the best idea, but hell, how do I plan without telling them why I'm planning?

Cooper has been gracious enough to watch Bella and Tristan at our place. Caleb, Bentley, Kaden, and Alex are all joining him to watch a UFC fight on pay-per-view. I don't really know much about Alex except that he goes to the gym and he's the one who took the picture of me at the club. You know, the one that almost blew my relationship up in smoke.

He did apologize and explain that he was just looking out for Cooper. I forgave him, but it still stings. He should've come to me before sending that picture to him. However, I'm not about to hold a grudge. That brings us back to the present.

Hayley, Kayla, Ashley, and I are all sitting at Hayley's place, giving each other homemade facials, manis, and pedis while listening to Iggy Azalea's *Fancy*. That girl can seriously rock those lyrics.

Hayley gets up and dances to the kitchen, bringing back a bottle of Jack in one hand and Coke in the other. Now is probably a good time to let them know I'm preggers.

She passes out the glasses and dishes out ice into all our cups, and then begins to pour the Jack.

"Just coke for me," I say.

"Excuse me?" Kayla cuts in. "Since when are you going sober?"

"Since I'm pregnant and I'm not sure how much the baby will enjoy Jack Daniels."

Everybody goes silent and then cheers erupt. They all take turns congratulating and hugging me.

Ashley finishes pouring everyone's drinks, but Kayla says she'll remain sober with me.

Ashley raises her glass and we all follow suit. "A toast. To the new precious little miracle."

"Here, here," all the girls say.

"So, does Cooper know? How far along are you?" Hayley asks.

"Not far at all, only six weeks, and no, Cooper doesn't know yet."

"How is he going to feel?" Kayla asks. She almost seems despondent about my news. I give her a quick look, silently asking if she's okay and she nods.

"I'm hoping he's going to be ecstatic since it was his idea. Back in October, he told me he wants another baby and we decided I wouldn't get the shot. I didn't think it would happen so soon, but I'm excited. Speaking of the shot, we never ended up going together. Did you go get yours done?" Kayla nods, but something is off with her.

"So, anyway, I want to come up with a cool way to tell him. Whenever I ask him what he wants for Christmas he says he has everything he could want."

"I got it! You can plan a family weekend away, like to Disney and say it's the last trip before you're a family of four."

"Oh, I like it, Hayley! Yes, that's what I'll do, and it'll be a Christmas present to Bella as well. Yay! I'm so excited! You guys can't say anything to anybody. It would break Cooper's heart if he found out he wasn't the first to know."

All the girls vow to keep silent and I'm ready to plan our trip.

Thirty-Seven

COOPER

ALL THE GUYS ARE HERE, WE'VE ORDERED PIZZA AND WINGS, the pay-per-view fight is on, and Bella and her friend Tristan are running around playing. I'm thinking tonight is the night I'm going to let the guys know I'm going to be taking a break from fighting.

"So, I've decided something..." The guys all turn to me, but when I see Bentley, he looks like he's a hundred miles away.

"Yo, Bentley! What's up with you?" I ask.

"Women, bro. No, not women. One woman. One stubborn damn woman that is going to be the death of me."

We all laugh and nod because we've been there.

"Kayla?" Kaden asks.

Bentley just shakes his head and we wait to see if he's going to explain. Finally, with a deep sigh, he says, "We had sex in Boulder."

We all congratulate him. Because really, that's what men do...A guy gets laid and you say, *Congratulations.* Yep, we suck.

"So, does this mean you two are together now?" I ask, remembering he said the next time they have sex would mean they're together.

"No, we aren't. Not only are we not together, but she's barely talking to me. She knew if we had sex it meant we would be together, but once it happened she said she made a mistake and left. I really care about this girl, but I don't know what to do anymore. I think it's time to move on. I'm already almost thirty years old. I want a family one day. I want a wife and kids, and I don't want to wait until I am too old to enjoy all of that. There's a girl I've been talking to, so we'll see…"

Because he hasn't been kicked down enough, Caleb adds, "She actually mentioned she might be moving out soon. I'm sorry, Bentley."

"Well, screw her then." And with that he gets up to clear his head.

I decide to hold off on my news for now.

A few hours later, and I can hear loud screeches and yelling from outside the house. When I look outside, I see Liz and her friends walking up the steps to the front door.

Ashley and Hayley appear to be drunk ,while Liz and Kayla are both sober.

"Hey, baby." She gives me a soft peck on the cheek and walks in with Kayla, while everybody else stumbles in loudly. It's actually quite amusing.

"What's with only half of you being drunk?" Bentley asks. Kayla turns her attention to him, and if looks could kill, he would be dead and buried six feet under.

"Not that it's your business, but I wasn't in the mood to drink and either was Liz. Is that okay with you?"

Bentley puts his hands up in surrender and turns back to the fight.

"Sorry to ruin your little fight party," Hayley says as she plops down next to Caleb and pats him on his leg. He blushes. The fool actually fucking blushes. Then he gets up immediately, like her hand set his leg on fire, and Hayley frowns at his reaction.

"I have to get to work," he says, and without saying goodbye to anybody, he's out the door.

Tristan and Bella come running down to say hi to their moms and tell them about all the Halloween candy they've been eating. *Damn traitors.*

We all find a seat and watch the fight. Liz is in my lap with Bella passed out next to us. Eventually everyone heads out. Kaden gives Ashley and Tristan a ride since her car isn't here and she's been drinking, and Kayla gives Hayley a ride home. Liz and I put Bella to bed and then head back to finish watching the main event.

"Are you going to miss this?" Liz asks as we sit back down on the couch.

"Miss what? The fighting?" I ask, stalling before I answer the question I know she's really asking. She wants to know if a few years from now I'm going to resent her and Bella. I've thought long and hard about this and I know this is what's right for my family and me. I would never turn around and blame Liz for my choices, but she needs to hear it so she doesn't feel like I'm making a rash decision.

"No, baby girl. I'm not going to miss it. I'll still be fighting. I'll fight at the gym every day. The only difference is I won't be fighting professionally. My contract ends in February and I'm okay with that. It's time to move forward."

Liz climbs into my lap, placing a leg on either side of me. I look up at the stairs out of habit and she slowly shakes her head. "She's fast asleep."

Taking the bottom of my shirt in her hands, she raises it over my head and throws it on the floor.

"Do you know how beautiful you are, Cooper?" *Maybe she is drunk after all.*

"Um, Liz, I'm not sure you should be calling a man beautiful. Do you want to emasculate me?"

She ignores my question and starts to kiss me. First, she kisses me on my lips but pulls away quickly. "You have beautiful lips. They were made for me. They kiss me with such passion and emotion, and the words that come out of them are just as beautiful."

Next, she kisses the tops of my eyelids. "You have the most amazing eyes. When you're happy, they are bright green, full of life, like the grass after it's been raining for days. And when you're angry, they go dark. I don't like it when they go dark. Bella has the same eyes as you. Every time I would look into her eyes, it gave me butterflies because it brought back the brief time we shared together."

She trails her lips down my neck, over to my chest, and stops right over my heart, placing multiple tender kisses there. "And your heart. It's so full of love. Whether it was for thirty-hours in Miami or every day since we reconnected, you give me your entire heart and trust me with it. The way you instantly fell in love with Bella. Many guys might have thought I got pregnant on purpose or they might have accepted her but they wouldn't have gone out of their way to make her feel so loved and cherished. You didn't just give us a place to live, you made sure we felt at home."

A lump in my throat forms. This girl is my entire fucking world. I'm going to marry her some day and she's going to have more of my babies, and we're going to live happily ever after.

She doesn't stop at my heart, though. She kisses her way down to my stomach and stops at the center of my abs. She's now kneeling on the floor between my legs. "Mmm...and this body. Cooper, do you have any idea how beautiful your body is? You treat it with such care only putting healthy foods in it. It's such a turn on, and I love that this body is all mine."

She moves on from my abs and unbuttons my jeans. Thank God because my dick is so hard it needs to be released from its confined space. I lift my ass and she pulls down my jeans, taking my boxers with her. I go to touch her and she shakes her head.

She gives my dick a kiss on the top of the crown, sucking on it lightly with her lips and then pulls back. *Holy Shit, this woman is going to be the death of me.*

"This is probably one of my favorites parts of your body." I lift one of my brows up. I mean, I know it's one of my favorite parts of my body, especially since it's the part that goes inside of her, but I wasn't expecting a woman to think it's her favorite. She giggles under her breath at my reaction. "Not for the reasons you probably think... Well, actually, kind of. I remember the first time I saw your dick. I thought it was crazy to think it was beautiful. I haven't seen any others to compare it to."

I growl at that. "And you never fucking will."

She giggles again, but continues. "It was so hard and thick, and when I felt it, it was smooth. Then when I tasted it, I thought it would be gross but it wasn't. It tasted like you." She puts her mouth back on my dick to give it another wet kiss, then she starts stroking it up and down slowly.

"But aside from its physical appearance, the reason it's one of my favorite parts is for a few reasons." She kisses it again, and it takes every ounce of restraint not to take her by her hair and push her beautiful mouth onto my erection.

"One, is what I feel when it's inside of me. I feel so close to you, like we're connected. When our bodies are skin to skin and you're pushing it inside of me, hitting me so deep, I feel like we become one."

This time she takes her entire mouth and covers my dick from root to tip with it then drags her mouth back up slowly. "The other reason it's my favorite body part is because of what it's capable of. Not only does it bring me an extreme amount of pleasure, but it's how we created Bella."

"That's really fucking sweet, baby girl, but you can't be bringing Bella up while your hands are stroking my dick."

She laughs at that and then puts her mouth back on me. This time she doesn't remove her mouth. Her tongue slides down with her mouth wrapped around it and she begins to move it up and down, fucking my shaft with her greedy mouth, and I can't take it anymore. I need to touch her. It's like she senses what I need because while keeping her mouth wrapped tightly around me, she grabs my hands with her own and moves them to her hair, giving me permission to touch her.

What started out slow and sensual, turns into rough and crazed. Her mouth starts to move faster as I entwine my fingers into her hair. I don't push her head down, though. She doesn't need me to. She's deep throating me like a champion and within minutes I'm tapping her to let her know I'm about to come. Of course, it only spurs her on, and within seconds, I'm shooting my seed down her throat. She slows down but keeps licking until my dick is licked clean.

"Damn, baby. I've changed my mind. You can emasculate me any time you want."

Thirty-Eight

LIZ

IT'S LESS THAN A WEEK UNTIL CHRISTMAS, AND I CAN'T believe I haven't told Cooper that I'm pregnant yet. My next appointment isn't until December 30th, so I'll be able to wait until Christmas to tell him when I give him and Bella their gift together, and he'll be able to go to my appointment with me.

Normally I keep the office door open, but I shut it today so I can finish planning our trip to California to Disneyland. I've figured out that we'll go in March during Bella's spring break, so she doesn't miss any school. We're going to go to all the parks and stay at a resort near Disney.

I'm making sure to put it on my personal credit card just in case Cooper decides to look at our joint account. I'm researching online the best hotels to stay at when a site pops up for the cheapest motels in the area. I go to click out of it, but of course the stupid ad opens up. *So freaking annoying.*

I hear a commotion outside the office, so I run out to see what's going on. When I get out there Kayla and Bentley are in the middle of a screaming match.

"I don't give a shit what you think. I'm moving out and you can do whatever you want," Kayla screams at the top of her lungs. Cooper looks at me to do something. This might be a gym, but it's still a place of business.

Bentley looks pissed as hell. His fists are at his sides, knuckles white like he has to hold himself back.

"Okay, I don't know what is going on here, but you guys need to take this to a private area. This is a place of business."

They both look over at me. I place my hand on Kayla to silently calm her down, and Bentley shouts, "Fuck this!" as he storms out of the room.

When I look at Kayla ,she has tears in her eyes. I brush her hair back out of her eyes and suggest we get out of here. Cooper hears me and nods his head slightly, letting me know he heard me.

We get to one of our favorite coffee shops and order ourselves each a hot peppermint mocha. It's only a few days until Christmas and then the delicious taste of peppermint will disappear until next year.

Kayla hasn't said a word since we left and it's killing me inside. "Kayla, I feel like we've grown apart." She attempts to argue, but I raise my hand for her to let me finish.

"I know this isn't about us, but at the same time it is because it's about you, and for the last eighteen years we've had each other's back. So, when you have something going on, so do I."

She slumps over and puts her hands in her hair and shakes her head. I think she's going to tell me what's going on, but when she raises her head, all she says is, "I've decided to move back to Florida. I've been thinking about it for a little while now, but I've decided for sure."

That takes me for a loop because Kayla knows I can't move anywhere. Bella and my home is here with Cooper, and if she moves to Florida we'll be a long ass plane ride apart.

I choke up and try to hold it in because this isn't about me. "Are you serious? Like your mind is made up for sure? I mean, your parents and brother are there, but you aren't really close to them. Bella and I'll miss you like crazy. We've never been apart since the day we met in Kindergarten."

She sighs and looks absolutely defeated. "Is it something I did, Kay?" I don't think it is, but I need to make sure.

"No, Liz. It's nothing you did. I'm just going through some shit and feel like I need a break from it all."

"So, take a vacation, but please don't leave me. I need you. You know I'm pregnant. I can't do this without you." I know it's selfish to say this to her, but it's the truth. I need her so much. I can't imagine going through this pregnancy without her.

"Liz, we aren't eighteen anymore, and you won't be alone this time around. You have Cooper now."

I don't even know what to say. "Can you at least wait until after Christmas? I'd like to have one last holiday together." She nods, and I get up and hug my best friend. I can feel her sobbing and in turn I'm crying. I can't help but feel like this is the end of our friendship. She wouldn't do this unless she really felt like she needed to leave, though.

All I can do is respect her decision and be there for her.

"Do me a favor, Liz. Please don't tell anybody yet, including Cooper." Even though I'm not okay with any of this, I agree.

"C'mon, chick, let's go pick up Bella and have a girls' afternoon," I say as we walk out the door with our arms around each other.

Thirty-Nine

COOPER

After Bentley walks out of the gym and Liz takes Kayla out to let shit cool down, I take advantage of the fact that Liz's computer is free. I've found Bella's puppy on a local animal rescue shelter website. The mom is a German Shepherd-Lab mix who was found pregnant under a bridge after giving birth to several puppies. The puppies are now eight weeks and can be adopted out. I put in a request to adopt one and was approved several weeks ago. I'm supposed to be getting an email from the shelter today letting me know when I can pick the puppy up. Since it's only a week until Christmas, I'm having Kaden keep the pup at his place until Christmas Eve. He's agreed to bring the little mutt over late at night after Bella and Liz have gone to bed.

I walk around to her desk, sit, and shake the mouse to wake the computer up. There are several webpages open, but the one that catches my eye is the top page. It's an ad for some sleazy motels in the area. I look on the desk and find Liz's personal credit card sitting atop it. Why the hell would she be booking one of these motels? And to top it off, she's using the credit card she keeps for emergencies. It's the only card that we don't have a joint account on. The only reason she would do something like this is if she doesn't want me to know.

My mind starts wandering to the last few weeks. She's been nervous, but nothing that would make me believe she's cheating or wants out. When we got back from Florida, she went out that one time and never told me where she was going, but she's been happy since then.

The last time I assumed the worst, I made her believe I didn't trust her. I sure as hell won't be doing that again. This time I'm going to just come out and ask her. Liz doesn't lie, and if something is going on, she'll tell me.

Quickly exiting out of all the windows, I pull up my email. The shelter says I can pick up the pup today, so I shut down her computer and leave to go pick up our new puppy. Once that's taken care of, Liz and I will talk.

I get home to Bella watching a movie in the living room and Liz in the kitchen making dinner. She doesn't make eye contact with me so I walk over to her and turn her around to face me. When I look at her, I can tell she's been crying.

"Baby girl, what's wrong?"

She just shakes her head. Well, that shit isn't going to fly.

"I can see the dried-up tears. Please tell me what's wrong. Does it have something to do with you booking a sleazy motel with your card?" Okay, well that wasn't how I planned to broach the subject, but now that it's out there...

Her eyes go wide for a second, but she quickly reins her shock in. "Were you seriously going through my computer, Cooper?" Damn it, leave it to a woman to turn it around on the guy like it's his damn fault.

"No, Liz, I wasn't. I got on to pull up my email and it was on the front screen."

"Oh, well no, I'm not booking a motel. It was just an ad that popped up."

"So, why was your credit card out? The one you only use for emergencies?" I force the issue because she isn't giving me much and something isn't adding up.

She looks at me and then loses it. She starts bawling her eyes out. I'm talking full- on crying. I don't even know what to think. Is she leaving me? What the fuck happened to make her cry like this?

I do the only thing I can do and move closer to hold her. She wraps her arms around me and bawls her eyes out. I can feel the snot dripping off her onto my shirt but I'm not about to say anything right now. It's breaking my heart to see her this emotional, especially since I don't know what's going on or how to fix it.

Bella walks in at this moment and I can tell from her soft voice she heard her mom crying. "Mommy, Daddy. Are you okay?"

Liz sucks in her snot and picks her head up to wipe her nose, trying to get herself together. "Nothing is wrong, Angel, I promise. I'm just really tired."

Bella looks from me to her mom and says, "When I'm so tired that I cry you always tell me to go to bed. Maybe you should go to bed." God bless our sweet daughter. May she always stay this innocent.

Liz nods her head in agreement and says to me, "I think I'm going to go lie down. Dinner is done. Can you take it out of the oven in fifteen minutes and give some to Bella?"

One, I don't like how she never acknowledged the issue of the credit card, and two, I definitely don't like that my girl looks like the world has beaten her up and thrown her out into the cold. However, now is not the time to get to the bottom of this, especially with our four-year-old in front of us. So, I agree and let her walk away from me.

When the food is ready, I dish it out, and Bella and I eat together in front of the television, finishing up her movie. It's something her mother barely ever allows, so I know it'll keep her entertained because she feels like she's getting away with something.

After the movie's over, I give her a bath, read her a story, and put her to bed. Liz still hasn't come out of her room, so I tell Bella I'm giving her two kisses, one from me and one from her mom. This makes her think. "Wait, if you can give me kisses from Mommy, can you give me kisses from other people?"

You'd think after living with a four-year old the last few months I would see what's coming, but I don't, and I fall right into her trap. "I guess."

"Great! I want a kiss from grandma. Oh, and a kiss from grandpa. Then I want a kiss from Auntie Kay..."

Twenty minutes and fifty kisses later—from everybody my four-year old knows to some people she doesn't know like Cinderella—and she's down for the night.

I walk into our dark bedroom to find Liz sound asleep. I want to ask her what's going on, but I don't have the heart to wake her up. So instead I strip down to my boxers and wrap my girl up in my arms, praying whatever's wrong doesn't involve her leaving me.

Forty

LIZ

HOW I HAVE MANAGED TO AVOID THE CONVERSATION with Cooper the last four days I have no clue. When he said he saw the motels webpage and credit card I thought for sure I was screwed. Luckily, when he mentioned them, it reminded me that I'm hiding my pregnancy from him, which reminded me that Kayla won't be there for me because she's moving, and then I remembered I'm not allowed to tell Cooper, and so I lost it. Poor guy had no clue what to do. He definitely handled it like a trooper though, accepting my snot all over his shirt like it wasn't even a big deal.

I can see it in his face that he wants answers, but dammit, I've made it to Christmas Eve, and I'm not going to give in now. After he gave me back my credit card, I was able to book the flights and hotel, and purchase the Disney theme park tickets. I even had matching shirts overnighted that have our names on them: Mommy, Daddy, and Bella, and for the surprise, I had put on mine below my name an arrow pointing down that reads, "Plus baby".

Everybody came over for Christmas Eve dinner and I have to say it was a bit awkward. I don't know what has happened between Bentley and Kayla, since neither of them are talking, but man their emotions are flying high. It probably doesn't help that Bentley brought a guest.

After everyone left, Bella set out cookies for Santa and carrots for the reindeer, along with a note telling Santa to fly safe. Now the three of us are sitting in Bella's room while Cooper reads *The Grinch That Stole Christmas* to her. I had asked Cooper about the swing-set she wants and he said he has it covered. I haven't seen anything in the backyard, but if he says he has it covered, I trust him. When he's finished reading the book, we both give her kisses and tell her we'll see her in the morning.

We go downstairs and begin setting out all the presents we've kept hidden in the gym. I'm pretty sure there's double the number of gifts here than I bought. It's Cooper's first Christmas with Bella, so I let it go.

I'm kind of shocked about one thing, so I decide to bring it up. "You know, I thought for sure you would have had that puppy under this tree, but I'm pretty sure I don't hear any barking."

He just chuckles and shakes his head. *What is he up to?*

Forty-One

COOPER

OH BOY, IF ONLY THIS WOMAN KNEW WHAT I HAVE BEEN UP to these last few days. She's not the only one who can keep secrets. When she decided she wasn't going to talk to me, I had two options: Freak the fuck out and assume the worst or go all in. I chose the latter. If she has any intention of leaving me, I'm going to make it hard as hell for her. I meant it when I said I'm going to fight for this second chance, and if I go down, at least I'll go down swinging, knowing I've done everything in my power to show her how much I love her. So, this is the part where I should tell you everything but...Nah. You'll have to wait to find out like the rest of them.

Forty-Two

LIZ

"MOMMY! DADDY! SANTA CAME!"

Cooper and I finished putting the presents out at almost two in the morning. Of course, I never learned where the swing-set or puppy is, or if there is even one. *Sneaky bastard.*

"What time is it? I don't even think the sun is up." Cooper moans and places a pillow over his face before throwing it to the side and getting up.

"It doesn't matter what time a child normally wakes up. On Christmas, their brain wakes them up before five, always."

We make our way down the stairs and Cooper puts some coffee on and makes Bella a hot chocolate. We sit on the couch, while she opens up her stocking first, and she's in heaven! There are new nail polishes, and candy, and tons of Barbie accessories.

Once she's done with her stocking, she moves on to her presents. She gets excited about every single one and thanks us for the ones that have our names on them. I don't think there is a single toy this child didn't get for Christmas, thanks to Cooper.

When she gets to her last present, her smile falters for a second. I don't care how good of a kid you have, when they realize they didn't get the couple items they asked for they're going to be sad. It doesn't make them spoiled...it makes them human. She opens the present and says thank you to the both of us.

Cooper looks way too happy with himself when he asks if she had a good Christmas. Bella says yes, and then he tells her he has one more gift, but it's for all of us and it's not here. I can see she gets her hopes up, but she doesn't mention it or ask.

"Before we get to your gift for all of us, I have one for all of us as well," I say.

I pull a box from the back of the tree and hand it to Cooper and Bella to open. Bella smiles as she tears apart the wrapping paper and shakes the top off. Nestled inside are the three shirts I ordered. I made sure to put mine on the bottom.

Bella pulls them out and attempts to read them. She's not a great reader yet, but she's definitely improving. "Bella," she reads the first one. It has a picture of a Minnie mouse with a crown under her name. She doesn't understand it yet, but I think Cooper does because his lips curl into a huge grin.

Next, she reads Cooper's shirt. "Daddy." This one has a mickey mouse on the front as well.

And finally, she reads mine. "Mommy. And there's an arrow pointing down. It says pl...us plus b.a.by. Plus, baby?"

Cooper whips his head around to me, and with wide eyes, asks,

"Are you pregnant?"

Forty-Three

COOPER

IT KILLED ME TO WATCH BELLA OPEN ALL HER GIFTS, knowing the only three she asked for aren't under the tree. I was able to take care of two of them, but the baby part is unfortunately out of my control.

Liz telling us she has a gift for us definitely peaks my curiosity. This is the happiest I've seen her so it must be good. Bella opens the box and begins reading the name on the shirts. I see Bella's shirt with her name on it and Minnie Mouse, and I know right away we're going to Disney. Not only am I excited to experience this with my two girls, but it also makes sense why she was using her credit card and looking up hotels. Although, hopefully she has better sense than to book one of those nasty motels that were up on her page. She pulls out my shirt next which has *Daddy* written on it with a mickey mouse under it.

Bella gets to her mom's shirt and she's struggling to read it, but we both let her sound it out. "...plus, baby?"

Putting all the pieces together, I go into shock. "Are you pregnant?"

Excitedly, Liz nods, and Bella starts going nuts, singing that she's going to have a baby brother or sister.

Grabbing her by her waist, I give her a kiss then move down to her belly and lift her shirt. It's too soon for there to be a bump, but I still have to kiss it. I look up with blurry eyes from the unshed tears and say thank you. This woman has just made me the happiest man in the world.

I stand and ask how far along she is. She laughs and says, "I'll be nine weeks on the thirtieth. I suspected I was pregnant on Thanksgiving and had it confirmed the day we returned. I thought it would be fun to surprise you for Christmas along with a family trip for just the three of us, but I didn't realize keeping a secret from you for a month would be so difficult."

Damn, now it all makes sense. The secret phone call and outing by herself, the way she's been up and down with her emotions, and going out of her way not to talk to me about her credit card. I'm so glad I chose to have trust in us instead of flipping out. Now it's my turn to give them my present, and with a baby coming, it makes the present even better.

"Okay, you two get dressed. We're leaving in fifteen minutes." They both look at me like I am stupid. Yeah, I know they will never get out the door in fifteen minutes but I still keep saying it in hopes they will one day get ready in under an hour. *Please let this baby be a boy.*

An hour later we're in my SUV driving towards the surprise and I text everybody to meet me there. This is more like four surprises in one. We pull up to the gated community and I pull my resident card out to swipe so I can be let in. It's a temporary one until we get our barcode decals. I look over at Liz, and she looks utterly confused.

Forty-Four

LIZ

WHEN WE PULL UP TO A BEAUTIFUL GATED COMMUNITY I think maybe we're going to visit someone, but then Cooper pulls out what looks like a resident pass and I'm back to square one. We drive down a few roads until we get to a massive house on the left and Cooper turns into the driveway. Parked along the road are our friends' vehicles. *Maybe there's a Christmas party going on here?*

We all get out and Cooper takes a key out of his pocket to unlock the door. When he opens the door, the cutest brown and black little puppy comes barreling down the hall and straight into Bella's arms. She scoops her up and looks at her father with hope in her eyes. "Is she mine?"

"Yes, Princess, she's yours. Merry Christmas." He kisses her on her forehead.

"Does she have a name?"

"She's yours, so you can pick the name."

She thinks about it, and when she figures out the name she wants, her entire faces lights up. "I know! I want to name her Princess!"

"But that's what I call you."

Bella pouts, but thinks of another name. "Okay, how about Elsa?"

We both laugh. "Elsa, it is!"

"Can I bring her home with me? Why wasn't she at my home?"

"This is her home, Bella. Do you like this house?" Bella looks around, and I do as well. The home is gorgeous. We're only standing in the foyer, but even from here I can see the spacious living room and the beautiful staircase that leads to the upstairs. Off to the side is what looks like a beautiful kitchen with a separate dining room. The floors are all hardwood, and the home is empty, but it's still stunning.

"Yes, I like this house. But why does she have to stay here? I want her with me."

Cooper looks at me as he answers Bella's question. "I bought this home for all of us. I was hoping we could all live here together as a family. I didn't know about the baby, but now it's even more perfect. I figured it would give us more room to grow as a family. It's empty so we can furnish it together."

He gets down on one knee and my breath hitches. I look around, realizing we aren't alone, which makes sense because all of our friends' cars were parked along the road when we pulled up. But now that I'm looking, I see that my parents and brother are also here, as well as Lauren, Cooper's mom.

Turning my attention back to Cooper, I see he's holding up a tiny box with a sparkly ring nestled inside of it.

"Lizbeth, when we met five years ago in Miami at that club it was lust at first sight." Everybody laughs, and I can feel the tears coming. "When I walked away from you, it was the hardest thing I ever chose to do. The only thing I can think of is that everything happens for a reason and maybe it just wasn't our time yet. Seeing you that night at my fight, I knew we were meant to be together. It took me a couple tries, but I finally came around. You have been so patient with me. Even when I didn't deserve a second chance you still gave it to me, and when I didn't have enough trust and belief in us, you did for the both of us. When I felt weak in this relationship, you held me up with your strength. You are an amazing mother to Bella and you're going to be just as amazing to this new baby. I want to spend the rest of our life reminding you why you will never regret giving me that second chance. Will you marry me?"

"Yes!" is all I can say before he's back on his feet, putting the beautiful ring on my finger. I don't know much about rings, but it has one big princess cut diamond in the center with smaller clusters of diamonds around the edges, and it fits me perfectly.

Cooper cups my chin and kisses me softly. "Thank you, baby girl."

Everyone watching takes that as their cue to come over and congratulate us. "Oh, sweetheart. I am so happy for you. A new home, an engagement, and a baby on the way! This is quite the Christmas for you. Congratulations," my mom says as she hugs me.

Everybody takes turns hugging us and when Kayla gets over to me we hug extra hard. "Please tell me you've changed your mind," I say quietly, so only she can hear.

She pulls away, but stays looking into my eyes. I already know the answer before she gives it. "No, Liz. I'm still leaving tomorrow, but I'll visit often, and I'll definitely be back before the baby's here. I just need to go. Please understand that."

"Okay, but please know I'm only a phone call and a plane ride away. Does Cooper know you're quitting?"

"Yes, I told him yesterday. He said he doesn't need two weeks' notice, so I'm flying out tomorrow night."

We hug again and then I watch Kayla slip out the door. I look over at Bentley and see him watching her leave as well. He's showing no emotions, but I know he cares. And if I'm honest, I hate him a little bit right now because I believe whatever is going on with them is the reason she's leaving me.

Cooper announces there is one more present and asks for everybody to join us in the backyard. When we walk out the backdoors, Bella goes running straight to the swing set. I don't even think you can call it that, though. The word swing set doesn't even begin to do this thing justice. It's an enormous pink and purple princess castle with a rock wall, swings, a slide, and of course attached to the end is the cutest little picnic table and benches.

"Look Mommy, Daddy. Santa brought me my swing set just like I asked! He must have known this was going to be our new house."

Cooper holds me in his arms and nuzzles his face into my hair. We just stand like this for a while, just letting it all soak in. It may have taken a little longer to get here, but I wouldn't trade our journey for anything, because every step we took led us to this moment right here, right now, with our friends and family. And these people mean everything to me.

COOPER

Two Months Later

I'M STANDING IN THE CENTER OF THE OCTAGON AT THE MGM Grand Garden Arena in my hometown city of Las Vegas. My eye is swollen so it's hard to see, and I'm pretty sure I have at least two fractured ribs, but it's all worth it because at this very moment the referee has my hand in the air, announcing me the new UFC Champion. They hand me my belt and it feels damn good to know I've finally made it to where I wanted to be.

The crowd is going crazy, chanting my name. I've worked my entire life for this moment, but more importantly, it signifies the end of one chapter and the beginning of a new one.

"Tell us, Rage, now that you're the new UFC Middleweight Champion, what's next?"

I knew this question was coming. There have been rumors flying and tons of speculation as to what I'm going to do next. People want to know if I'm going to fight to defend the title, or if I'm going to retire as the champion. The UFC has offered me a healthy contract to stay on board and nobody knows what my decision is except my fiancée.

Looking out at the crowd, I see my entire world sitting in the first row closest to the octagon. Liz wasn't thrilled about letting Bella come to the fight, but our daughter is less like a princess and more like a warrior than Liz cares to admit. She loves watching these fights, and I would bet money that one day she becomes the UFC Champion in the Women's Bantamweight Division. Liz is looking at me through shiny eyes, clapping, and Bella is screaming at the top of her lungs for me.

I crook my fingers for them to come up and join me. When they get up to me, Liz gives me a soft kiss on my lips, afraid to hurt me as Bella grabs the microphone.

"My daddy is retiring," she says clearly, so everybody can hear. The crowd boos and she gets mad. "That's not nice. My mommy is having a baby and my daddy is going to work at the gym and train me to be a UFC Champion just like him." And...the crowd goes nuts.

I throw my head back in laughter at my crazy daughter and then take the microphone from her. "My little girl is correct. I'm honored to be the new UFC Champion. I want to thank everybody who has supported me over the last fifteen years..." I go on to name my friends and family, my trainer, the gym, the UFC, and when I'm finally done, I walk hand in hand with my fiancée and daughter out of the octagon for the last time.

Today isn't just a great day because of my win—today is also my daughter's fifth birthday. Earlier in the week we had a huge party for her. She wanted a doghouse built for her puppy and we all know whatever Bella wants, Bella gets. Sitting in the backyard in matching colors to her princess play set is a doghouse fit for a puppy princess.

It's also Valentine's Day, so this morning when the girls woke up I made sure to have lots of chocolates and stuffed toys for them, along with breakfast in bed. I bought Liz a charm bracelet that has the same boxing gloves as the one on her necklace. It also contains a heart charm with Bella's birthstone. She cried her eyes out when I put in on, not that it surprised me. The woman cries over everything these days. She's sixteen weeks pregnant and is due July eighteenth. I've been going to her doctor appointments with her and even got to hear the heartbeat and see the baby in an ultrasound. A-maz-ing. One thing I've noticed is the farther along she gets, the hornier she gets. I might just have to keep her knocked up the next few years.

"Everybody ready to party?" Bentley yells as we get off the plane in Palm Beach. Everybody gives a, "Hell yeah." We decided there was no better way to celebrate Caleb and my win than to go to the place where Bella and I first met: Miami.

We drop Bella off with her parents and head south. Liz is a bit upset because Kayla is in Florida, but is refusing to join us. I'm definitely not getting into the middle of all that drama. I'm about to spend the weekend with my woman at the resort we spent together five-and-a-half years ago. Life can't get much better than this.

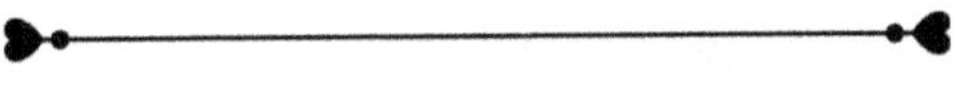

LIZ

WE GET TO THE RESORT, CHECK IN, AND HEAD RIGHT TO

our room. Everybody wanted to go out, but Cooper wasn't having it, so he told them all they can go without us.

We walk into the room that looks identical to the one from five years ago and Cooper leads me straight to the bed. He takes my shirt off and reaches behind me to take my bra off, so I'm lying in the center of the bed with only shorts on. Of course, those don't stay on for long. He removes my shorts and panties and, leaning over me, runs his eyes down my body.

"Like what you see?" I tease.

He takes his hands and rubs them over my belly. It's not big yet, but there's definitely a visible bump that you can see. If you didn't know me, you might think I was just bloated, but those who know I'm pregnant can tell it's from the baby growing in me.

"Yes, I do like what I see, very, very much."

"And what do you see, Mr. Cooper?"

He continues to rub his hands over my belly then bends down to give it a kiss. "I see the most beautiful woman carrying and protecting our baby."

He lifts his hands up from my belly and moves them to my breasts, gently palming them. "I see beautiful, voluptuous tits. They're preparing to one day nurse our baby." I squirm at his touch. Pregnancy has definitely made my body more sensitive.

He moves up to my face, putting his arms on either side of my head and kisses my eyelids. "I see the most amazing brown eyes that look at our daughter and me with such love."

He kisses my lips softly. "I see the most kissable lips. These lips are mine." And with that, he presses his lips back to mine, pushing his tongue through and sucking on my tongue. Our lips move together like they're puzzle pieces that fit together just right.

Too quickly, he pulls away and moves back down my body. "Mmm...and this sweet pussy. I'm definitely looking at this." I can feel my cheeks blush. I don't know how, after all this time, this man can still make me blush but he does.

He licks up my center from bottom to top. "I want to taste you, baby girl. I want to make you come on my face." And who in their right mind would argue with that? *Not me.*

Cooper continues to lick and suck, devouring my pussy until I'm at the brink of an orgasm. My legs tighten and my muscles clamp down on him, and I moan loudly as my climax barrels down on me.

He pulls his body back up mine, and places his arms on either side of my head with his fingers threading through my hair. His hard length is pushing into me as he slowly enters me. Looking into my eyes with so much love that I want to pocket it all and store it away, he says, "I'm looking at my entire world. Thank you for giving me a second chance. I love you so much."

"I love you, too." And for the rest of the night, Cooper makes love to me, showing me why giving him a second chance was the best decision I ever made.

The end!

About the Author

Reading is like breathing in, writing is like breathing out.– Pam Allyn

Nikki Ash resides in South Florida where she is an English teacher by day and a writer by night. When she's not writing, you can find her with a book in her hand. From the Boxcar Children, to Wuthering Heights, to the latest single parent romance, she has lived and breathed every type of book. While reading and writing are her passions, her two children are her entire world. You can probably find them at a Disney park before you would find them at home on the weekends!